THE AMBER CRANE

MALVE VON HASSELL

ODYSSEY
BOOKS

Published by Odyssey Books in 2021
www.odysseybooks.com.au

ISBN: 978-1922311221 (paperback)
ISBN: 978-1922311238 (ebook)

A catalogue record for this book is available from the National Library of Australia

"Sometimes, beach watchmen and guards in search of treasure notice lovely huge pieces of amber floating in the water close to the shore. However, when they row their boats closer so they can lower their nets, it all turns out to be nothing but an illusion, vanishing in the froth of the sea."

— Excerpt from a collection of German legends (Ludwig Bechstein: *Deutsches Sagenbuch*. Ed. Karl Martin Schiller, Leipzig: Georg Wigand, 1853.)

CRANES IN FLIGHT

PEOPLE WERE HANGED FOR LESS.

Peter Glienke stomped along the field path toward the shore, flicking a willow switch back and forth with jerky movements, swiping at the tops of thistles and nettles on the edges of the path. *Whack.* Hanged for less. *Whack.* Just for looking at someone the wrong way. *Whack.* For failing to take off one's hat in respect. *Whack.* With angry fascination, Peter began to recite to himself all the horrible things done to people for the most insignificant of offenses. Hanged on the gallows. *Whack.* Head cut off. *Whack.* Drawn and quartered. *Whack.* Tossed into a rat-infested jail. Spread-eagled. Run through with a sword. *Whack, whack, whack.*

Stealing. Murder. Pillage. Destruction. Peter could understand punishment for those crimes. But walking on the beach? Picking up a piece of amber, something nature spit onto the sand after a storm?

A hoarse rattling sound made him look up. A flock of cranes was taking off into the sky. They were free, he thought. If only they did not screech so much. Usually, he liked cranes. At least they did not fly in regimented formation like silly geese without a mind of their own, but rather in a raggedy shifting V spilling across the sky like droplets of ink. One still sat in a clump of grass, apparently undecided whether to take off after his mates. That young crane was like him, stuck, unable to move.

Stupid birds. They were ungainly, with a tail and beak too short for its elongated shape. Yet, when Peter gazed at the glowing evening sky, he could not help but be bewitched by their wildness, silhouetted against the light, flying with high-pitched whistling and loud rattling calls, without any discernible pattern.

In the distance, on an elevated stretch along the shoreline, he could make out the gallows, dark and threatening in the dusk, a rough-hewn pole with a crossbar. In his lifetime, no one had been executed there, but still the sight made Peter uncomfortable. He averted his eyes and focused on the silvery tips of the churning sea below.

Something urged him on. He wanted to get closer to the water. After a moment's hesitation, he scrambled down, leaving the path behind. Once on the beach, he continued along the shoreline, relishing the bracing smell of the sea and the spray of the incoming waves. But his sense of pleasure did not last long. He could not keep from thinking about all the things that had been going wrong lately.

Until last year, he had been content and satisfied with his life.

Of course, war continued to rage across his homeland—as it had done since long before his birth fifteen years ago. But now, in 1644, the twenty-seventh year of the war, Peter could not imagine life in any other way. He cared little whether the Swedes or the Imperialists were in control. It made no difference to the horrors and arbitrary punishments they inflicted on the populace. They simply took turns pushing and shoving their way into town and devastating fields and villages all around. In their wake, sad throngs of people shuffled along dusty roads in search of food and shelter.

People bit their lips and shook their heads when yet another one of the sons of Stolpmünde died on a distant battlefield. They turned away when refugees with grey, weary faces traveled through the town, walking silently, their feet wrapped in rags. They shrugged when fields lay fallow because there were not enough people left alive to plant them. That was life, the citizens said. There is nothing we can do. Maybe the war will end one day, but we have to take care of our own, they said, sighing and going on with the business of the day.

Peter did the same, shrugging and turning away from what he could not change. Together with his friends, he skipped stones at bends of the Stolpe and stole pasties from stalls on market days. He dared others to run along the forbidden beach and made jokes about girls, pretending not to be interested. He paid little attention to his sister, tugging on her braids and cuffing her affectionately before forgetting about her. He rarely gave any thought to the fact that Effie was frail and inexplicably locked in silence and jerky movements as if her body was a cage. His parents would take care of her.

Peter was content in his apprenticeship. He loved amber. He loved the translucence of polished pieces, soft to the touch, yet solid and firm, and the colors, ranging from tawny gold to dark reds and rusty browns. He loved the feel of the tools in his hand and the scent of resin permeating the workshop.

However, last year, Peter's brother Lorenz, a soldier in the Swedish army, lost his life, and everything changed. Peter's mother died shortly after that, and his father spent most of his waking hours in his study. Effie spent most of her time in her room. The only sounds relieving the silence hanging over the house came from the kitchen where Clare banged pots and sometimes hummed as she worked. Peter began to avoid going home. Master Nowak's house had become a place of refuge, warm and welcoming. And yet, there as well Peter felt stifled and restless, chafing under the rules and regulations imposed by the guild, and impatient to be done with his apprenticeship.

With a frustrated sigh, Peter tugged on his jerkin. It was too tight around his neck. He would have to ask his father for money to buy a new one. Gloomily he kept an eye on the foamy surf close to his feet as he continued along the shore and thought about the humiliating afternoon in the workshop.

"Well, you will have to rework that on Monday," Master Nowak had said. "See the crack?" His face stern, he twisted the small piece of amber in his hand. It was supposed to become the mouthpiece of a pipe. "You forgot to place it in water before heating it. You have been an apprentice for almost three years now. I should not have to tell you something that basic."

Peter opened his mouth to protest that he had too many other tasks that day to concentrate, but he stopped himself. Master Nowak was right after all. Scowling, Peter gathered his tools and cleaned up his workstation before setting out for his father's house.

Master Nowak's house was at the southern edge of the harbor town Stolpmünde, while Peter's family lived northeast of the harbor. Peter did not mind the long walk. It gave him time to think.

Absorbed in his thoughts, Peter walked with his head bent, picking his way past refuse and ruts in the street. He was oblivious to the familiar sight of timber-frame buildings with sagging windows and walls blackened by fire. After all his mistakes, Master Nowak would never let him take the exam. He did not even allow Peter to accompany him to the amber market in Königsberg in the summer. Peter had pleaded with him, but the answer remained the same. "It is not a good time," Master Nowak had said. There never would be a good time; the war would go on forever.

When he crossed the central square, he glanced at the row of stately patrician houses. Marthe Neuhof, the mayor's daughter, lived in the one with the grey-green façade. This portion of the town had escaped the ravages of the war. Both Swedish and Imperial Army officers liked to be quartered there and made sure those houses were protected. Hunching his shoulders, Peter continued on his way. Marthe would never even notice him anyway. He walked past the familiar red brick church and storage buildings along the harbor, and crossed the river to the northeastern side of the town.

At the turnoff toward his parents' home at the edge of the town, Peter looked back to see whether anyone was watching. Then, with an angry toss of his head, he headed toward the shore. He did not have a beach permit, but he was tired of all the rules and regulations. What did he care about a distant duke's claim to all the amber along the Baltic Sea? This was his town, his home, his beach.

When Peter was younger, he and his friends had sometimes dared each other to sneak into the dunes, pretending to search for amber and being chased by the beach watchman, thrilled by the danger of being caught.

"Do not ever pick up amber and think you can keep it," Master Nowak told him when Peter started his apprenticeship. "All amber must be surrendered to the guild. They have not hung anybody for stealing amber for some time, but still, the punishment is severe. You could be thrown into the town jail or expelled from the city. Besides, whatever you do reflects on my position in the guild."

"Why do we have to put up with the guild?"

"The restrictions are imposed by the Duke of Prussia, and the guild administers them," Master Nowak responded, his grey eyes without a hint of impatience. "More importantly, the guild protects us. It regulates the market and supports us when we purchase amber. It helps apprentices find work. We need the guild."

"But why can we not just do our work and sell it without the guild?"

"That is the way it is." Master Nowak sighed. "We cannot operate outside the guild. Nobody would buy from us."

"It is not fair. The guild sets the prices. The guild controls what we sell and to whom. The guild tells us what methods of working with amber we should use. And we are not even allowed to walk on the beach—our beach, in our land. It is like being in jail."

"Better this 'jail' as you call it than being out there, all alone, without the protection of the guild. Think of all the guild does. The guild helps when there is a fire or a flood. It builds hospitals, schools, and orphanages. The guild even pays for funerals and masses. Without the guild, you might as well become a *Bönhase*."

Peter shook his head in frustration as he thought about what Master Nowak had said. Bönhase came from a word meaning "a hare hiding in an attic." A Bönhase was a worker who crafted and sold amber in secret. Operating outside the law, without guild certification as a journeyman or master, a Bönhase was always at risk of being found out—a hunted hare, with hounds right behind it. Then again, it had to be wonderful to be independent.

Peter pulled his coat tighter around himself against the wind. Occasionally he stepped into a depression filled with water, but it did not bother him. The sound of the waves soothed him; he felt as if he could breathe more easily. He dreaded the weight of his father's unhappiness, the lingering sadness over his brother's death, and the weaving and rocking from side to side his sister engaged in when she was upset. There was no room for Peter in any of this.

To get out of the wind for a while, Peter crawled into a little hollow beneath exposed roots of a stand of scraggly pine trees. Riding along a path on top of the dunes, the beach watchman would patrol the area, on the lookout for people gathering amber. The tide was going out but the sea was churned up by the storm, and gusts of wind continued to whip across the water. Occasionally the spray from breakers hitting the beach tickled his face and his lips tasted salty. The smell of the sea and the incessant slap of the waves onto the shore gave him the feeling of being worlds away from Master

Nowak's disapproving frown or his father's gloomy dissatis-
faction.

Absorbed in watching the shimmer of the water in the glow
of the setting sun, he felt his thoughts calm down. Perhaps he
could find a way to escape from all this. He began to dream of
journeying far away, perhaps to the city of Königsberg, the heart
of the amber trade. It would be marvelous to come upon a
hidden cache of amber somewhere along the fabled amber
beaches outside of Königsberg. Of course, he knew there was
nothing more unlikely. He thought of the tales told by amber
fishers who claimed to have seen large chunks of amber floating
in the waves. Whenever they got closer, reaching out with their
nets, it all vanished.

Peter ran his hand back and forth over the sand and the
exposed gnarly pine roots near his legs, then stopped, wincing.
He had cut the sensitive area between thumb and index finger.

Thumping sounds made him raise his head. The silhouette
of a horse and rider loomed against the darkening sky—the
beach watchman, cantering along the path on top of the dunes.

Peter squeezed farther back into his shelter, his foot digging
into the sand. The ground reverberated as the rider thundered
past his hiding place. Sliding down as if a sinkhole had opened
up beneath him, Peter grabbed onto an exposed pine tree root to
keep from making noise and attracting the watchman's attention. The horse started and snorted as if sensing Peter's presence.
The rider cursed, kicking the horse, and within moments, passed
by. The sounds of the hooves in the sand faded away.

Peter was still clutching the root with one hand when he felt
a lump underneath the other. Slowly he sat up and tried to pull
his find out of the sand, tugging until it was free. He shook it to
dislodge some of the sand. The clump smelled bad; it was
nothing but rotted netting, with barnacles and small shells
caught in its coils. Disappointed, he raised his hand to toss it
away.

Then Peter hesitated. The dark stringy strands reminded him

of the nets used by the amber catchers. He could feel something firm inside the tightly twisted mess of rope and knots, and worked his fingers into the tangle, pushing and pulling until he was able to pry it apart. A salt-crusted stone with a rough, cracked surface fell onto the sand in front of his feet. He picked it up to take a closer look. There actually were two pieces, a longer one, about the length of his palm, curved around a smaller one, like a mother cradling a baby in her lap. When he prodded the clump with a little twig, the pieces came apart. These were not stones. They were too light.

Amber.

Instinctively Peter closed his hands over his find and glanced around to see whether the watchman was coming back. The tops of the distant pine trees waved in the wind. The beach was deserted, and the only sound other than the surf was the raucous screeching of the cranes.

After a moment, Peter relaxed, opening his hands to study the lumps. Dull, crusted with salt, unpolished, they did not look at all appealing. But he had worked with Master Nowak long enough to know at least one of them to be a unique and unusually large piece of amber. On the amber market, it would fetch a high price.

The smaller piece was just large enough for a lady's pendant. Peter could see it with his mind's eye as clearly as if he had spent hours working on it—a perfect little heart with a warm dark golden glow. He put it down and picked up the other one.

It was almost as long as his hand and half as wide in the middle. In the workshop, he rarely handled or worked on pieces larger than those used to make rosary beads. He poked at the crusty surface with his fingernail. He turned it this way and that. It made him think of a tall bird, perhaps a crane. Its oblong shape seemed curiously alive, as if a bird was waiting underneath the crust, dreaming inside its dark golden nest.

It rested on the palm of his hand, its secret hidden. He should throw it back. Someone might have seen him walking toward the beach. It would be awful if he were caught. He would have to count himself lucky if he only got flogged. He should throw everything back into the sea immediately. The watchman might come circling back any moment. He closed his hand firmly on his find and lifted his arm. Then, as if pulled down by a tremendous weight, his arm dropped. *Just for a night.* He would keep it just for a night. Tomorrow he would take it back.

✿ 2 ✿

SHADOWS

RAT-A-TAT, RAT-A-TAT. SHARP RAPID BANGS IN THE distance. Peter raises his head. He must have fallen asleep.

Another *rat-a-tat*, closer this time. Cannons? Not like any cannons he has ever heard. Have the imperialists returned to take over Stolp?

Peter blinks in disbelief. The beach is gone. The ocean is gone. He sits in a ditch, water seeping into his shoes. Next to him, the stinking bloated carcass of a horse. He flinches and tries to shift away. It is as if he is stuck. Unable to move, he peers over the top of the ditch at a hayfield.

This field and the gently rolling hills in the distance covered with dense stands of trees do not look anything like the land around Stolpmünde.

Where is he? What's happening to him? His mouth is dry. The hayfield appears unkempt. Someone apparently began with the harvest and then abandoned the work, having finished just a small area and leaving behind piles of hay and a mess of stubble and dust. At least that's familiar. All the villages around Stolpmünde suffered over the last years. Swedish and Imperialist troops took turns pillaging, burning, and looting over and over again. Many fields have the same look of neglect as this one.

Peter rubs his eyes. Everything is flat, as if taken out of the pages of a book—a world leached of all color, leaving behind just shades of black and grey.

Another *rat-a-tat*. A humming sound far above in the sky makes him glance up, squinting to avoid the last rays of the setting sun. Light-headed and dizzy, Peter stares at something monstrous and utterly impossible—huge, bird-like shapes, with snub noses and blades whirring in front that streak across the horizon and disappear behind a bank of clouds.

Shaken, Peter turns and gazes over the top of the embankment on the other side. People walk in a steady stream along a road. Old people, women, children grabbing on to their mother's skirts. Heads bowed. Silent. They pass a large metal box with wheels, with doors left open. Nobody glances at it. Horse-drawn wagons with tent-like covers. Horses coated with mud, heads bent, hooves dragging. Bundles, bags, boxes held together with rope, a few handheld carts.

A young man with a dark cap, long baggy breeches, a jacket too big on his slender frame, and a bag slung over his shoulder walks next to a horse-drawn cart. With one hand, he keeps pushing a bulging sack in place as the vehicle wobbles precariously in the rutted street. A woman sits on top, the reins in one hand, the other gripping a small child on her lap, two children next to her, their faces blank. When the young man passes, he briefly turns his head in Peter's direction, glancing at him with large light-colored eyes. Then he walks on.

Another rapid *rat-a-tat* in the distance. Peter feels himself slide into the ditch.

❧ 3 ❧

EFFIE

A BREAKER CRASHED ONTO THE BEACH.

Peter jerked upright. He shook his head. What a strange dream.

It was late. He must have slept longer than he realized. His hand was stiff and cramped from holding on to the amber. He glanced around to see whether the beach watchman had come back, but all he could see was the gleam of the sea in the moonlight and the dark expanse of the shoreline. Quickly he stuffed both pieces into his pocket and stood up, brushing the sand off his clothes. Just for a night, he repeated to himself. He would toss them back into the sea the next day. Nobody would see him.

Quickly, he retraced his steps across the dune toward the path back to town.

Rustling in a clump of trees just ahead of him. A blur of movement. *A fox? No, this was too large.*

Peter's steps faltered. Then he softly moved to the side, away from the moonlight that made the sandy path look like a band of silver. He could not let anybody see him here, so close to the beach. He tried to quiet his breathing. There was a swishing sound, evoking the soft folds of a woman's skirt, followed by a chuckle, loud in the darkness. A whiff of scent reached him, spicy, with a hint of roses. It stirred a thought, but then he forgot about it. Two shapes melted apart and made their way down the hill. Peter could hear low murmuring as they walked in the direction of the town. He shivered. Had they seen him? It seemed unlikely. The moon had disappeared behind a bank of clouds and he could barely see the path ahead of him.

Peter started jogging toward the road that led to his father's house at the edge of town.

He slowed down as he got closer. The next day was All Hallows' Eve, and he dreaded the tramp to the cemetery to pray over his mother's grave. His brother was not buried there. He had died far away from home.

Lorenz had always been the favorite son. Taller than Peter by half a foot, with broad shoulders and a head of golden reddish curls, vivid and full of laughter, he had charmed everyone. His parents' eyes had lit up whenever Lorenz had come home. Peter might as well have been invisible. Next to Lorenz, Peter had felt puny, with his mousy brown hair and slender frame, and his habit of running into things and stumbling as he walked along the road, lost in thought.

Sometimes when Peter thought about his brother, he was close to tears. He would give anything to again hear his brother's baritone, which stood out among other voices during the Sunday church service, and to see his wide-open smile, changing to exuberant laughter at the slightest provocation. He missed the warmth that stole over him when Lorenz would sling an arm around his shoulders and cuff his head. Since the news of Lorenz's death, it was as if storm clouds had blotted out the sun.

Lorenz had served in a regiment of Queen Christina of Sweden. In the room they had shared, he had often talked to Peter about great armies of the past and shining heroes who died for their cause. He had revered King Gustav Adolph, the father of Christina, who had been killed in the battle of Lützen in 1632.

Over and over, he told Peter the story of the king's final battle and death on the field after he rode astray behind the enemy lines in the mix of fog and gun smoke from the burning town of Lützen.

Lorenz apparently considered this the pinnacle of glory. It made no sense to Peter, but he did not say that, bewitched by his brother's passion and even slightly envious. He had never himself felt such zeal and enthusiasm.

"I wish I could have been his flag bearer," Lorenz exclaimed, his eyes burning. "I would not have gotten separated from the king on the field of battle."

However, Lorenz had not died in battle as he had envisioned. Bitterest of ironies, he died in an accident. His regiment had been crossing a stream when the rickety bridge collapsed. He and other foot soldiers fell into the stream below. Knocked unconscious, Lorenz drowned in the shallow water of the stream before his comrades realized what had happened.

His parents only knew he was dead because one of his friends in the regiment had come back to tell them. Peter's mother had listened to the young soldier without showing any reaction. When he stopped speaking, she said, "Thank you," and slowly climbed the stairs to her room. She never came down after that.

She died within a few months after news of Lorenz's death had reached them, overcome by fever and coughing.

"She died of grief," the neighbors said, nodding sagely as if that would make it better.

Peter cringed when he heard them. It was such a pointless thing to say. Perhaps grief played a role, but the food shortages, rampant diseases that seemed to strike so many people, and sheer exhaustion from years of war certainly had a lot to do with her death. She was hardly the only one who died recently.

Peter's father was a shipping merchant. Several years ago, he had suffered several losses—two ships had sunk and all merchandise they had carried in their holds was lost.

Even so, Peter could not understand why his father dismissed one of their two servants last year. Jenrich Glienke was one of the most successful merchants in the town. Surely, he could afford another servant. He was too stingy and careful.

Fortunately, Clare Betke, who had worked for the family for years, stayed. She cooked and cleaned tirelessly, and she kept an eye on Effie.

The roadway was badly rutted, and Peter cursed as he stumbled into a mud puddle. Most of the houses appeared drab and unkempt. After years of war, people had given up trying to take care of them. It seemed a waste of time and energy since, at the next moment, either the Imperials or the Swedes could come pouring into the town, destroying everything all over again.

His father's house, imposing with its sturdy walls of red brick held together with timber beams typical for buildings in the area, looked out onto a large front yard with a storage house where, in better times, merchants would come with their wagons to discuss shipping charges with his father. Several times soldiers had broken into the storage house, taking whatever they found useful and callously destroying the rest. At least his father's house had not been burned down. When the Swedish troops had forced the Imperial soldiers out of Stolp, they had gone on a rampage, destroying, looting, and burning down houses to drive home they were now in control.

Today, it was quiet. Peter opened the gate and headed for the main door. Before he could walk through, he heard Clare call to him from the servants' entrance.

"Where have you been?" Her headscarf had loosened, releasing strands of greying hair. She rubbed her hands on her apron.

"I walked around." For a moment, Peter's hand touched the amber in his pocket. "Anyway, I'm here now. What's the rush?"

Clare came toward him, leaving the door to the kitchen open behind her. Peter could smell barley soup and cabbage.

"You're covered with sand." Clare reached out and brushed

her hands over his coat. "You went to sit on the beach again. One day, the beach watchman will find you and teach you a lesson." She talked as if her mind was on something else. "I have to go back so your supper will not be burned. Just go inside. Your father will be glad to see you safe and sound."

"I doubt that," Peter muttered.

Reluctantly, he opened the front door and walked into his father's study. His father did not look up from his desk, sitting slumped over with his head resting on his hand and his eyes closed.

For a moment, Peter gazed at him.

Throughout Peter's childhood, Jenrich Glienke had been an imposing figure, solidly built, with broad shoulders that belied his short stature, the bearing of a tough captain from his seafaring days. Relentless and unforgiving of weakness in others, he frequently admonished Peter about his posture. "You slouch too much, son. People will not respect you when you slouch." Holding himself with rigid discipline, he had never shown any tiredness, despite the unending struggle to keep the business going throughout the war years.

His father seemed to have shrunk into himself. With a pang, Peter realized he had gone grey. His formerly thick, glossy brown hair had thinned and faded to the color of cold ashes in the hearth.

"Father?" Peter asked hesitantly.

"Peter." His father raised his head and rubbed his hands over his face.

One word only, and yet there was something in his voice Peter had never heard before. His father sounded glad he was home.

"What is it?" Peter was shocked by his father's lined face.

"Something happened to your sister. She came back from a walk this afternoon, completely disheveled and dirty, and now she just sits in her room, staring at the wall."

"Shall I check on her?"

"Yes, please do."

Peter put his hand on the doorknob.

"Peter, wait."

He turned back.

"I know the last year hasn't been easy." His father's voice faltered. "Since your mother died, it all has been a bit of a struggle."

"I know," Peter muttered, embarrassed and uncomfortable. He waited to see if his father would say anything else, but there was nothing.

The floorboards creaked as he walked upstairs. He told himself that he was trying to tread lightly so as not to make too much noise, but he knew it was reluctance more than anything else.

Effie was one year younger than Peter. When she was a little girl, she had had a series of seizures. That's what Mother had told him. Those seizures hurt her somehow, even though one could not see it from looking at her—large for her age, with thick brown tresses of shiny hair, curling generously when not pinned back under a scarf, and dark eyes with thick lashes. She never talked, moving about the house and the yard like a ghost. When she got frightened, she rocked, weaving back and forth for hours on end.

Lorenz used to read to her. Humming contentedly in response, she stabbed her fingers at images in the books. Sometimes her eyes wandered, seeming to disappear into her own world. Lorenz would nudge her gently and wave the book in front of her eyes until she resurfaced.

Lorenz was fiercely protective of Effie. She was the only person whom he never treated dismissively. With a gift for biting comments, Lorenz was frequently careless and quick to mock people, but his parents did not mind. His laughter charmed them, and it was as if they and everybody else fed on his vivacity. But when he was with Effie, he was quiet and patient.

Suddenly Peter remembered something, and it filled him

with longing for Lorenz. Not long before his brother's death, during his last visit home, the sound of cannon fire had gone on for several days near the town. Effie had run into her room and sat on the floor, rocking back and forth with her eyes closed as if trying to drown out all other sensations of sight and sound. Peter had watched her from the doorway, fighting an urge to laugh—to no avail—when Lorenz stepped up behind him and cuffed him, pushing him out of the way.

Ashamed, Peter watched Lorenz go into the room and sit down on the floor right next to his sister. Without saying anything, he moved his torso alongside Effie, matching his rhythm to hers. He began to hum. It was one of the songs of their childhood. Maybe it was just as well he did not say the lyrics—all about the three riders leaving for war and their girls gazing out of the window, weeping. Meanwhile, the melody was cheerful, almost bouncy.

Three riders passed through the gate, farewell!
Their lady loves looked out of the window, farewell!
If we must be parted,
Then give me back your golden ring!
Death drives us apart, farewell!
Leaving breaks our hearts!
Farewell! Farewell! Farewell!

Effie gradually slowed down her rocking motions and then joined her soft light voice to Lorenz's baritone, humming contentedly.

Since Lorenz's death, Effie spent a lot of time sitting on the floor, her face closed and inward as if waiting for something. After their mother died, it got worse. At the cemetery, at first, she stood quietly next to her father as the minister intoned the committal prayer. But when the townspeople filed past, shaking her father's hand, she began to moan, weaving back and forth until Clare quietly drew her away and brought her back to the house.

Peter clenched his hands in his pockets as he watched. His father appeared oblivious to this byplay. He was living as if surrounded by demented people, Peter thought bitterly. He could hardly wait to get back to Master Nowak's house after the funeral.

Clare was the only one who managed to coax Effie out of her room.

"Come, Effie, you can help me cook," she would say. "It is warm in the kitchen." Clare would give her a bowl of peas to shell, beans to trim, or carrots to peel. Sitting at the big wooden table and humming softly, Effie did as she was told. Sometimes, Clare fetched a brush and patiently untangled Effie's hair. Several months after Mistress Glienke's death, Effie began to venture outside and occasionally accompanied Clare to the market in town.

Now it appeared that Effie's fragile calm state had come undone.

Reluctantly, Peter pushed open the door to his sister's room.

Effie sat on the carpet, her arms tightly wrapped around her torso as she rocked back and forth without making a sound. She always wore her shiny brown hair in a neat braid, but today, the thick, glossy plait had come undone and strands hung loose and matted on her shoulders. Bits of dirt, leaves, and twigs clung to the curls. From where he stood, he could see one side of her face. A bruise encircled her left eye and her cheekbone was bloody. Several buttons on her stained jacket were missing and the shoulder seam had split.

"Effie?"

Nothing indicated his sister had even heard him. She continued rocking back and forth.

Peter stepped closer to get a better look at the bruise but stopped when Effie flinched and scooted backward away from him, rocking faster.

Helplessly, Peter glanced around the room. There was something different about it.

Effie liked to keep her room meticulously organized. Her clothes were always put away in the cabinet, the bed made, the shoes lined up like soldiers in the army, and the washbasin, cloth, and brush neatly arranged on the table. Pewter jugs on the windowsill were filled with purple and blue dried asters and strawflowers, and papers on the desk for what Peter thought of as Effie's scribbles were laid out on the table next to a pen and ink set and a box of chalks sorted by color and length. His mother had made a point of getting Effie all sorts of pens, charcoal, and colored chalks. She hummed when she sat over her papers, scratching with the chalks. When anyone entered her room, she would quickly push everything out of sight into a large leather folder.

Now the blanket from the bed was bunched up, the pewter jugs had fallen over, spilling the dried flowers on the floorboards, the shoes and clothes lay in a heap near the bed, and the box with the chalks was upended, its contents spread out on the table.

At least there was something he could do. He moved around the room and put everything back where it belonged, straightening out the blanket on the bed, arranging the shoes, hanging the clothes over the chair, and gathering up the chalks and placing them back in their box. When he bent to pick up the dried flowers, he realized Effie had stopped rocking. She sat still, hunched over and her arms folded around her body as if to hold it in place.

She seemed to listen to his movements.

Moving slowly, he placed the flowers back in their mug. A few of the petals had fallen off. He swept them up, put them in his pocket, and took a step toward his sister.

Effie immediately resumed her repetitive weaving back and forth. Shaken, Peter backed out and ran downstairs.

"Effie looks awful," he said to Clare. "I wonder where she went to come home in that state."

"Really, is it not obvious?" Clare's voice was biting. "She was raped."

"What?" Peter shook his head in disbelief. "That is ridiculous. Who would rape a poor dim girl like her?"

"You think that matters to those who rape? Poor, rich, old, sick, pretty, ugly, sane, dimwitted—it does not matter." Clare was wiping the table with furious motions. There were red splotches on her cheek. "Of course, she was raped. Figure it out. She came home dirty, bruised, disheveled, and terrified." Clare put down the rag and stood in front of Peter, her arms crossed. "So, you want to know what happened to her. There is your answer."

Effie was raped. Peter clapped his hands over his mouth and rushed to the scullery where he retched over the slop bucket. Nothing came up other than green slime. Perhaps it was just as well he had not eaten all day. He dipped a beaker into the water bucket to rinse the foul taste out of his mouth. Then he went back to the kitchen and sat down on the bench.

"Maybe there is some other reason," he said, a note of pleading in his voice.

"Not likely." Clare shrugged. "Let me know if you have any ideas."

Peter ran his fingers through his hair. "What can we do?"

Clare glanced at the pot on the stove and gave it a stir. Then she turned back to the table, her face slightly flushed from the heat. She no longer seemed angry, just tired and sad. "I do not know if there is really anything anybody can do. Time might help."

"Is she ..." Peter hesitated. "Is she going to have a baby?"

"I hope not. But we will not know for another month or so."

"And if she is?"

"Well, she certainly is not the first. I would not say anything to your father just yet."

"Of course not." Peter could not imagine telling anyone about this.

"I thought she had gone for a walk." Clare wiped an old rag back and forth on the same spot of the wooden table. "I was so happy she started going outside by herself again. I never thought anything wrong in that. Everybody knows her. I cannot keep my eyes on her all the time."

"I know," Peter said quickly. "It is not your fault."

But it was someone's fault. Who would have done this to Effie? Everyone knew her in Stolpmünde; many of the townspeople were protective of her. Strangers must have done this, perhaps refugees traveling through the town.

Peter's thoughts were in a jumble, a mix of revulsion and pity. It was hard to think of Effie. It was as if she no longer was his sweet little sister. But it was not her fault. He blamed himself for never being around and forgetting about her for the most part. But he had his apprenticeship. How could he be home often enough to have prevented something like this?

"She has a big bruise on her cheek," Clare said and sighed. "I tried to wash her hands and her face, but she would not let me. I figured I would let her be until she calmed down."

"We cannot just let her sit like that. It is horrible."

"You try then."

"Me?" Peter took a step back.

"Is there anybody else I could be speaking to?" Clare glared at him. "She is your sister."

"I do not know what to do. Lorenz would have known. Please, Clare?"

Clare put down the knife with which she had been peeling carrots. Deftly, she tipped the chopped-up carrots into the pot and gave it a stir. "Fine, let me try again. But you can help." She filled another bowl with water. "Here, take this." She took a washcloth from the shelf and a soft brush.

Reluctantly, Peter followed her up the stairs. Some of the water sloshed out of the bowl.

"Sorry."

Clare shook her head.

Effie had not changed her position, still on the floor and rocking steadily. She smelled of sweat and something sour and rank.

"Put the bowl on the dresser," Clare said, speaking softly.

"What are you going to do?" Peter whispered.

Clare held a finger to her lips. Thus silenced, Peter watched —repelled and fascinated in turn.

Moving slowly, she approached Effie and sat down on the floor next to her. Effie flinched and rocked faster.

Clare began to move along with Effie—just as Lorenz had done when he was alive. Without looking at her or touching her, she rocked alongside the girl while humming familiar childhood tunes and then gradually slowed down.

To Peter's amazement, Effie slowed down as well. It was as if her body listened.

When Clare reached for the brush, Effie flinched again but did not pull away. With slow, even motions, Clare brushed out the tangled mess, all the while crooning softly. She made a sign to Peter to bring over the bowl and washcloth, and began to wipe off the dirt from Effie's hands and face. Finally, she helped her up from the floor and to her bed. Obediently, Effie laid down, and Clare covered her with a blanket. Immediately, she started rocking from side to side, her eyes closed.

"I think that is all we can do right now," Clare whispered and picked up the bowl and washcloth. "I hope she will sleep. Poor mite."

Peter followed her back downstairs. "I could not have done that," he said.

"You never tried. You are still waiting for Lorenz to come back."

"That's not fair." Clare had never been so harsh with him before.

"There is not much that's been fair in the last years." Clare's frown lines stood out on her pale face. She placed two bowls on a tray, ladled barley stew into each, and added some slices of bread. "Here is your supper."

Peter took the tray from her hands and entered the study.

His father had just finished with his accounts and closed his books. "Why is supper so late?" he asked as he pushed back his chair, got up from his desk, and went over to the table where they usually ate their meals.

"Clare helped Effie get cleaned up."

"I see. I suppose we will never know what happened." He sighed. "Not that it matters all that much. Your sister has always been frail. I do not think that's ever going to change. Of course, it would all be different if your dear mother or Lorenz would still be with us." Slowly, he crumbled a piece of bread into his bowl of stew and began to eat.

Peter opened his mouth to speak but stopped himself. It wouldn't do any good to say Effie had been raped. It would just make his father feel more helpless.

The wind had picked up and the shutters rattled. The amber pieces in Peter's pocket felt huge all of a sudden. He should have thrown them back into the sea right away. The wooden carving of the chair's backrest dug into his shoulder and he shifted, crossing and uncrossing his legs. He could hardly swallow anything. Restlessly, he moved his spoon around in his bowl.

His father's grey hair drooped over his forehead, hiding his eyes. All Peter could see was his nose, thickened, the red veins along the sides more prominent than ever before. His hands, once so sure and steady, seemed shaky. Perplexed, Peter watched the knobby fingers gripping the spoon. His father had gotten old.

"Father," Peter blurted out, unable to bear the silence any longer. "I think I will put my name in for the exam at the next guild meeting." Perhaps his father would be pleased. Each apprentice had to pass an exam to prove that he had successfully completed his apprenticeship.

"So, Master Nowak thinks you are finally ready?" His father raised his bloodshot eyes. The lines around his mouth and the sagging jowls were more pronounced than ever.

"I think so." Peter felt deflated. Why could his father not for once say he was pleased with something Peter did? Nothing would ever be good enough.

"You said that six months ago." His father drew down the corners of his mouth.

Peter scowled. It was true. He had asked several times if he could take the exam. "You are not ready yet," Master Nowak had told him again and again.

That evening Peter made no other attempt to get his father to talk. Finally, he put down his spoon. "Shall I clear the table?"

"Yes," his father grunted, pushing away his bowl and the breadbasket. "Remember, tomorrow we go to the cemetery."

"Yes, Father." Peter took the remnants of their meal to the scullery and went up to the room he used to share with Lorenz.

A shelf in the corner held a few books about seafarers and explorers Lorenz had read over and over again. Between them, acting as a bookstand, was a wooden ship model. He had made that model himself, carving for hours, meticulously gluing together the masts and attaching tiny bits of scavenged lace for the sails. "That's the *Katten*, a Danish yacht," he had told Peter. "It was well named, fast and nimble just like a cat. I wish I could have sailed on it."

The *Katten* had been used in expeditions by King Christian IV to seek out the lost Norse settlements of Greenland. Lorenz's eyes had sparkled when he talked about those ventures to distant lands. Lorenz had yearned for exploration of unknown shores and dreamed of searching for silver and gold ore, supposedly found in Greenland during the first expedition. Lorenz had planned to serve on one of his father's ships. But then he was recruited to serve in the Swedish army and his dreams of glory came to a bitter end when he drowned in a shallow stream. Perhaps it was just as well that Father had never realized his beloved son had had little intention of settling down to become a respected shipping merchant.

Peter sat down on his bed. He missed Lorenz every single day.

Then, he remembered his find. He took out the two lumps. With his nails, he removed as much of the encrusted surface as he could.

The smaller one was lighter in color. Peter dried it off and held it up against the candle. It was shapeless, unpolished, and rough, but it glowed.

He picked up the other one. Again, he thought of a bird with folded wings. It was almost as long as the base of his thumb to his index finger. He traced its contours and then closed his hand, gripping it tightly. It was special. He had never felt that way about a piece of amber.

It had been a long day. He pulled off his boots, blew out the candle, and stuck his find under the pillow. Although he was tired, sleep eluded him for a long time.

❦ 4 ❦

STRANGER IN A BARN

IT SMELLS OF COW DUNG AND ROTTED HAY, AND IT IS PITCH
dark.

Peter stretches out his hand uncertainly and winces. He has
stubbed his fingers on a wall of rough bricks. A gust of wind
wraps itself around a chimney, whistling through the flue. A
shutter blows open. Light from the moon picks out the low
enclosures of sheep pens.

Peter takes a tentative step forward when a soft snuffling
sound freezes him in his tracks. He is not alone. When he peers
over the low wooden barrier next to him, he makes out several
shapes, rolled up inside a stall. Another is on the ground in the
passageway, leaning against a hay bale and covered by a blanket,
with a long slender foot sticking out. The sleeper stirs restlessly
and the blanket slips down, revealing an odd-looking men's shirt
and a woolen cap pulled down over the ears. Something rustles
in the scattered hay next to the sleeper. A long snout emerges,
topped by a slightly domed head covered with silky grey fuzz
and slanted eyes blinking at him.

Peter moves backward and trips on the tines of a pitchfork.
It falls over, clattering loudly in the dark. The beast rises up on
long legs, bits of hay clinging to his fur, his body tensed as if

ready to jump. Then, a tremor goes through the entire body. The creature lifts its long nose and sneezes violently.

The sleeper sits up, dislodging the blanket, eyes distended in fear. It is the same young man whom Peter has seen in the other dream.

"I do not mean any harm." Peter raises his hands. "I am sorry I woke you." He hears his own voice as if from far away and it sounds tinny. Then everything fades into darkness.

ALL HALLOWS' EVE

When Peter woke up, he was clutching the large amber piece in his right hand. He rubbed his eyes. He had slept all through the morning.

"Peter, hurry up," his father shouted from the hallway.

"I am coming." Quickly he put his hand under the pillow, found the smaller piece of amber, and stuffed both in his pocket. He ran his hands through his hair and pulled on his shoes.

Clare came out of the kitchen, drying her hands on her apron. Swiftly she brushed her hands over his jerkin and straightened out the collar of his shirt. Stepping back, she slipped a slice of bread into his hand.

Peter glanced at her gratefully. "How's Effie doing?"

"Quiet right now," Clare said. "When are you coming back?"

"I do not know. Soon." Peter looked down. All he had thought about this morning was to get away from the house and back to the workshop. It was not as if he could help his sister. "I will try. It depends on Master Nowak."

His father was wiping the tops of his boots with a cloth. He had put on his best coat and had even trimmed his hair.

It always happened like that. Jenrich Glienke might be lost in gloom for days, but when called upon, he resurfaced, neatly dressed, stern, and disciplined. This was a formal occasion, and he would honor it.

"Clare, where is the basket?"

"Outside where it is cool. I wanted the flowers to stay fresh."

"Fine, fine," his father said impatiently. He pulled open the front door, grabbed the basket standing on the steps, and handed it to Peter. "Here, you carry it."

This was the first All Hallows' Eve since his mother's death. Peter hadn't visited the cemetery for a long time. He knew his father went every week after church. So many people had died in the last years that the church had given permission for a new cemetery on the hill above the old one.

As they walked uphill, they were joined by others carrying baskets with plants, wreaths, and bunches of flowers. At the cemetery, people were busy scrubbing gravestones and raking the soil around the graves. Henrietta Glienke's resting place was still just a bare mound with a wooden cross at the head.

"When will we get a stone for her grave?" Peter asked.

"It is not something I can afford right now," his father said. "Maybe next year."

Peter pressed his lips together. How much could a stone cost? How could his father be so stingy? Every year, his father became more reluctant to give Peter money for even the basics, and Peter hated having to ask. At least, Cune and Anne did not tease him about his worn tunic. Peter silently promised himself the gravestone would be one of the first things to take care of as soon as he was a journeyman and had some income.

His father opened the basket and pulled out a trowel and several little pots of white and yellow chrysanthemums. Clare had also created a bouquet of purple and blue asters from the yard, tied together with reed grass.

"Do you need help?" Peter asked reluctantly.

"No," his father grunted as he began to push away the soil and stick the plants into the hollows.

Peter wandered around. Everywhere people raked, scrubbed,

and planted. Many of the mounds were bare, like skin rubbed raw. Every single year since he was born, he had watched people from his town, silent and clad in dark clothes, hovering over row upon row of new graves. His father insisted there had been at least twice as many people living in Stolpmünde before the war started. Peter found that hard to believe. Still, at times, it seemed there were more new graves than children being born in the town.

The last time Lorenz had been at home, his voice had been flat and dull as Peter had never heard it before. "It is not like anything you can imagine," he told Peter at night when they sat in their beds in the darkened room. "People just die along the road, and the soldiers march past without looking. I have seen bodies of horses in the field, bloated and covered with flies. At least in the winter, they will be buried under the snow."

Sometimes Peter was afraid all he would remember of Lorenz was this—images that made his stomach churn.

Meanwhile, until last night, the war had never entered his dreams. Of course, during his waking hours, it was unavoidable. Its traces were everywhere he looked, in the sad, strained faces of the people around him, the damaged buildings and ravaged landscape, and the absence of so many. But it had started long before he was born. It was a part of life. That was the way it was. There was nothing he could do about it. So why did he have those odd dreams? About those people walking along the road, just like the throngs of refugees who came through Stolpmünde? What about that girl hiding in a barn? It was unsettling.

"Peter," his father shouted. "Come and stand with me while I say a prayer."

Reluctantly, Peter joined him and stood with a bent head in front of the grave, his eyes on the chrysanthemums. His father had planted them too deeply in the soil; they looked as if they were about to drown. The bouquet of asters had begun to wilt despite Clare's care of them.

"Our Father, who art in heaven," his father began to recite

the Lord's Prayer. "Hallowed be Thy name, Thy kingdom come ..."

Peter forced himself to chime in, although a malicious spirit inside his head shouted out some of the popular sayings and rhymes people wrote on town walls, drowning out his father's voice.

"War feeds on itself."

"Fresh, undaunted, spirited, and brave, the sharp saber is my field, loot the aim of my plow; that's how I will make plenty of money."

"The devil may get the one who is merciful, the one who does not kill, the one who does not take all, the one who does not curse or drink, the one who prays, the one who is the most pious, the one who goes to church, the one who gives to charity."

The devil would get them all, Peter thought grimly.

His voice blended with his father's as they reached the last line. "Forever and ever, Amen."

His father picked up the basket. "I am tired. I am not going to the bonfire, Peter. You go ahead. Will you come home before you return to your master?"

"No, Father, Master Nowak expects me."

This was the first time Peter was going to the bonfire by himself. He was relieved he would not have to worry about his father's disapproval if he had a good time. Of course, it wasn't a proper bonfire. His father had told him of the ones in his childhood where there was plenty of wood available. Nowadays, people just collected piles of twigs, pinecones, and small branches.

He ran down the hill toward the field near the edge of town. He could smell the smoke from the fire. Then he heard voices and laughter ahead of him and slowed down.

In a copse of oak trees next to the field path, two apprentices stood around a tree trunk on which perched a young woman, her ample skirts spread out around her. It was Marthe Neuhof. Everything about her was large—tall, with an ample build, a thick golden braid wrapped around her head, enormous blue eyes, and full lips. She had draped a dark green shawl loosely around her shoulders so one could see the gold-embroidered brocade vest and the delicate lace around her neck and her wrists.

The apprentices were older than Peter, but he knew them both. Thomas, an apprentice mason, had been friends with Lorenz. Tall, with a shock of blond hair and broad shoulders, he exuded the kind of confidence Peter could only dream of.

Lars Steiner, another apprentice mason, hovered behind Marthe with his arms folded, frowning at Thomas and pushing out his lower lip. His limp, greasy brown hair reached below his collar, only partially disguising his thick neck. A big heavy boy with a lumbering gait, he frequently barreled into Peter, knocking him over. "Oops," he would say, "I did not see you there." Peter avoided him as much as he could.

Marthe held a bouquet of light blue fall asters in her hands. She pulled off the petals from one of the flower heads, flicked them into Thomas's face, and laughed.

Her father, the mayor of Stolpmünde, owned one of the most imposing Patrician buildings at the edge of the town square as well as some other buildings. He also held shares in the weekly publication and had interests in a growing trade in book printing. Rumor had it that he sold armor to the Swedes as well as the Imperialists.

"Mayor Neuhof has got it made," Master Kruse from the brewers' guild once said in Peter's hearing. "He might as well put up a sign, 'battle-to-grave services rendered'. First, he sells you the armor and then, if you are lucky, you get a death notice in the *Stolp Observer*."

Peter cared little about any of that. The mayor's wealth did not interest him. The mayor's daughter, however, was another matter. Lately, whenever Peter saw her, he forgot everything else. He could not stop watching her when she walked through town, swinging her skirt. He strained to hear her low chuckle when she raised one of her perfect little round hands to pat one of her admirers on the sleeve just like one might pat a little lapdog.

Peter straightened his back and held his head high, trying to appear relaxed and unconcerned as he passed the three young people. In truth, he knew he had no chance with her—she could have her pick from among the finest young men in the town. She wouldn't have time for someone like himself.

"I am tired of all of you." Marthe stood up, scattering petals in the air and brushing her skirts. "I am going for a walk." With a few quick steps, she caught up with Peter as he was making his way down the path.

"How are you, Peter?"

He almost stumbled into a cluster of thistles next to the path in his surprise and felt his cheeks go red as he turned around to face her. Now that he had her attention, he could not get a word out.

"What, cat got your tongue?" Marthe raised her eyebrows.

"Very well, thank you." Peter felt like kicking himself for his stiff response. Lorenz would have made her smile with a comment about the flowers or the sunshine that brought out the shimmer of her hair.

"You must miss your brother."

"You knew Lorenz?" Peter was taken aback. It was as if she had read his mind.

"Well, yes. A bit." Marthe was twisting and untwisting her scarf and then tossed it back over her shoulder.

Of course, Lorenz and Marthe had known each other. Why was he surprised? Lorenz had been popular with all the girls. Marthe was not interested in Peter at all. She just wanted to talk about his brother. Peter kept his eyes on the path, stepping around muddy hollows and ruts.

"You like the bonfire?" Marthe asked after a few moments of silence.

"Yes, sure."

"Well, I do not." Marthe twirled the bouquet of asters. "It is dusty and smoky, my hands get sticky from the roasted apples, and I hate chestnuts."

Peter almost laughed at this outburst. "So, why are you going?"

"My father wants me to be there," Marthe said glumly. "He goes on and on about how important it is the public sees us at events like this."

Peter glanced at her from the side. She sounded sulky, like a little girl. It made her seem less intimidating.

They had reached the field where the bonfire was. People milled about, and young boys carried branches and baskets with twigs toward the fire. Others sat on blankets nearby. He could see Master Nowak with his daughter Anne, and Cune, the other apprentice, next to him. Anne raised her arm as if to wave at Peter but then turned away, absorbed with something in her basket.

"I wish it were dark. Everything is so much prettier in the light of a full moon. I love listening to the waves at night." Marthe smiled at him.

Peter did not know what to say, confronted by her shining eyes and the dimples on her cheeks as she smiled. Something in her expression made him think of a cat. He shrugged, trying to cover his embarrassment.

Marthe reached out and stuck one of the asters into the top buttonhole of his vest. She was close enough for her scent to envelop him like a cloud.

His cheeks burned. "I am supposed to join my master," he mumbled and quickly walked on to where he had seen Master Nowak.

"Peter, come and sit with us." Cune's shirt was buttoned wrong, and his socks had slipped down. He had a smudge on his cheek. He was just a year younger than Peter, but sometimes Peter felt as if they were apart by many years.

"Nice of you to join us." Anne, sitting on a blanket, scowled at Peter. As usual, she had braided her long blond hair and twisted the braids into a bun at the nape of her neck. "Pretty flower you got there."

There was an edge in her voice Peter hadn't heard from her before.

"This?" He fumbled at the aster in his buttonhole and pretended to toss it into the grass before quickly sticking it into his pocket. "It is nothing, just a joke."

"Are you going to just loom over us?" Cune looked up. He was holding an apple impaled on a long stick over the flames, turning it slowly so that it got roasted on all sides. "You cannot expect us to do all the work."

"Really, sit down," Anne said, no longer with that odd tense note in her voice. "We brought enough cider and bread to feed an army, not to mention beer from Father's brewery." She held out a piece of bread with a slab of cheese.

"Thank you," Peter said, crouching next to her and taking the bread. For a moment, he was content. Children roasted apples and fished for chestnuts in the ashes amidst squealing and laughter and gruff commands from parents to pay attention.

"Did you just come from the cemetery?" Anne asked. "We were there earlier, but Father wanted us to come here. He said he has had enough of mourning to last a lifetime."

"I suppose we all have." Peter munched on his bread. He did not feel like talking. All his misery came flooding back as he thought of his sister. He never thought one could feel disgust, pity, and embarrassment all at the same time. Mostly he felt ashamed, ashamed for leaving her alone, for not having been there to protect her, ashamed for laughing at her. What if anyone found out what had happened? People would laugh. People would shun his family if she had a child.

"What is wrong?" Anne asked. "You look so troubled."

Peter blinked and shook his head. "There is nothing wrong. I am just listening to that conversation over there." He pointed toward Master Nowak, sitting on the ground with other guild members.

"I am getting so tired of the war," Master Hegemann, one of the oldest members of the amber guild, said in a low voice. Both his sons were soldiers in the Swedish army, and everyone knew how disappointed he was neither of them had followed in their father's footsteps. Daily, he feared to hear news of their death.

"It is bad for trade, bad for the guilds, bad for everyone." Master Nowak rolled a chestnut in his hands as he gazed moodily at the fire. "Never mind all the poor and displaced people flooding into Stolp."

"I quit caring whether it is the Swedes or the Imperialists who will win," Master Sturm, an elder in the tailor guild, said. "Our houses get burned down, and our girls get raped either way." It seemed as if his craft did not extend to care for his own clothes. His coat was bedraggled and threadbare.

Peter shifted, moving away from the smoke drifting into his eyes. That must have been what happened to Effie. Someone from out of town.

"To be sure, the Hanse will never recover or regain its former glory," a town elder said.

Once they started to talk about the Hanse, it was going to get boring, Peter thought. He was tired of hearing about this trade association. Whatever they did would hardly make a difference in his life. Then a name caught his ear.

"It almost makes you wish for another Stoertebeker to shake things up, what with the Swedes and the Danes dominating shipping and trade." Master Gerke, one of the younger amber guild members, sometimes reminded Peter of Lorenz. They had the same tendency to be disrespectful and to question everything.

Peter knew all about Klaus Stoertebeker, the famous pirate of the 14th century. In fact, he had read many stories about his exploits and the ship on which Stoertebeker sailed all over the Baltic. Of course, it hadn't ended well. Stoertebeker was eventually caught and executed. However, even his death had become part of the legend. His last plea to the mayor of Hamburg was to spare as many of his companions as he could walk past while already headless. The mayor granted his request. The execution proceeded, and to everyone's amazement, Stoertebeker's headless body arose and walked past eleven of his men before the executioner tripped him with an outstretched foot. The eleven men were executed along with the others.

"Well, it is not as if Stoertebeker had been a friend of the Hanse. I doubt a firebrand like him would do us any good." Master Nowak shook his head. "We need peace more than anything. The war has been going on for twenty-six years now."

"Peace or no peace, the best days of the Hanse are over," Master Gerke growled. "And I am afraid the same holds true for the guilds."

"I could cry when I think of our harbor—if it continues to silt up as it has, soon ships will not risk pulling in for fear of getting stuck on sandbars in the shallow waters," one of the merchants said.

"At least the war has not reached the areas east of Stolp, so we can use the overland route from Königsberg for our shipments. But you are right. It is a ridiculous state of affairs."

Peter started tossing twigs into the fire. War was all he had ever known. He got tired of the incessant complaints. Anyway, the older amber guild members had no reason to complain. They got their yearly supply of amber and did well financially. They were among those least affected by the ravages of the war.

"I am getting tired of Königsberg getting the lion's share of the amber." Master Gerke stuffed his pipe with impatient movements.

"Well, it is better than the monopoly the towns of Brügge and Lübeck had until the beginning of the century." Again, Master Nowak was the voice of reason. "At least we do not have to contend with the Order anymore or with the Jaskis."

The other masters sitting near the fire continued to argue while Master Nowak focused on peeling the blackened skin of the chestnuts he fished out of the ashes.

"Hah! From the fire into the frying pan. Danzig merchants or Duke Frederick William—what difference does it make? We are just as powerless as we were before. Duke Frederick William is hardly an improvement."

"I am not sure how he managed to get out of the contract with the Jaskis. He must have paid a lot of money. He is certainly not wasting any time in taking control."

"Too true. Soon, the duke will have every man, woman, and infant swear on their mother's soul not to even so much as look at the ocean, never mind setting foot on the beach. It is bad enough that we have to listen to the dreary proclamation every year."

"If you keep talking like that, you will end up like another Wullenwever, inciting a revolution."

Lorenz had told Peter about the revolt against the patrician regime in Lübeck in 1533, led by Jürgen Wullenwever, one-time mayor of the city. The war with Denmark ended that rebellion, and Wullenwever was put to the sword as well as drawn and quartered on the wheel for his pains. Peter admired Wullenwever, but it was so long ago, and besides, he could not see how a rebellion would help now.

Peter stopped listening. His thoughts circled back to Marthe. He wanted to bask in the recollection of her interest in him, but something about the encounter made him uncomfortable. Then he dismissed that thought. He just wished she had not mentioned Lorenz.

"Hey, be careful!" Peter jumped up and grabbed a little boy who had gotten too close to the fire.

"I want to get my chestnuts." The boy tried to wriggle free from Peter's hold. "Let me go."

"Here, this is how you do it." Peter grabbed a long branch and started poking at the glowing embers. Several blackened chestnuts rolled free. Peter scooped them up and placed them in the boy's basket. "Wait a bit. They are still too hot to peel."

"Thank you." The boy rubbed his hand over his face, leaving it smudged. Then he grabbed his basket and walked away.

Peter smiled as he speared an apple and held it over the embers, turning it slowly until the skin began to burst. He pulled it back and blew on it energetically. After a few moments, he risked a small bite. His mouth was flooded with the sweet hot juice of the apple.

"I saw your uncle. He is talking to some town elders over there," Anne said, pointing with a small knife toward a group of men sitting at a distance from the bonfire. "Why isn't your father here, and how is Effie? I thought your father would bring her to the bonfire." She used the knife to peel the sooty skin of a chestnut, revealing the white flesh inside. "Ah, this is always the best," she said, nibbling on it daintily like a cat.

Peter watched her slender hands flicking back and forth. He finished his apple and tossed the core into the fire where it vanished with a hiss.

"Father left her with Clare." He hesitated, reluctant to say anything. But this was Anne, after all. She knew everything, and he trusted her. "Something happened to her. She is doing all that rocking again."

"Poor Effie," Anne said, her eyes wide and anxious. "Did someone hurt her?"

"I do not know." Peter shifted and pretended to be absorbed by the flames. He could not bring himself to tell Anne that Effie had been raped. It was too difficult to talk about.

"I will visit her soon. I will take Inga. It might cheer her up." Inga was Anne's little sister. Inga and Effie liked to sit together on the floor for hours with balls of yarn, rolling and unrolling them.

"Oops." A large boot kicked over the basket filled with chestnuts next to Peter. "Really, you should know better than to put the basket right where people are walking. I hear stupidity runs in the family."

Peter looked up to find Lars looming over him and hastily got to his feet. Clenching his fists, he glowered at his tormentor.

"Your sister is a bit soft in the head." Lars grinned, twirling his index finger against his forehead suggestively. "What about you? Want me to test it?" He made a sweeping movement as if trying to knock on Peter's head.

"Do not dare say anything about my sister," Peter shouted as he charged.

Lars was taller by a head, but Peter went straight for his stomach, bending down and barreling into him with his head. It was like charging into a flour sack.

"Oomph," Lars grunted and fell backward.

Peter landed on top of him. "Do not"—he slapped him in the face—"speak"—another slap—"about my sister"—*slap*—"ever again."

"Stop this immediately," Master Nowak growled. He pulled Peter up. "And you, young man, get up," he said to Lars. "I saw everything. Be gone."

With a grimace at Peter and mouthing the word "later," Lars sauntered off.

"You have no business getting into a fight with this young hoodlum." Master Nowak glared at Peter. "Why do you let him goad you into reacting?"

"Sorry, Master Nowak." Peter glanced down, distracted by an acrid smell. It came from his shoe. He must have stepped in the fire and singed the sole. Angrily, he stamped his foot on the ground as if he could undo the damage. Maybe the cobbler could mend it. The shoes had already been resoled more times than he cared to count. "I think I will head back to the house, Master Nowak."

Peter walked quickly as he made his way down the hill. He was still angry. Lars had deserved every slap. Then, he felt ashamed. Not so long ago, he had run around with Lars and his friends Gregor and Urban, and had joined in when they made fun of Effie.

A few months before he joined the army, Lorenz had come upon Peter and his friends sitting on a stone wall and aiming rotten apples at Effie as she walked past.

"Do not ever let me catch you treating your sister like that," Lorenz hissed as he dragged Peter home. "She cannot fight for herself."

Now, with the memory of Lorenz's voice ringing in his ears, unsettled and restless, Peter continued on the road into town.

"Peter, wait."

He turned around. Uncle Frantz was trying to catch up with him.

"I guess your father decided against joining us."

"He said he was tired." Peter shrugged.

"He should get out more." Uncle Frantz sighed. "But listen, I wanted to talk to you. Could you walk back with me before you return to Master Nowak's house?"

Peter nodded and followed his uncle toward his house, which was located south of the harbor on the western bank of the river Stolpe.

"It is time to show you something," Uncle Frantz said portentously. "Of course, your father knows about this, and so did Lorenz. I need not tell you it must stay that way. Come."

Uncle Frantz led Peter around the house and toward the riverbank, glancing up and down the gently flowing stream. There was not a boat in sight. "You are so much like your brother," he said, putting an arm around Peter's shoulders. "Lorenz never talked about this to anyone else. I could always rely on him."

That was a first. Nobody had ever told Peter he and his brother were alike in anything. "Lorenz did not tell me anything about whatever it is you want me to see."

"No, I knew I could trust him. It has become a bit of a rite of passage. My father told me about it when I was about your age."

Intrigued, Peter followed his uncle as he made his way

through the shrubbery and climbed down onto a small sandy area.

"Mind the brambles." Uncle Frantz led him around a clump of dense shrubs. They had been planted in such a way as to obscure a path curving around the thicket up to a large wooden door. The door, set into the hill, was framed by fieldstones. Vines and brambles reached down from the top like a mop of hair. Carefully, his uncle shifted some branches out of the way. "I never trim these; they help to hide the entrance. Even if you steer your boat directly into that little bay, all you can see from the river are the shrubs." He pushed the door open with barely a squeal. "I keep the hinges well-oiled at all times."

Peter looked around in amazement. The wide opening led to a cavernous space in the front and several other chambers further back. It was cold and clammy.

"What is this place?"

"It is an ice cellar. At least it started out that way. My father began enlarging it, and I added more chambers in the back. One chamber I still use as an ice cellar. I just added more ice. It should keep things cool through the summer months. Now, I mostly use it to hide things. This has been a lifesaver during all the bad years. It is the only way I could keep going."

"You could put a fishing boat in here." Gazing at the empty space, Peter shivered. He felt disoriented as if he had seen something inexplicable in the half-light. Then he shook himself and tried to focus on his uncle's voice.

"You are right. I have done that a few times. That is why I widened the opening. Lorenz suggested this. Fishing boats can come and unload directly from the river, and the ice cellar can be used for storage—if this damn war ever ends."

"What is this?" Peter pointed at a hole with a bit of metal grating over it.

"That was another of Lorenz's ideas. He thought it would be good to create drainage for those times when the river floods."

On his way across town, Peter pondered what he had seen,

flattered by his uncle's trust and fascinated by this glimpse of a parallel life. He had always thought of his uncle as kind and reliable, but hardly exciting, much less someone with secrets like hidden storage cellars.

Peter was tired by the time he reached Master Nowak's house. It smelled stuffy inside the little attic room, which he shared with Cune, and he had to duck his head to avoid hitting the beams as he crawled into his bed.

Something niggled at his thoughts—Marthe's scent. Peter felt his cheeks grow hot at the memory of her sticking the aster into his buttonhole. He tried to picture himself wandering around town with Marthe. He grinned, remembering Thomas's and Lars's annoyed faces when she had walked off with him.

Suddenly he sat up, throwing off his blanket. That scent—that was what he had noticed in the woods near the beach. Roses and something spicy. Thoughts raced through his head. Had she been at the beach? Had she seen him? No, it was not possible. A wealthy and protected young woman like Marthe would not be at the beach in the dark. It seemed unlikely. Whoever it was hadn't been alone.

All his tiredness was gone. Restlessly, he got up and straightened out his clothes, thrown on the floor in a careless heap earlier. He took the amber from his satchel. He had to find a hiding place. There was a blanket chest, but that was hardly safe. Sometimes, Mistress Nowak opened it. Stuffing them under the mattress was not going to work. That's where Cune hid his sweets and other food he brought with him after visits to his family, and Peter's mattress would be the first place Cune would search if he became suspicious. Peter looked around the small room. No place seemed safe. Beginning to yawn, he put the amber pieces under his pillow and pulled the blanket over himself. He would think of a better place tomorrow.

❦ 6 ❧

GIRL WITHOUT A NAME

PETER SHIVERS. HIS BED IS GONE, AND HE IS STANDING IN a strange room.

Light comes through a small opening. The air feels cold and clammy. He rubs his eyes as he takes in his surroundings. A bed stands at a slant in the middle of the room, bare, with its mattress slashed open like a gaping wound. As his eyes adjust, he can see a chest of drawers, two of the drawers pulled out, the top one hanging crookedly in its tracks, its contents spilled onto the floor. A cast-iron stove is covered in dust, and a chipped white enamel pitcher and bowl have been upended and tossed onto the floor.

On a big chair in the corner, someone is curled up underneath a green and red-checkered woolen covering.

On the floor close to the chair sits the same beast Peter remembers from the previous dream, its head raised and growling softly. The fluffy hair around its ears, combined with its impossibly long slightly curved snout, gives it a curiously bird-like appearance, a grey raptor ready to pounce on its prey.

The sleeper is awake, staring at him and clutching the blanket with one hand, the other hidden in its folds.

"You are a girl," Peter exclaims as he takes in the sleeper's face and the long thick braid resting on top of the blanket. His voice sounds muffled as if he is talking through thick cloudbanks.

The girl moves her arm and pulls out an odd-looking pistol from beneath her leg. She points it directly at him, scowling furiously.

Peter gulps and takes a step backward. "I am not going to hurt you."

"Don't come any closer." Her voice is scratchy as if she has not spoken in a while. "I'll shoot, I promise you that." Then she adds with a note of puzzlement, "Who are you? You don't sound Russian."

"Russian? Are the Russians fighting against the Swedes?"

"Are you daft?" She still holds on to the pistol. "Where are you from? Are you a refugee?"

"I live in Stolpmünde."

"Stolpmünde? Why are you here? Shouldn't you be going west?"

"What is 'here'? And what do you mean going west?"

"Elbing, or at least somewhere nearby. I lost track."

"We have not seen any refugees for a while," Peter says slowly, shaking his head. None of this makes any sense. Elbing— that is almost halfway to Königsberg. "With Denmark out of the war, it has been quieter." This strange girl must be confused. "Will you stop pointing that pistol at me?"

"Denmark?" She frowns at him. "What are you talking about? Denmark is occupied, and they aren't fighting at all. And Swedes? Pistol? Are you serious? And why are you wearing such strange clothes?"

"What do you mean? And what about Russians?"

"I saw you the other day. You were in a ditch, watching me," the girl says accusingly. "And last night, I dreamed of you. Wait." Her voice grows faint. "Come back."

7

PATERNOSTERMAKERS

PETER SHOOK HIS HEAD AS IF TO CLEAR THE FOG FROM HIS mind, but only ended up banging it against a wall. He blinked and moved his hands, touching a familiar mattress stuffed with straw and a woolen blanket. He was in his bed, Cune snoring gently in the bed next to him.

After that, he had a hard time getting back to sleep. When he woke up in the morning, he felt groggy. Confused, he gazed at the blues and reds of his blanket, the solid brown of his shoes, the dark floor planks, and the familiar walls, scuffed and gone yellow-grey from the candlelight. He lifted his hands and scrutinized them as if he had never seen them before, the pink tones under the nails, the blue veins on the inside of his wrist standing out, the white edges of his nails. Everything was blurred. In his mind, he was still in the flat black and white world of his dream. This was the third time it had happened.

"Are you falling asleep again?" Cune stuck his head in the door. "Come on, breakfast is on the table."

Hurriedly, Peter pulled on his clothes and brushed his hair before making his way downstairs.

In the kitchen, Mistress Ottilie Nowak was pulling a loaf of bread out of the oven and placing large mugs of ale on the table. Small and slightly built, she rarely seemed tired.

Sometimes Peter would watch the fine lines around her mouth and remember that her two older sons had died a few years ago in a battle near Leipzig, fighting in the Swedish army. Her youngest child had died soon after birth. But usually Peter did not think about that. She was just the mistress, always ready with a warm meal and a comforting smile.

"Anne," Mistress Nowak shouted. "Would you get the butter out of the pantry?" Her daughter complied with her usual morning grumpy expression.

"Oops." Inga giggled. Anne's little sister was playing with her spoon and some of the porridge from her bowl had splattered onto the table. Master Nowak had built a highchair for her so she could sit with everyone else.

"Stop that." With deft motions, Mistress Nowak tied a towel around her little daughter's chest and tucked it into the collar.

"Good morning." Master Nowak walked in the door, returning from buying the paper. He never missed a single issue and insisted the apprentices read some of it. "You should be proud we have our own weekly paper," he reminded them when they grumbled. "I expect my apprentices to be informed."

Cune obediently stuttered his way through the main stories, sometimes asking Peter to help him. "He will ask us about it, Peter."

Impatiently, Peter scanned the pages. "It is always the same —another battle, thousands killed, this time around the Swedes beat back the Imperial forces. It makes no difference. The war will just keep going until there is no one left alive to fight." Then he relented and helped Cune decipher some of the words.

After eating their bread, Peter, Cune, and Anne started their day in the workshop. Master Nowak was working on his accounts that morning. Peter was relieved to be able to work for a few hours without his stern eyes on everything he did.

Peter drew the master's attention almost every day. He

worked too fast. His work was chipped or cracked. It needed more polish or hadn't been soaked sufficiently. The holes were drilled off-center, or the rosary beads were not evenly sized. Master Nowak was never satisfied. He would never think Peter was ready for the exam.

Just yesterday, Peter had failed to soak a piece of amber sufficiently, so it cracked while he worked on it. He also managed to break off a chip on another one just because he was distracted. His thoughts wandered as he remembered walking past Marthe and two other girls on the market square whispering to each other. Marthe caught his eye and winked. He felt his face grow hot. They were talking about him, he knew it.

Peter's file and other tools tumbled to the floor with a clatter. He winced, not realizing he had been leaning against the narrow workbench until it had tipped to the side. He bent down and retrieved the amber he had been working on, the mouthpiece of a pipe, which had rolled under his chair. Dismayed, he saw there was a new chip along its edge.

Master Nowak came over. "You were not paying attention again," he said mildly, taking the piece from Peter's hand and looking at it carefully. "You are in luck. The chip is not too large; you can sand it down and polish it."

Peter bent over his work, his cheeks hot. Master Nowak never raised his voice in the workshop. Sometimes Peter wished he did. It would be easier to bear than having to listen to his quiet voice, tinged with disappointment. Anne and Cune did not glance his way, seemingly absorbed by their work.

Today, Anne quietly headed to her work area, as usual neatly organized, clean, and swept free of all debris, where she picked up a small basket of beads that needed to be polished. Her braid was pinned back, so it did not interfere with her work.

Cune set to work drilling holes into beads, and Peter began the tricky process of filing away the outer layers of small rough pieces of amber.

Anne was the best of the three apprentices even though she

had started a year later. Peter and Cune knew that perfectly well. She picked up new skills with ease. Peter thought her father should be proud of her, but instead, he criticized her every move. Anne never appeared to mind. Cheerfully flinging back her braids, she absorbed everything he said to her and carried on. Eagerly, she badgered her father for answers for everything.

Did people in the east really dig up amber from mines in the ground? How could amber be used to make eyeglasses? How old was it? Hundreds of years? Thousands of years? What was the biggest piece of amber he had ever seen?

Master Nowak was reluctant when it came to trying new methods, but because of Anne's questions, he had begun to teach them how to fit different colored slivers together like a mosaic or inlay and how to carve more complicated shapes without cracking the amber.

Cune worked steadily and calmly. He always finished the work Master Nowak gave him, and he was patient. Master Nowak praised his diligence and rarely found fault with his work. He would be the first to be allowed to take the exam.

Cune hummed while he drilled holes into beads. Several polished beads lay on the low table in front of his workbench. It had taken hours to get to this point. First, the raw nuggets had to get soaked so they would not crack during the work. The outer layer had to be filed away, turning the pieces into perfect rounds. Then came the tedious task of smoothing them with a pumice stone, rubbing them down with shavings. Finally, they had to be polished with slaked lime, also called whiting, or Tripoli, a porous rock. The final step was to drill a hole into each bead for the string.

"Do you not get tired of making these beads?" Peter stretched his back, stiff from leaning over the workbench. His thoughts confused, they traveled somewhere along torn-up fields to a girl in long trousers, with her thick hair hidden under a cap.

Cune shook his head and continued drilling.

Peter kept thinking about what he had seen in his dream. It

had felt real and immediate, even though everything had appeared flat—like pictures pressed between pages of a book— and devoid of colors. Now, glancing at the pile of amber beads, butter yellow and dark golden, the tools in front of him, the brown floorboards, and Cune's carrot-colored hair and light blue eyes, Peter was overcome by a sense of disorientation. His own world had become strange to him.

"It is not as if we use these beads ourselves," he said peevishly. The biggest market for the rosary beads was in the south. "For all you know, Imperial soldiers will be praying with these rosary beads."

Peter had always hated the name for amber workers —*Paternostermakers*. Catholics referred to single beads on a rosary as a *Paternoster*. The beads were used for counting the prayers. Some of the rosaries made in Master Nowak's workshop were more elaborate, including marker beads made of silver in addition to the regular counting bead. Sometimes, these marker beads were fashioned into shapes based on the Passion story: the hammer, the three nails, and the crown of thorns. Terminal beads, larger than regular ones, might be fashioned into a small flask for holy water or a pomander holding scent.

Peter put down his drill and flexed his hands before picking up the next bead. Cune worked steadily, humming softly. Irked by Cune's contentment, Peter started the laborious process of polishing the amber while reciting the *Paternoster* as if it were a marching song. Admittedly, the prayer made for a nice solid rhythm for working.

Pater noster, qui es in cœlis;
sanctificatur nomen tuum;
Adveniat regnum tuum;
fiat voluntas tua,
sicut in cœlo, et in terra.

It always sounded better in Latin than in German. "Our Father, who art in heaven …"

Cune looked up with a puzzled expression on his round face. "You should not be so disrespectful about the Lord's Prayer."

Peter shrugged. Cune was right to chide him, but he did not want to admit this. "I want to do more. I want to create beautiful pieces, not just a bunch of marbles."

"I do not mind this work. At least I know what I have done at the end of the day." Cune picked up a pumice stone and began sanding.

Anne was quiet, working steadily.

Peter glanced at her, so calm and neat. All he could see of her face was the curve of her cheekbone. Suddenly he remembered Effie. What if someone attacked Anne? But she was never alone. Mistress Nowak made sure of that. Effie should never have walked around by herself. Maybe she had done something to provoke someone into attacking her. Then he was ashamed all over again. How could he blame Effie? He shook his head. All this thinking would not do any good.

Trying to focus on his work, Peter breathed in the spicy scents of heated amber and amber dust. Usually, he loved the workshop with its stools and workbenches in front of long narrow tables, with wooden bars above on which they hung strings of finished beads. In front of each workstation was a box of tools, neatly organized. Every evening, Master Nowak ran an experienced eye over the workstations, reprimanding his apprentices when they failed to put their cleaned tools back into their proper places.

Now, Peter was restless and irritated by everything. "I just get so annoyed sometimes," he grumbled. "Remember the other day when Master Nowak told us about his idea to use linseed oil for making amber more transparent?"

"Yes, so?" Cune raised his eyebrows.

"It was brilliant. You would simply soak the amber in heated linseed oil for a little while. That's all. But can we use this? No.

Of course not. The guild hasn't approved it, and they have to approve every little bit of innovation. This is so infuriating."

"I am sure the guild will introduce some of these innovations soon."

"Why should we have to wait for them? Besides, we are stuck with these old tools." Peter waved his drill around in his frustration. "In Paris, they use all sorts of new tools to produce the finest work. And then the guild members are shocked when we can't compete in the markets. That is what they get for obsessing about tradition and protective tariffs."

"Oh, Peter, stop whining," Cune snapped. "Just do your work. Master Nowak will be upset if we do not finish what he gave us for the day."

That night, after he was sure Cune was asleep, Peter got up. He had gone to bed without undressing so that later he would not make any noise searching around for his clothes in the dark. Peter navigated his way to the door, tiptoeing carefully. It made a creaking sound as he pulled it open. He stopped and held his breath, but Cune just sighed and turned over in his bed, pulling the blanket over his ears.

In the hallway, Peter made his way down the stairs to the workroom, located behind the kitchen. He lit a tallow candle, taking care to use one already burned down to a mere stub. Tallow candles were less expensive than beeswax candles but smelly, and he would have to open the window for a while when he was done so the smell could evaporate. Master Nowak would hardly miss a few stubs. Anyway, for now, he just wanted to be able to take a proper look at his find.

He soaked both pieces in warm water and cleaned them thoroughly with a stiff bristle brush until all the grit and sand accumulated over centuries was gone. Then he placed them on the table close to the candlelight.

He sucked in his breath. None of the pieces Master Nowak had let him work with had looked anything like this. Even rough and shapeless, they were beautiful. The smaller one, with a color that promised to be a dark reddish gold once polished, fit just inside the palm of his hands like a robin's egg, warm, almost alive. There was something darker inside its core. Intrigued, he held it up to the candle. It looked like a bubble. He would have to work on it more to see it better. He had heard of inclusions— insects and pockets of air trapped in amber. They were especially valuable.

He put it down to examine the other one. As long and almost as wide as his hand, with an elongated shape, this piece of amber was dark honey-brown with tinges of red. He turned it over and rubbed the long shank sticking out. It reminded him of a crane, with its wings furled, one leg hidden inside the feathers, as if asleep just before setting out for the long journey south.

He weighed the raw amber in his hand, staring at it. He could not give it up. Besides, if he did that now, he would already be in a lot of trouble just for walking on the beach. Of course, he should return the pieces to the sea, but the mere thought of watching them disappear in the waves made him feel a sense of loss. It was not as if he had gone searching for amber. These pieces had literally come to him. They were his.

A creaking sound somewhere in the house startled him out of his absorption. It was getting late. He had to get back to bed. He put away the bowl of water and snuffed out the candle after making sure there were no drops of wax on the worktable. The window hinges squeaked when he pushed it open to let in the cold night air for a few moments and get rid of the scent of candle wax. Then he closed it again and snuck up the stairs in the dark. Back in the attic room, he listened to Cune snoring in his bed and thought of a place to hide the amber. No, he would keep the pieces with him. That was safest. He crept into bed. For a long time, he shivered under the blanket while thinking of what he could create.

8

LIOBA

Peter bumps against a wall. It is dark. Feeling around with his hand, he touches a metal knob. He twists it, and a door opens.

Peter stares at the sight in front of him, faintly illuminated by early morning light from a window. It is a room filled with rows of wooden tables and chairs. Peter's eyes are drawn to a huge picture on the wall. A face with a mustache, shiny black hair combed to one side, and piercing eyes looms over the room. On a big blackboard, he can just make out two lines on top in a scraggly script, the last word missing where someone had started to wipe the board.

Oh, stranger, when you arrive in Sparta, tell of our pride
That here, obeying her behests, we—

"That here, obeying her behests, we died," he completes the line in his mind. He had heard the lines often enough from Lorenz, who had learned them from his tutor. He had recited them to Peter over and over again at night when they sat in their beds and talked. Three hundred Spartans had died there at the battle of Thermopylae, the narrow pass where they made their last stand against tens of thousands of enemies.

Maybe this is a schoolroom, albeit an elaborate one. In the school in Stolpmünde, where Peter and Lorenz learned their letters, there are only benches without tables and a plain lectern for the teacher. Still, this space somehow smells like a schoolroom, stale and musty, evoking bored students waiting for the droning voice of the teacher to come to an end.

Startled by a soft rustling, Peter whips his head around.

The girl from his dreams is sitting on the floor with her back against the wall, wrapped in a ratty-looking blanket. She is awake.

"It's you again." The girl pulls up the blanket. "Are you in my dream, or am I in yours?"

"I honestly do not know," Peter says slowly. "This is not like any dream I have ever had."

"Well, at least you're not a Russian soldier. Anyway, they haven't gotten this far west yet. Are you going to vanish again in mid-sentence?"

"I do not even know how I got here. Why do you talk so strangely?" He could understand her, but it was like listening to someone through a thick blanket. She seemed to swallow many of her words. "Why do you keep talking about Russians? Where is this?"

"Somewhere east of Danzig." The girl frowns at him. "You sound like someone reciting the Luther Bible."

Peter stares at her, bewildered and shaken. The bread from his supper sits in his stomach like a rock. The long-legged beast he remembers from before gets up from behind the desk and stretches.

Peter backs up.

"Don't worry, she won't bite you."

It is the tallest dog he has ever seen—if it is a dog. It comes up to Peter and starts sniffing him vigorously. He can feel its breath. Then it evidently loses interest and lies down again, its legs stretched out in front like those of a crane. The matted fur smells like a sack of dirty woolens, but it is a warm and comforting scent.

"Your dog seems real," Peter says, eyeing the beast nervously.

"So do you—for someone in a dream." The girl studies him. She does not seem afraid any longer. "My name is Lioba. What's yours?"

"Peter."

"Well, Peter, are you going to vanish again, or can we talk a bit? This is actually nice. You are the first person I have talked to in a while." She starts to laugh. "Since you aren't real, it's not as if you are going to hurt me." Then she wipes her face roughly as if irritated.

"You are crying," Peter says.

Lioba's hands are long and slender, but her nails are ragged and dirty.

The dog lifts its head as if in response to her distress and pushes its long nose against her leg.

Uncomfortable with Lioba's evident anguish, Peter tries to distract her. "What sort of dog is that?"

"I think it's a *Borzoi*." Her voice sounds muffled.

"A what?"

"You know—a Russian wolfhound."

"What do you mean, you think? This is not your dog?"

"She has been following me for weeks. You don't have anything to eat, by any chance?" The dark shadows under Lioba's eyes emphasize her broad cheekbones.

"Sorry." Peter thinks of the loaf of bread Mistress Nowak had cut up for supper. Maybe the next time he goes to sleep, he should try to keep a piece of bread in his pocket.

Lioba drops the blanket and gets up. She closes the shutters of the windows and fastens them. She pulls the two panels of black fabric together, plunging the room into total darkness.

"Why are you doing this? I cannot see you."

"Haven't you heard of the blackout?" she scoffs.

Blackout? Bewildered, Peter hears the girl move toward the wall near the door. Suddenly, light streams from a strange lamp. At least, he thinks it is a lamp. Definitely not a candle or an oil lantern. "How did you do that?" he asks.

"Really?" Lioba scowls. "Are you making fun of me?"

"No, of course not. What is that? How did you make it glow?"

"Electricity, stupid! What century are you living in?"

"What do you mean, what century?" How dare this girl call him stupid? Clearly, she was confused. "Everybody knows that. This is the year of our Lord 1644."

Lioba stares at him. Then her lips widen into a grin. "I don't believe this. I am talking to someone in a dream, and he is not even from my own time."

"Your own time?"

"Right. I don't know about the year of our Lord 1644. This sure isn't that. This is 1944. But I would gladly trade with you if I could."

Three hundred years into the future. Peter reaches out to touch the wall next to him. It feels solid. The dog's smell certainly feels real. Nothing else does in this strange, flat, dark grey world. It is as if he is standing outside, looking through the frame of a window.

Lioba frowns, folding her arms across her chest.

There is a roaring in his ears. A door bangs loudly somewhere, and everything goes dark.

❧ 9 ❧

IN THE LAND OF PLENTY

"WHEN DID YOU LAST GO HOME?" ANNE SCRUTINIZED Peter with a slight frown. "You should check on Effie."

"I am going today." Peter did not meet her eyes. He had avoided going for the last few weeks. It was not as if there was anything he could do for Effie, and he dreaded watching his father crumble his bread into his soup in morose silence. With a sigh, Peter cleaned up his workstation and left Master Nowak's house.

Passing across a small square, he noticed several apprentices at the corner where they liked to meet when they were done with their work. They were smoking. He liked Urban and Gregor. Lars was there as well and another apprentice whom Peter did not know.

I could stay with them for a while. Peter walked toward the group.

Urban and Gregor glanced at him and then turned away as if they had not seen him.

Shocked, Peter watched them pass the pipe around. He could hear them chuckle. He bit his lip. His shoulders hunched, he walked on.

"That sister ..." Peter heard one of them. Another laughed.

"Yeah, a bit free with her favors, I hear."

"Just a slut."

"And dimwitted to boot."

"What did you say?" Peter swung around, clenching his fists.

Gregor and Urban avoided meeting his eyes. The other two smirked at him.

"Oh, nothing," Lars said. "We did not say anything."

Out of the corner of his eye, Peter noticed the town guard in front of the bakery. It would be bad if he were caught brawling. Besides, there were four of them. Sticking his hands in his pockets, he went on.

They were gossiping about his sister. How did that happen? How could anybody know what had happened to Effie? And he had thought they were his friends. Of course, not Lars, but the others?

Shaken and distracted, he continued on his way.

"Peter, where are you off to?"

Startled, he turned to see Marthe's beaming face, her dark blue velvet cap framing her glowing cheeks. Peter caught a whiff of her scent.

"Hello, Marthe." Again, he found himself helpless when confronted by her presence. "I am going to my father's house. What about you?"

"Oh, I am on my way home," she said with a satisfied smile. "But I like walking. Maybe we will meet sometime." Her eyes studied him intently.

Peter flushed under her scrutiny. "I better get going," he said awkwardly. Did she just ask him to walk with her? Her soft chuckle followed him as he continued on his way, flattered and unsettled at the same time.

Once he reached his father's house, he hesitated before going inside. It was an unusually mild November, and Peter sweated in his jacket. Voices came through the open window of his father's study.

"You have to face facts, Jenrich!"

"Oh, Frantz, let me be."

"You know perfectly well why your storage house is empty."

Peter could hear his uncle walking restlessly back and forth in his father's study.

"You are deluding yourself if you think business will come back as it has before."

All the trade talk was boring. What difference did it make if a few barrels of silk and spices floated away in the rough waters of the Baltic Sea? His father would be fine. He just needed to quit drinking and sitting at his desk. Anyway, he had promised to have the money for Peter's exam.

If only he could finally tell his father that Master Nowak had given him permission to take the exam. Instead, it seemed as if he could not do anything right anymore. Master Nowak gave him a lot of work. He appeared disgruntled and dissatisfied with Peter's work, often hovering over him at his workbench to see what he was doing. It made Peter nervous. A few times the drill slipped, once he knocked over the bench so all the finished beads rolled around on the floor, and he cut himself on the saw.

His uncle's raised voice pulled him back into the present.

"You are close to being bankrupt. Your shipping trade is in terrible shape just like everyone else's thanks to this blasted war, never mind losing your best ship with all its cargo."

Peter moved closer to the window, careful to avoid the rambling vines of the old rosebush. His mother had planted the bush years ago, a pale pink damask rose that sometimes bloomed in the fall. She had been very proud of it. Now it was scraggly and unkempt, with a few late buds, tinged brown and flattened from the first frost.

Was his father really in trouble? Over the years, Peter had so often been annoyed by his father's frugality that it had never occurred to him his father actually might not have enough money.

His uncle's voice had become almost shrill. "You cannot sit

around forever, waiting for the insurance payment. Why will you not accept Heintze Mathis's offer for the *Kranich*?"

The *Kranich* was the smallest of his father's ships and now the only one left. It appeared unimposing when in the harbor, but was nimble and fast once underway, like the cranes after which it was named. His father liked to keep its sides painted in a light silver grey with white trim as if to emphasize its name.

The last time Peter remembered his father laughing out loud was during a week onboard the *Kranich*, just after Lorenz had joined the army. His father had shown Peter everything, the darkest corners of the hold filled with merchandise, the bunks shared by the sailors, the galley, and the captain's quarters. He even took him up to the crow's nest, the lookout platform high above the deck of the ship. Peter caught himself feeling glad Lorenz was not there with him.

Peter helped the sailors load the rowboat with herring, dried peas, and beans, as well as beer and water for an upcoming journey. When trying to negotiate the rope ladder to climb back onto the ship, he slipped and tumbled into the chilly Baltic waters. Seaweed and barnacles from the ship's keel clung to his hair and drooped over his face. When he could open his eyes, he saw his father almost weeping with laughter. "Our very own Medusa from the deep," he exclaimed while the sailors fished Peter out of the water and propelled him up the ladder.

In the cabin, Peter, wearing one of his father's shirts, tried to shake the water out of his ears.

"It happens to everyone who goes to sea." His father smiled at Peter and handed him a mug with hot, spiced cider and something sharp he added from a flask. "You have done well on your first journey. I am proud of you. Maybe you should consider this rather than starting your apprenticeship with Master Nowak."

"Thank you," Peter mumbled, sipping from the mug. Warmed by the cider and the novelty of his father's praise, he imagined himself as a captain, standing on the bridge of a large merchant vessel. Lorenz would be impressed. For that matter, it was easy to picture Lorenz as a captain, with his wild hair and bold features, undaunted by the dangers of the deep.

But he knew it was not right for himself. He took another swallow of the translucent, golden liquid, savoring the heat in his stomach. The fumes made his head spin. "Thank you, Father," he said again, shaking his head slowly as his thoughts became hazy. "But I love amber. I really do." He felt his father's hand take the mug from his hand and cover him with a blanket. The topic never came up again. Sometimes Peter wondered whether his father had been disappointed, but that would hardly be anything new.

Now, standing underneath the window outside his father's study, Peter was overcome by a sense of desolation at the thought that the *Kranich* might be sold. He heard his father mutter something, then the clinking of a carafe followed by the sound of wine being poured into a glass.

"If you did that, at least you would be able to take care of your daughter." Uncle Frantz sounded almost desperate. "Your son will manage, but Effie will always need someone to look out for her." A chair scraped on the floorboards. "I am going home now, Jenrich. Think about what I said. Remember, I have my own family. I can help you only so much."

"How can I possibly forget? You remind me every single time," Peter's father muttered.

Uncle Frantz did not respond as he banged the door shut behind him.

Peter stepped back behind the rosebush. He watched as his uncle came out of the house, with his shoulders hunched, head bent, and walked away.

The midday meal was a silent affair. Peter did not want to admit he had heard his father and his uncle arguing. His father was even more glum than usual as he ate his soup, oblivious to the bits of barley stuck to his chin.

Peter was used to this. Over the last year, since his mother had died, his father hadn't said much at all. The silence was easier to bear than being harangued by his father for all his inadequacies. Peter tried to concentrate on the barley soup with just a few bits of carrots, cabbage, and turnips relieving the congealed mess. He missed Mistress Nowak's meals.

Then his father's hand fumbled, and his glass fell over, rolled off the table, and shattered as it hit the floorboards, spilling the golden ale. The pale green Römer with its wide knobby bowl had been his mother's favorite glass.

Peter stood up to fetch a rag from the kitchen. When he returned to the room, his father sat slumped over the table. "I do not know what to do," he mumbled, his head buried in his hands. "What is going to happen to us?"

"It will be all right." Peter reached out to put his hand on his father's shoulder, surprised at his own daring.

"You do not understand." His father shook him off. "I do not know how we are going to manage in the long run. I cannot expect Clare to take care of everything in the house and yard and keep an eye on Effie forever. I do not even know how much longer I can pay Clare's wages, given how things have been going."

Appalled, Peter stared at his father. Nothing had prepared him for this outpouring of despair. His father actually worried about feeding them all.

"Father, I will be a journeyman soon. Maybe that will help."

His father shrugged, stood up, and walked out of the room, leaving Peter alone with the sad remnants of their meal, breathing in the smell of the spilled ale.

Perhaps his father would not even have the money Peter would need for his exam. Before he set out for the walk back to Master Nowak's house, he went to the kitchen to talk to Clare.

It smelled of fermenting yeast and of bread baking in the oven. Clare's sleeves were pushed up, a large towel wrapped around her skirt, and her hair tied back in an untidy bun. She was kneading dough. Using a rolling pin, she spread it out on the large wood table. She gathered it up again into a ball, punching the air out and slapping it. Then she started all over, rolling it out again. Several times she spread a thin layer of flour on the table to keep the dough from sticking to the surface.

"There," she said, blowing wisps of hair out of her flushed face and punching the dough into a big ball. "That should be enough."

Peter placed the plates from the midday meal into the scullery and then sat down at the table. "You are making a lot of bread."

"Some of it is for my family. I am going there tomorrow for a visit."

"Oh." Peter had forgotten all about Clare's family. "How are they?"

"Fine, thank you. My sister-in-law is expecting another baby. She's got her hands full." She brushed the remaining flour and dough off her hands and reached into the oven to pull out a long wooden board. "That's the first batch. I think they turned out pretty well."

Peter stared at the fragrant golden shapes. "What are these?"

Instead of regular loaves, Clare had shaped little fat men with arms and legs sticking out and faces marked by nuts. She had cut grooves into the dough, so it looked as if some of the rotund figures were smiling, while others grimaced.

Peter wrapped a towel around his hand and picked up one of the bread-men to examine it more closely. "You gave them beards or at least stubble," he said, chuckling. Clare had used sesame seeds for blond beards and poppy seeds for dark ones. "Where did you get the seeds?" he asked curiously.

"From your uncle. He got a shipment of spices and other things recently." Clare glanced at Peter thoughtfully. "Sometimes I wonder how he does this. There is hardly any merchant as successful as your uncle is at always having some merchandise despite the Swedes and Imperialists rampaging all over the land over the last years. He has been providing grain and dried fish at times when nobody else had anything after soldiers went through the region, rampaging and pillaging to their hearts' content."

Peter shook his head, pursing his lips, as if he also had been puzzled by this but did not comment. He knew now where Uncle Frantz kept his stash. Again, he wondered about Lorenz. It was odd to think of Lorenz as practical or discreet, and yet he had kept the secret of the ice cellar for several years, never even hinted at it. What else had Peter not known about his brother?

"Why are you so sad all of a sudden?" Clare asked.

"I just remembered something." Peter mumbled, reluctant to explain. He regarded the dough figures in front of him. "They could audition in the Shrovetide play. They look so fat and pleased with themselves."

Last year, the town had put on a play about the so-called land of plenty, the *Schlaraffenland*, the home of the lazy bums.

"It is not *Schlaraffenland* this year," Clare said as she worked on shaping the dough. "Do you know what they will perform?"

"No, and I am truly not interested. But why are you doing all this extra work?"

"I was getting tired of sadness. Besides, you should see my nephew when he gets one of these." Clare reached for the bowl with the remaining dough.

"Can I do some?"

Clare squinted, wiping flour from her face with the back of her hand. She turned, grabbed a towel from the shelf, and handed it to him. "Here, wrap this around your front so you do not get flour all over your clothes." She divided the remaining dough and gave him half.

It was warm in the kitchen. Peter relaxed as he listened to the crackling from the oven, the occasional gurgling from a pot of soup on the stove, and Clare humming as she worked. Handling the dough reminded him of playing with mud when he was a child. Only, this springy lump could be pulled and twisted and flattened. His first little bread-man was misshapen. Peter rolled the dough out again. Then he had it figured out, getting more adventuresome once he realized he could make long stringy pieces with which to shape hands and feet, and even ears. He used a knife to score lips into the faces. "It would be great if we had raisins."

"It would be great to have a lot of things, but I think we will have to wait for the end of the war."

Wind beat against the window and the kitchen felt colder all of a sudden. Peter bent his head in silence, trying to focus on giving his bread-man ears. "Do you use sesame seeds and poppy seeds for the hair?" he said to change the atmosphere.

"Yes." Clare smiled at him. "Just press them into the dough lightly, so they do not disappear during baking." She studied his creations. "Not bad." She fetched an egg from the pantry, added a bit of water, and stirred it up with a fork. "Here, take this brush and coat them. It will make them nice and shiny."

Peter carefully painted the little bread-men with the egg liquid. He glanced at Clare from the side. He wondered whether she knew about his father's troubles. Where would she go if his father could no longer pay her?

"Clare, why did you never marry?"

She turned away from him, reaching for the small lump of dough that remained. Something about her hunched shoulders and the stiff motions of her hands made Peter wish he could take back the question.

"I was going to get married, but he was killed," she said after a pause. With a hard slap on the dough, she started kneading the last bit before beginning to shape it into a small loaf. "Perhaps just as well. It would have been hard to explain to my family I was about to run away with a Swedish soldier."

She brushed off the large wooden board and placed the bread-men on it. "Time for these to go into the oven." With practiced, fluid moves, she opened the oven door and slid the board inside. Then she began to clean up the table.

"How is Effie?" Peter asked hesitantly.

"Oh, you remember your sister, do you?" Clare scowled at him.

"Clare, I heard some apprentices in town talking about her," Peter blurted out. "I do not know where this is coming from. I did not tell anybody. I mean, Anne knows something happened to Effie, and so does Cune, but truly, I told no one else. And Anne and Cune would never talk about her like that."

"What did they say?" Clare asked, narrowing her eyes and frowning.

"Awful things. One even called her a strumpet. I just heard them whispering when I walked by. I was so mad, but then I was afraid of making trouble for Master Nowak, so I let it be." Peter felt his cheeks burning. It was not entirely true. He had been afraid, but it had little to do with Master Nowak.

"Ah."

"What do you mean—ah?"

"That kind of talk is what happens to girls who get raped. Word gets around, do not ask me how, and people love to gossip."

Clare glanced into the opening of the oven to check on the bread and then turned back to face Peter.

"So, how is she?" he asked again. "Should she not be getting over this? It has been four weeks already."

"Get over this?" Clare put her hands on her hips and glared at him furiously. "You try getting over something like this quickly. And you are not even troubled and frail like she is."

"Sorry," Peter said. "I do not know what it must be like."

"I know that." Clare no longer looked angry, just tired and sad. "I have cut Effie's hair, and it is not so ragged anymore. She let me do that, but other than that, I cannot get her to do much of anything. Mostly she just sits in her room, rocking back and forth." She picked up a linen towel, folding it and unfolding it, her brow wrinkled by her concern. "I will get some lavender for her pillow. That might at least comfort her in the evening. My grandmother swore by amber, but of course, that is impossible to get."

"Amber?" Peter asked. "What do you mean?"

"You work with this all day long and you do not know what it can do?"

"Like what?"

"It has always been used for healing. Oma said if you wear amber on your skin, it will protect you against jaundice, a sore throat, stomach griping, and all sorts of other illnesses. Some people grind amber into a powder you can take with water or honey. Oma even claimed there is an oil made of amber used for scents and for healing, but I never heard about that anywhere else. Anyway, she swore it made her arthritis better."

Master Nowak had never talked about this. Peter had heard Mistress Nowak mention something to Anne. But it had not interested him, just as he had no use for all the teas and powders Mistress Nowak had in her cabinet for healing.

"But it is not as if Effie has jaundice or arthritis."

"No, of course not. Still, it might help. You better get going." Clare grabbed a few wrinkled winter apples from the pantry and two loaves of bread. "Here, do you have room in your satchel?"

Peter made a quick grab for the satchel to prevent Clare from seeing what was inside. "Let me do that." He relaxed when he remembered he had put the amber pieces in his pocket earlier. That still seemed the safest place for them. "Sorry," he added to cover for the awkward moment. "Master Nowak had me fetch something for him, and I do not want it to get squished."

Clare glanced at him from the side but refrained from commenting. "Wrap the bread in a towel. Take this one and bring it back next time."

The wind had picked up and it had begun to snow. Peter pulled up his collar and started out. It was a long walk toward Master Nowak's house.

His thoughts were racing. His father's business in trouble. Effie raped on top of her general helplessness. Peter thought about what his father had said. Until his brother's death, his parents had always relied on Lorenz. Peter could not help feeling a twinge of pride that his father appeared to now look to him for support. At the same time, he felt trapped. He would have to be responsible for his sister in the future. A lifetime of making prayer beads. A lifetime of taking care of his sister while tolerating the jeers and snide remarks from others. A lifetime of trying to catch up to his dead brother.

For years, he had dreamed of finishing his apprenticeship. He looked forward to traveling all over the land as a journeyman. Sometimes, he had even pictured his life as a master craftsman with his own shop in Stolpmünde. Now, all he could think of was a heavy door closing on his future—his life defined forever by the rigid rules and regulations of the guild and the demands of his family. If only he could run away. For an instant, he had a vision of himself as a sailor onboard a Hanse merchant ship. Yet, how could he even think of something like this when his family needed his help?

Then he remembered he could not possibly put his name forward. There was no way he could ask his father for the money to purchase the pound of amber a candidate had to provide for the exam.

The sun was already setting. Peter hated how quickly the days grew shorter. He marveled at the glow in the sky, just like a perfectly polished, translucent piece of rose-colored amber.

His thoughts began to wander. His mother had told him an ancient Greek tale of a wondrous bird from India whose tears at the death of one of the Argonauts had turned to amber. His favorite story was the one about the magical amber bear that supposedly brought good luck to its owner. In another story, amber was created when the ancient gods wept and their tears washed into the waves.

"Hardly tears of the gods," Master Nowak scoffed when

Peter had asked him about that tale at the beginning of his apprenticeship. "Amber is the result of resin and sap from trees that have washed into the sea, where it hardened over thousands of years," he said. "Not all amber comes from the sea. Amber is also found deep in the ground where it is dug up like precious minerals. Of course, some say amber comes from the sperm whale or rather the sperm whale's excrement." Master Nowak laughed. "Likely story. Just goes to show you should not believe everything people tell you."

One day he brought in fresh globs of sap he had picked up in the woods to show his apprentices, proudly displayed on a piece of wood. "See, here it is. It is just beginning to stiffen."

"It smells nice." Cune reached out to touch it.

"Watch out," Master Nowak said. "It is sticky and hard to get off your hands. If you throw this in the ocean, many years from now, you will have a lovely solid piece of amber. That is one of the most remarkable facts about amber. It does not sink." He had a strangely wistful expression, surprising for someone usually so dry and businesslike. "Some people say amber is restless and that is why it does not stay in the sea but washes up on the shore."

"Maybe it has a soul," Anne said, seated on a little stool in the back of the workroom, knitting a woolen cap for a baby cousin. She looked like a miniature Mistress Nowak, so busy and intent on her work. That day, Anne had not yet started formally as an apprentice. She had been too young, but she often sat in the back when her father talked to Peter and Cune about amber.

"That is ridiculous." Peter laughed. "It is just sap."

Master Nowak did not comment on this.

Now, with the amber in his pocket preying on his mind, Peter was not sure of anything anymore.

It was snowing more heavily. Peter trudged along and thought of amber floating on top of the waves. He loved the story of the Indian bird. He pictured it with long tail feathers, graceful and elegant, but with sad, glowing eyes out of which the amber tears spilled faster and faster as they rolled toward the sea.

Snow flurries were swirling almost level with the ground. Peter squinted to keep them out of his eyes. Yet, he could not help staring at the glittering flakes, mesmerized by their unrelenting movement toward him.

The houses around him had vanished in billowing swathes of snow. Scrunching up his eyes to keep out the flakes, he continued, stumbling over the uneven bumps and hollows in the road. Fortunately, Master Nowak's house was just a ten-minute walk from the town square. The snow was blowing into Peter's collar and he felt a layer settling on his eyebrows. Suddenly, he lost his footing and pitched headlong into a snowdrift.

10

REFUGE IN A STORM

His face is wet.

Peter blinks at the large snowflakes drifting toward him, settling on his eyebrows and cheeks. He shifts, trying to stand up, when he touches something soft. A furry back, another body next to it, snuffling sounds.

He shrinks back. Then he recognizes the elongated snout. The dog lifts its head, the golden eyes almost shut with snow and ice hanging off the lashes and the long-matted fur.

"Lioba, what are you doing?" In a panic, Peter starts to pull on the lump next to the dog. "Get up."

No response. Peter takes a handful of snow and rubs it over the girl's face. "Wake up. You are going to freeze to death. You cannot stay here."

"Why do you have to bother me?" Lioba groans. "I was just getting comfortable."

"Exactly," Peter says. "That is what makes it so dangerous." He pulls on her arms and tries to shake her into action. The dog barks at him and at Lioba. "That is right dog, keep it up."

Finally, Peter manages to pull Lioba to her feet. "Move your arms and move your feet," he commanded.

"It hurts," she complains.

"Keep going. It gets better."

"What makes you an expert on snow?"

"Ah, you are getting angry now. That is good. I know because my brother told me about soldiers freezing and what to do to prevent it." He squints across the glittering field. Nothing is remotely familiar. Fortunately, it has stopped snowing. "Do you have any idea where we are?"

"Not really," Lioba says. "Somewhere near Danzig."

"Danzig," Peter exclaims. He has never been in Danzig and feels a curious lurch in his stomach at the thought that he is in a completely different area of Pomerania, but there is no time for worrying about this now. Shielding his eyes with his hands, he scans the snow-covered fields. "See over there? Just at the edge of the woods? I think there is a house."

Lioba does not appear interested in that or in anything else. She looks as if she is about to sit down again.

"Come on," Peter shouts at her, grabbing her hand.

They stumble across the field until they reach the little house. The door opens with a creaking noise to a room as big as his father's study, a comfortable space complete with benches along the walls, a table and chairs in the center, and a cast-iron stove.

The dog walks around sniffing at all the corners.

Lioba has started shivering. Through stammering lips, she says, "I suppose there isn't any wood." She sits down on a bench and rubs her arms.

"I saw some just outside." Peter quickly pulls the door open and turns to the neat woodpile underneath the overhang. After brushing the dusting of snow from the top layer, he grabs a few logs and an armful of kindling. Back inside, he sets to loading the stove. It is no different from the ceramic one at home, just smaller. "Right," he says, "you do not happen to have a fire striker on you?"

"A fire striker?" Lioba begins to laugh.

"Why are you laughing?" Peter glares at her. "I am just trying to help."

"Sorry, but you have to admit this whole *time* thing is funny." Lioba reaches into her bag. "Here, use these."

"What is that?" Peter studies the little box doubtfully.

"Matches. Fine, I'll do it." With a swift movement, she swipes a tiny wooden stick along the side of the box, producing a flame. She sticks it into the middle of the kindling, but the flame dies. She lights another one, and that one catches. "Nice," she says. "You lay a good fire."

"Why for the love of God were you sleeping in the snow?"

"I didn't mean to. It wasn't snowing when I sat down to rest for a bit. I suppose I fell asleep."

"If the dog had not stayed with you, you would have frozen to death."

"See, she's a good dog."

"What is this place? It does not look as if anybody lives here."

"It's a hunting lodge. My grandfather had something like this."

"A hunting lodge?" Peter raises his eyebrows. "Your grandfather sounds like the Duke of Prussia."

"Well, he did own a lot of land," Lioba says thoughtfully. "I loved going to the hunting lodge."

Peter shakes his head. None of this makes sense to him. It is as if they speak different languages.

"When I was a little girl, I was sometimes allowed to help on the day of a hunt. We'd bring pea soup for the hunters and spiced hot wine. At the end of the day, they lined up all the animals they had shot and spoke a blessing over them. I always loved that moment." She looks wistful. "Some pea soup would be nice right now."

"Pea soup! I do not have that, but I do have something else." He takes off his satchel and opens it.

The dog walks up to Peter and tries to push her nose into it.

"Hey, stop that." Peter pulls out the bundle Clare has given to him and folds back the cloth. He can smell the yeasty scent of the bread-men. Bizarrely they are still warm. He hands one to Lioba. "Here."

Her eyes grow large. "What, you have a *Till Eulenspiegel* in your house?" She laughs until she almost chokes.

Peter begins to smile. He remembers his mother reading them stories about the legendary prankster. Till Eulenspiegel played tricks on everybody. One day he amused himself by breaking into the baker's shop and turning all the dough into sculptures of the mayor and various other town elders. He arranged them neatly on the counter for all to see when they came in the morning to buy their daily bread.

Lioba wipes her face, still giggling. She starts munching on the bread while breaking off a leg and throwing it to the dog.

"Hey, that was for you," Peter protests. This girl is strange. Starving, wandering around the countryside, almost freezing to death in the snow, running away from dangers he could not even begin to comprehend—after all that, she feeds the dog, and she is laughing.

The dog gulps it down and sits on her haunches, looking at Peter and Lioba expectantly.

"She is hungry just like me, and besides, she is a good dog." Lioba sniffs at the bread. "It's not like the bread we have—this is a lot darker and denser." Then she takes another bite and begins chewing more slowly. "It's not bad," she mumbles, her cheeks bulging. "Odd, but not bad."

"That is what we eat," Peter says defensively. "Here, have an apple. If you chew the bread and the apple together, both become sweeter."

"My uncle's cook used to say that." Lioba throws another piece to the dog. "Can you bring more?"

"How? I just happened to have this in my pocket. It is not as if I have any control over when I appear in your time. Anyway, we are not exactly living in the land of plenty."

Lioba grins at him. "The land of plenty? *Schlaraffenland*? I guess we read the same stories."

Peter frowns at her. He isn't sure if she is mocking him. "The town performed a play on that, *The Schlaraffenland*, last February."

"Oh, yes, the land where the rivers flow with milk, wine, and honey, and where fish and fowl fly through the air, fully cooked and deliciously roasted, and where the houses are made of cake, and stones are made of cheese," Lioba intones in a gravelly voice as if on a stage.

"Exactly." Peter laughs and continues, "Where the roofs of houses are covered with dishes of pie, doors are made of gingerbread and floors of spicy bacon bread, and the fences around the yard are lined with links of sausages."

Lioba shudders. "We better stop this. It's making me hungry." She leans back against the wooden slats of the hut, one leg pulled up onto the bench, the other stretched out.

Peter has never seen any girl sit like that or one who wears trousers. Girls are supposed to sit with their skirts modestly covering their laps. Perhaps occasionally they might cross their ankles.

Wisps of hair stick out of Lioba's long light-colored braid, and her face is smudged with dirt. She appears relaxed, contentedly munching the bread. One final piece she throws to the dog. "Here, Natasha."

"Why do you call her Natasha if she isn't your dog?"

"Oh, it seemed fitting. Natasha from *War and Peace*."

Peter stares at her blankly.

"Never mind. Not your time."

Natasha has apparently realized she will not get anything else. With a sigh, she lies down close to the stove, her long snout on her paws. The damp, musty smell from her fur is beginning to permeate the air.

This is the longest time yet Peter has spent with Lioba. Now that the stove is starting to warm up the room, it feels almost cozy.

In his other dreams—that is the only word he could think of to describe these strange times in another reality—the landscape had looked flat, all in grey and black tones. Now it does not appear so flat anymore, and the outlines of things are less blurry. There are even tinges of brown and red in some of the furniture and the floor. This dream world seems to get more real every time. *Perhaps eventually I will not return to my own time anymore. I will be trapped here.* Then he shakes his head. Sometimes thinking does not help.

Lioba stretches and then slips off her coat, spreading it out on the bench next to her so it can dry out. Underneath she wears a woolen tunic with long sleeves. Wisps of hair from her braid curl softly around her cheeks, in contrast to her prominent, slightly hooked nose and high cheekbones. It is not a gentle face, even though right now, her expression is pensive, and her full lips pursed as she runs her hand through the dog's fur.

"Maybe I could just stay here for the night and then go on," she says finally, with a resigned expression as if reluctant to return to her present problems.

"Why are you traveling on the road?"

"To try to get away from the Russians."

"The Russians?" Peter shakes his head in confusion. "I guess your Russians are like our Swedes or the Imperialists depending on how the war is going. Mostly we get refugees from the west, though."

Lioba smirks. "Right now, I wish I could trade you—your Swedes against my Russians."

"Oh, I am not so sure it would be an improvement. But you cannot just keep wandering around. Where are you going to go?"

"Muttrin."

"Muttrin? That is southeast of Stolp, is it not?" He tries to think what he knows of Muttrin. The villages in the region have suffered terribly over the last years, and much of the land is lying fallow because there are not enough people to work it. In several villages like Lübzow, where Clare's family lived, the Swedish soldiers have used manor houses and other buildings for temporary lodging, leaving everything in shambles once they go. The forests are laid to waste, and people have taken to gathering wood from collapsed houses and barns.

Muttrin probably suffered the same fate. Vaguely, he remembers a conversation between his uncle and his father about a dispute of the lord of the manor in Muttrin and the town of Stolp about using the Stolpe River for transporting timber toward the harbor.

"These damn landowners always think they can do anything they damn well please," his father had complained.

His uncle had been more conciliatory. "You have to admit they have been trying to help with food during the awful years lately."

"What about you?" Lioba raised her eyebrows. "Where do you live?"

"In Stolpmünde."

Lioba beams at him. "That's where we go swimming in the ocean."

"We are not even allowed to walk on the beach," Peter says enviously. "Why do you want to go to Muttrin? Is your family there?"

"My aunt and uncle and my cousins—and my parents, I hope. They usually are in Muttrin for Christmas."

"Where are your parents now?"

"I don't know. I thought they would be in Stolp. I kept writing to them, but they haven't responded. Maybe they already left for the west. I thought they would have waited for me. My aunt will know."

"So why are you on the road at all and not in Muttrin? Where are you coming from?"

"I don't know where to begin. Let me see. I was a land girl. Now, I am trying to go home."

"What is a land girl?"

"The government requires everyone to complete at least six months of service labor. Often it's work in factories."

"Factories? What is that?"

"At this rate I'll never get to tell you anything." Lioba laughs. "Factories are places where things get built … Oh, I don't know how to explain. Take my word for it. Working in a factory isn't a whole lot of fun. My cousin had to work in a munitions factory making bullets. But many of the girls and young women have been sent to work on farms all over Germany while the men are in the army. I suppose I should be grateful I didn't get assigned to digging ditches like my cousin."

"Digging ditches?"

"Yes, well, the army had this idea that ditches would present an obstacle to the Russian tanks, but, of course, they roll right over the ditches. So, I got the better end of the deal. At least weeding and planting made sense, even if I hated every minute. They sent me to a place further east from here. I mean, I didn't mind working in the fields, but it was like being in the army— with early morning wake-up calls and forced singing and standing in line. But we were all dismissed suddenly. I suppose because of the way the war is going. So, I thought I would go home."

Peter puzzles over the word "tanks", but lets it go. "What about all those people on the road with you? They were also trying to get away?"

"Oh, that's right. That's where I saw you first. I remember now. You were sitting in the ditch."

"But why are you alone? What happened to the family with whom you were traveling?"

"Oh, that's not my family. I was just trying to help the mother. She was alone with three kids."

"And what happened?"

"She went to Elbing. She had relatives there and thought she'd be safe. I tried to get her to go on, but I gave up."

"Master Nowak knows some amber merchants in Elbing. He promised to take me along the next time he goes to Königsberg to the big market."

"Amber? Is that what you do?" Lioba looks at him curiously.

"Yes, I am an apprentice. Why?"

"Oh, I don't know. My grandmother told me many stories about amber. There even were a few amber merchants among my ancestors." She yawns, hunching her back and folding her arms across her chest. "I'm finally getting warm."

There is a roaring and rushing sound as if snow is sliding down the roof. Then everything vanishes.

11

PROCLAMATION DAY

"WAKE UP, PETER."

Peter opened his eyes to find Cune hovering over him and tugging on his blanket.

"Stop that," Peter snapped, snatching the blanket back. Panic-stricken, he felt around for the amber pieces. There they were, underneath his shoulder. His panic receded like the roar of an outgoing wave at the shore.

"Come on," Cune said, looking hurt and puzzled. "We're going to be late. Master Nowak already called from downstairs."

Peter hadn't been able to sleep much, thinking about Lioba. He remembered how he had woken up in the snowdrift, stunned and feeling very cold. When he looked in his satchel, the bread and the apples were gone, and there was just Clare's crumpled-up towel.

His head hurt. It was as if he was bewitched, catapulted by an unseen force into another world and then just as suddenly thrown back. It could not have happened. Surely it was a dream. Part of him wanted to go back, to talk to Lioba, to watch her face shift from lost and miserable to mischievous. He worried about her, but that made no sense. She was not real. She was not even going to be alive for hundreds of years.

Cune tried to brush at a stain on his shirt. As always, he appeared disheveled, and his hair was sticking up, but at least he was already dressed and had put on his best jerkin.

"Oh, I forgot. Proclamation Day." Hurriedly, Peter jumped out of bed. He pulled on his breeches and a clean shirt, tucking the amber pieces into his pocket while Cune's head was turned.

Usually, Proclamation Day was on the same day as the meeting of the guild masters on Michaelmas Day in late September. However, because of the war, everything had been postponed until after All Hallows' Eve. The town elders had used the defeat of the Danish fleet at the hands of the Swedish navy in October as an excuse to postpone everything.

Last year, Denmark had switched sides and joined the Imperial forces. "They probably regret that decision right now," Master Nowak had said with a grim laugh when the news came out. Peter had not paid much attention. It would make little difference. Refugees would flood the town, and soldiers would burn down buildings and devastate villages regardless of which army won.

"What's the matter with you these days?" Cune asked. "Half of the time you seem to be thinking about something else."

"Sorry, Cune. I just have a lot on my mind." Peter shrugged, avoiding Cune's concerned eyes. "Thanks for waking me up." He reached into the cupboard he shared with Cune and took out the grey jerkin his father had given him a year ago for special occasions. It felt tight over his shoulders. No help for it. Quickly, he buttoned it in the front, brushed a hand through his hair, and followed Cune downstairs.

Master Nowak was pacing back and forth in the hallway. He glanced at his two apprentices and narrowed his eyes, but then just shook his head without commenting. He wore his best doublet, dark grey with velvet trim, over a shirt with white linen sleeves. A white lace collar lay flat on his shoulders and chest. His black knee-length hose was puffier than his usual wear.

Anne, equally formally attired, wore a high-waisted black

dress, with a matching linen kerchief, and a lace-trimmed collar and cuffs. A white lace band encircled her head, holding her curls away from her face. Her formal clothes made her appear taller, even though she reached barely to Peter's shoulder. She scowled at him. "What are you looking at?"

"Nothing," Peter said hastily. "You look nice." In fact, he had never seen Anne dressed like this and he was perplexed by the transformation. He had thought of her as a little girl—good-humored, kind, and sensible, but a little girl. The two years that separated them had seemed almost like a lifetime. This elegant young woman was a stranger.

Under his scrutiny, Anne lifted her chin and drew herself up. Then the corners of her mouth turned up and she grinned at him.

"It is time to go," Master Nowak said, pulling on his formal robe. Carefully, he arranged the amber guild medal on its chain to rest on top of the velvet, displaying the principal tools of the trade—a scraper knife and a drawknife, crossed and overlaid by a caliper, with a rosary bead in the center. Then he placed his broad-brimmed hat over his grey curls. "I do not want to be late."

By the time they reached the square in front of the town hall, Peter was sweating in his tight jerkin. It was a mild day, and last night's snow was melting in the morning sunshine.

A crowd had gathered near the gate that led into the town hall's courtyard. A messenger of the Duke of Prussia, Frederick William, also known as the Elector of Brandenburg, stood in front of a pillar. His tunic, emblazoned with the bright red eagle of the coat of arms of Brandenburg, stood out among the subdued clothes of the townsmen. Two workers next to him had set up a temporary scaffold for a large board with a text affixed to it, while a third man used a hammer to drive nails into the board.

On a platform next to the pillar, the mayor, several town elders, and prominent guild masters waited, looking solemn and stern in their stiff robes. Mayor Neuhof repeatedly wiped his face with a large handkerchief.

A town drummer stepped forward. At a sign from the mayor, he began beating his drum until all eyes faced in the direction of the platform.

When the drumming stopped, the messenger read from a large sheet of paper he held in front of him like a shield. "Hear all of you citizens of the town of Stolpmünde assembled here," he shouted in a voice shrill and grating. "By the grace of the Great Elector Duke Frederik William of Brandenburg, hear his words sent to you today in affirmation of the relationship of trust and cooperation between him and the town of Stolp and its merchants. This is to restate the rules and regulations as they apply to the gathering of amber."

Peter glanced around. The little son of one of the town elders had climbed to the top of the lantern in the back of the square. From that vantage point, he smirked and stuck out his tongue, waving his hands in rhythm to the proclamation.

To keep his smile hidden, Peter turned his attention back to the platform.

The messenger stopped to gaze at the assembled crowd before he resumed. "We direct that no individual, amber craftsman or any other craftsman, merchant, or vagrant from Königsberg or any other city or town in our dukedom, will be permitted to walk on the beaches, shorelines, or any area in their vicinity. Any individual found on a beach without a permit is subject to penalties. No such individual may take home or keep overnight any amber found, gathered, or dug up, and must immediately surrender any such pieces to the designated beach watchman or his superior."

Peter put his hand in his pocket. The amber pieces felt warm and silky. He should go to one of the senior guild members and pretend he had just found them. There was no way he could ever keep them or work on them openly. He might as well surrender them before they caused any trouble.

He could not do this to Master Nowak and his family. It was all wrong.

"Furthermore, malefactors may be tempted to hide such pieces of amber in the countryside in shrubs or underground, only to dig up later to sell in Königsberg. Rest assured, any such persons shall be caught. You may only walk along the shoreline with a permit from the beach watchman. The watchman has been instructed to follow suspicious individuals along the beach, inspect their clothes, their wagons, and their belongings, and if found to have obtained any amber in contravention of these laws to arrest them and immediately surrender them to the Amber Court for investigation and punishment."

Peter's thoughts drifted again. Master Nowak had the apprentices recite the laws regularly. "Remember," he would say, glaring at them, "if you break the law, you put yourselves at risk as much as my workshop, my reputation, and my position in the amber guild."

Peter had known this all his life, and yet, he could not bear to give up his find.

Every night, he took them out and studied them in the flickering light of the lantern in the workshop. He had to find more beeswax candles somewhere. They were expensive, but maybe he could snitch some candle stubs from his father's study. The light from tallow candles was weak, and it stank. Everybody would know he had spent time in the workshop at night. Beeswax candles gave a better light and did not smell so bad.

It was as if these amber pieces had attached themselves to a corner of his heart. They spoke to him of the sea and the dune grass swishing in the wind, of rolling fields and woods along the Baltic coastline, and of cranes flying, their wings beating in rhythm to the strange hoarse chants of sorrow and longing.

The smaller piece was lovely in its simplicity, and he knew exactly what it would look like when finished. The larger one was different. It made him think of something secret that called to him. Sometimes when he examined it, it was as if he caught glimpses of its final shape, a crane about to leap into the air, and then it blurred again in his mind's eye.

So far, he had hesitated to work on the pieces in earnest. It was almost as if he was afraid of losing something, of breaking their curious spell over him once he started. His thoughts were splintered. When his eyes were fixed on the warm dark glow of the larger amber piece, he saw the grey and black people trudging along the road and the shadows underneath Lioba's eyes, her torn jacket, and her hands blue from the cold. He heard Lioba's voice and felt the intensity of her gaze.

"Ouch," Peter grunted in an undertone. Anne had jabbed a sharp elbow into his side.

When he glared at her, she lifted her chin in the direction of the platform. Peter bit his lip but heeded her advice. For the remainder of the proclamation, he looked attentively at the speaker.

The man went on to list the forms of punishment, ranging from fines to imprisonment and hanging on the gallows.

Peter shifted his weight from one foot to the other, biting his lip. Every year they seemed to add yet another regulation. It was ridiculous. Soon they would even punish hapless dogs wandering around on the beach.

"To prevent any possibility of collusion between the beach watchman and the local populace, your current watchman has been relieved of his duty, and a new one without any previous connections among the citizens of Stolpmünde has been appointed in his stead. The watchman will report to the Amber Controller once a month."

That would hardly make a difference, Peter thought. The current watchman was from Stolpmünde, but he was an angry, bitter man who discharged his duties with revolting enthusiasm.

Finally, the speaker stopped. He gazed around as if to impress his message on his audience once again. Then he nodded to the drummer, who played a few beats to signal the end of the ceremony.

A collective sigh went through the crowd, and people in the square began to talk again.

"Well, that's over," Master Nowak said to his apprentices. He bought each of them a fresh hot pasty from a stall at the edge of the square.

They stood together in companionable silence next to the town fountain, munching their pasties. Hungrily, Peter wolfed down the last bite; juice from the meat filling dribbled over his chin.

Anne ate hers as daintily as if she sat at her father's table with a fork and knife. With a contented sigh, she licked the last crumbs from her lips. "That was wonderful. Thank you, Father."

Her father smiled at her. "You are all free this afternoon. We will resume work tomorrow."

Cune immediately announced he would visit his family.

"Mother wanted me to pick something up from the tailor. I will walk out with you," Anne said.

Peter hesitated, reluctant to go to his father's house, back into the gloom and despair that seemed to ooze out of every crevice. Wistfully, he watched Anne and Cune as they walked off, chatting with each other. He wanted to go with them. But lately, it felt as if there was a barrier between him and his friends.

"I need to visit the brewery," Master Nowak said. "Do you want to come along?"

Peter had never been inside the brewery. He did not care for beer all that much, preferring to drink water if it was clean and fresh. On the other hand, visiting the brewery was better than sitting in silence in his father's study. Then he felt guilty. "I will walk with you part of the way. I should really go home."

Master Nowak was one of several senior guild members with beer brewing privileges and was proud of the beer that his brewery produced. Sometimes, at supper he let his apprentices have a measure of the latest beer, asking them to identify the different flavors—bitter and crisp, brown and malty, or full and rich like dark sweetened fruits. "It is not all that different from amber when it comes to colors," he would say with a laugh, pointing out the different shades from pale yellow to dark golden brown in his large glass mug.

"How is your sister?" Master Nowak asked as they walked out of the square. "Anne told me about her accident."

That was one way of putting it. Peter hunched his shoulders, uncertain how to answer when someone veered into their path.

"So, when are you going to sell me your brewery?" It was another guild member, Otto Roth. He was weaving back and forth like a stalk of corn in the wind as he grabbed Master Nowak's sleeve with a shaky hand.

Peter was not sure whether Master Roth did this to give more emphasis to his question or to keep himself upright. He was large and bulky with stained clothes that barely covered his ample midriff, and a whiff of stale beer that surrounded him like a cloud.

"Master Roth," Master Nowak smiled blandly, gently pulling his arm out of the man's grasp, "we have an urgent errand and have no time to chat." He sketched a partial bow and gestured to Peter. "Come, we must hurry."

"You would not believe it now, but there was a time when he was one of the best amber craftsmen in the region," he said in a low voice to Peter as they walked on.

"I will never drink beer if that's what it does to you," Peter said.

"I suppose all these years of war have gotten to Master Roth."

"But you, too, have lived through these years. And so has everyone else, and they do not all turn into a sodden mess like that." Peter was confused and irritated. Master Nowak had never tolerated anything bordering on sloppiness. Any apprentice caught drinking beer in the workshop would be dismissed before he could swallow the last dregs in his stein. Now he was lenient —just because it was someone from his own generation.

"Do not be so judgmental, Peter." Master Nowak gazed

down at him, his blue-grey eyes thoughtful and searching. "You need to walk in someone's shoes to really understand what they are going through."

Sometimes it felt to Peter like Master Nowak could see his thoughts, and it made him squirm.

"Why do you keep the brewery?" Peter asked.

"I like beer, and I enjoy experimenting with different flavors. It is profitable." Master Nowak smiled. "People will always drink beer, even during times of war."

Peter thought of his father—bent over, unkempt, and with the sour, unwashed smell of someone who hadn't gotten out in a long time. He could not remember the last time his father had smiled about anything. Master Nowak had lost so much, with only two of his five children still living. And yet he remained calm, kind, and serene.

"And it gets me out of the house—and that makes the mistress happy." Master Nowak's eyes twinkled.

Peter grinned. Then he thought of how Mistress Nowak's eyes lit up whenever Master Nowak returned home. There had to be other reasons. Peter never had the impression his master got much profit from the brewery, but then perhaps this was in part because he spread it around liberally. He had seen Master Nowak help out many a time when the guild funds were depleted, one of the members did not have enough to cover the costs of a funeral, or there was need of funds for rebuilding after a fire.

They were about to cross the bridge over the Stolpe when Peter saw Marthe, accompanied by an older woman, coming toward them.

"Master Nowak, how nice to see you again." Marthe beamed at them. "And Peter. How are you? Are you working on any new treasures? Could I come to your workshop and see what you are doing? I just love amber."

"Of course, Mistress Neuhof," Master Nowak said politely.

"You would always be welcome." He bowed toward the older woman. "And you as well."

"Oh, forgive me," Marthe exclaimed. "This is my aunt, Mistress Meyer. She has come to stay with us for a while."

The woman inclined her head, her lips pinched as if she had bitten into a sour apple.

"My father wants her to keep an eye on me," Marthe added, her expression demure.

Mistress Meyer whispered in her ear.

"We have to get going." Marthe smiled as she looked at Peter. "Peter, you promised to take me for a walk one of these days. I hope I will see you soon." With a wave, she turned, and the two women continued on their way.

Master Nowak raised his eyebrows. "You promised to take her for a walk?"

Peter shook his head, flustered and unsure of what to say. Working on a new treasure? Had she seen him on the beach? He watched her swaying skirts and the sheen of her hair as she strolled along, and thinking of her smile, Peter dismissed his fears. He was reading too much into her comments. She was just teasing him.

"I heard she is no longer walking out with young Thomas," Master Nowak said with a sly smile. "It is her loss. Thomas is a decent young man."

Peter shrugged, trying to hide his embarrassment as well as tempted to grin. Master Nowak listening to gossip and passing it on was a novelty.

"Still, I suspect her father would not be happy to know his daughter is walking out with all these young men. She makes me think of a child with a new toy. She is definitely enjoying herself. You better watch your step, young man."

They had reached the fork in the road, one leading to the brewery up on a hill, near a spring that provided clean water for the beer. The other fork led to Peter's father's house.

"I should turn off here." Peter avoided looking at Master Nowak's face.

At home, his father was bent over papers in his study and did not respond to Peter's hello.

Peter climbed the stairs and stopped outside Effie's room. He could not hear any sound from inside, not even the low humming his sister produced when she was comfortable. Maybe she was asleep. He sighed and made his way back downstairs.

Clare was in the scullery, bent over a tub of linens. "Ah, Peter," she said as she straightened her back, rubbing it briefly and wincing. Her hair was disheveled, and her hands were red from the water. "Would you like something to eat? This needs to soak for a while."

In the kitchen, she cut up a loaf of fresh bread. "Here." She put the platter in front of Peter and watched him wolf down a slice. "Sometimes I think you do not get any food at Master Nowak's house."

"Thank you, this is really good." He would try to grab some for Lioba.

"You should come more often," Clare said.

Peter kept chewing. He knew she was not talking about food, but how could he explain how much he dreaded seeing his father and how helpless he felt when watching his sister?

"So, what's this I hear about a certain girl being interested in you?"

"What are you talking about?" Peter felt his cheeks burn.

"Ah, you know whom I meant right away." Clare grinned at him. "I hear Marthe isn't so friendly to Thomas anymore—although someone said it was not her choice."

"She probably got bored with Thomas." Peter pretended to be absorbed with eating.

"Anyway, I ran into her on my way to the market. She was quite chatty. She asked about you and your sister."

"What did you say?"

"Not much. I'm not sure I would trust that one."

"Why?" Upset, Peter put his bread down.

"That girl talks too much."

"She is just friendly," Peter retorted angrily. "Why should she not like me?" Quickly, he bit into his bread and began to chew, embarrassed by his outburst. It was true that Marthe talked a lot. But she would not hurt him. It was upsetting that nobody appeared to think a girl like Marthe could be interested in him.

"Now, do not get all huffy with me."

"I hate this town," Peter growled. "All this gossip all the time."

"Sometimes it has its uses." Clare cut another slice of bread and pushed it across the table. "Peter, are you sure you told no one other than Anne and Cune about what has happened to Effie?"

"No," Peter said, looking up. "And they do not know she was raped. I just told them someone had attacked her. Why?"

"After you mentioned what you heard from other apprentices, I have kept my ears open. It's not just apprentices. Apparently, people say Effie is acting strangely. Some are afraid of her. Some even claim she is consorting with strangers at night. Until recently, nobody ever paid any attention to her. People in town always knew she was different, but nobody minded. I have a bad feeling about this. It is more than gossip, and someone is spreading it."

On the way home, Peter thought about what Clare had said. He was irked by her comments. People were just jealous of Marthe because she was so beautiful. Anyway, he should not read too much into her hints. Maybe she suspected he had been at the beach. But she was just curious and interested. Why would she want to hurt him? And those rumors Clare had mentioned? He could not believe Anne or Cune would have gossiped, and no one else knew something had happened to Effie. Then he decided to put it out of his mind. People were spiteful and loved to gossip. It would pass. They would get bored and move on to something else. It was more important to do something that might help Effie feel better.

Peter rubbed his neck as he walked, glancing back to see whether there was anyone on the road behind him. He could not shake the feeling that someone was watching him. Clutching the amber in his pocket, he quickened his pace and was glad when he reached Master Nowak's house.

That night, when the house had quieted down, and Cune snored in the bed next to him, Peter snuck downstairs to the workshop. He knew now exactly what he wanted to make for Effie—an amber heart to be worn on her skin, hidden by her gown.

He had not really needed to hear Clare's comments about all the ailments amber could cure. Having carried the pieces around with him for weeks had convinced him of their strange power. He could not understand it, but they affected him. He no longer worried that he might get caught. He was consumed by new, strange thoughts, reeling at the vision of different worlds out there. His own world could change. He felt invincible in ways he had never felt before. Some of this power had to work for Effie.

He made a sketch for the smaller piece. He did not really need one, but he wanted to get it right. Drawing one for the larger piece was harder. It was as if that chunk of amber had taken hold of his thoughts. He often felt for it in his pocket, tempted to take it out and look at it. It pulled him in and pushed him away at the same time. He loved it, and he hated it. He wanted to throw it into the fire, and he did not want to let it go. Frustrated at his inability to draw what he could see with his mind's eye—a young crane precariously perched on one leg, the wings folded, and the neck stretched out as if getting ready to take off—he gave up for now. He had to finish the heart first.

A small piece like the amber heart would not take long. However, since Peter had to do this at night, he had to break up the steps. He listed them in his mind.

Proper soaking. Scrubbing off all the remaining grit and dirt.

Sanding the surface until all of the weathered crust had been removed. Soaking repeatedly so the amber would not overheat. Taking care not to move too fast or getting too close to the tiny bubble. It would be just right of center in the finished pendant. Carving to bring out the shape of the heart—this would take the longest. Carving and cutting amber had to be done with great care so the piece would not break. Stopping frequently to allow heat to disperse and to rest one's eyes. More sanding down with a pumice stone. More soaking to prevent the development of a sticky surface when the amber gets too hot. Taking great care when sanding to avoid scratches. Polishing the piece with linen, impregnated with spirits of wine and slaked lime. Rinsing again. Polishing with soft leather to achieve the final silken sheen.

When he worked, he forgot about everything else. He no longer paid attention to the creaks and cracks of the old house in the winter nights. He did not notice when it got cold because he had forgotten to add wood to the stove. It was as if he was in a dream. This feeling did not leave him when he made his way back up the stairs to the little attic room, crawling under the blanket with a grateful sigh, his thoughts caught in the golden glow of the amber heart like a mosquito fluttering around a candle.

12

LINDEN TREE ON A HILL

"Stop!" Peter yells and starts to run. "Leave her alone."

Lioba stands in the middle of a road, surrounded by three men in bedraggled clothing. She has lost her cap, and her long braid hanging down over her shoulder has started to unravel. Natasha stands next to her, the fur on her back bristling, barking and barking.

"We got ourselves a little lady!"

"Would you believe it? Her daddy is probably a count something or other."

"Let's see how fine her skin is."

"Ah, yes, let me kiss your hand, milady." One of the men sketches a courtly gesture of bowing over a lady's hand. Then he makes a grab for her neck, trying to pull on something hidden by her shirt. "Now what's that pretty thing, a family heirloom?"

Lioba jerks back.

Just then, Natasha leaps up and sinks her teeth in his arm.

"Hey, get that beast off me." The man aims a kick at Natasha.

With a high-pitched yelp, she lets go and huddles on the ground whimpering.

"Leave her alone," Peter shouts again.

"Ah, and the little lady has a trusty servant coming to her aid." The man lets go of Lioba, turns around, and grins. "Isn't that sweet?"

There is nothing Peter can use—no stick, no stones to throw. He launches himself at the man closest to him, butting him in the stomach as hard as he can, and immediately turns to grapple with the other one. But he has lost the element of surprise, and the man is bigger than Peter, blocking his flailing fists with ease.

"Watch out, she's got a gun," someone shouts.

Lioba must have used the moment when her tormentor was distracted to pull the odd-looking pistol from her bag. Holding it with her two hands, she aims it at the man.

"Now, little lady, you wouldn't want to do that, would you?" He has a cajoling tone in his voice.

"Oh, I'll shoot, believe me." Lioba stands firmly, her legs spread out for balance, and her back straight. "I have done it before. Go."

The man Peter hit in the stomach is still doubled over, wheezing heavily. The other one, who appears to be the youngest of the three, stands still as if at a loss for what to do.

"We are hungry. We thought maybe you'd have some food or something we could sell." The young man looks ashamed. "We have been fleeing west for days."

"Go. This is your last chance." Lioba stares at the men over the barrel of her pistol.

The leader glances over his shoulder at the two others. After a moment, he shrugs. "Ah, whatever, let's go. Too bad—I hate to see things wasted. The Russians will be sure to get her sooner or later."

The three men walk off, heading down the road.

"Natasha." Lioba crouches next to the dog.

She whimpers and groans, trying to lift her head. Every rib stands out.

"Oh, God. I think those bastards broke her back." Lioba runs her hands over the dog's body and flanks.

"How do you know?" Peter asks.

"See, she can't even lift her tail." She sits back on her heels, one hand gently caressing the dog's head.

Peter watches helplessly.

Lioba keeps stroking the matted fur while reaching behind her with the other hand and retrieving the pistol she had dropped on the ground. She pats the dog, running her hands over her snout, rubbing her ears, and murmuring to her. Then, she puts the pistol close to the dog's head and pulls the trigger. *Bang.* The dog lies still.

"I can't leave her here like this." Lioba stands. Her face is pale and set like a mask. "Help me."

"What do you want to do?"

"Let's put her over there and pull branches over her." Lioba points at the bushes on the other side of the ditch next to the road. "We don't have a shovel, but we can at least make her look decent."

The dog is much heavier than Peter would have thought. Together they grab her and carry her across the ditch into the underbrush. Why would there be a ditch alongside the road? he wonders. But watching Lioba's rigid, angry movements, he stays silent.

With furious motions, Lioba begins ripping branches from bushes and small trees. Peter helps her, and they pull them over the grey body until the dog is completely hidden.

"That's it," she says, her face a rigid mask.

Together they climb back across the ditch.

"Your hands are bleeding," Peter says.

Lioba ignores him. "Let's go." She reaches for her bag.

"Let me get that."

They bump heads, both bending down.

"You've got to stop doing this," she hisses.

"What did I do?" He is surprised by her reaction.

"Stop interfering. Stop messing up my life. I had it well in hand until you showed up."

"But I tried to help."

"Yes, well, stop it." She rubs her hands over her face. "Stop showing up and vanishing again. I can't bear it."

Peter is silent. There is really nothing he can say.

Without talking, they walk along the road until they reach a village. There are no people in sight anywhere.

"Where is everybody?" Peter gazes around, fascinated by several metal structures in a farmyard next to the road. They make him think of crouching monsters. Their wheels are as big as a cart, and they look like a cross between siege engines and plows suitable for giants.

"How should I know?" Lioba snapped. "Maybe they decided to evacuate already, or they got tired of putting out welcome mats for treks coming through."

"Treks?" Peter blinks at the strange word.

"You know, refugees from the east with horse-drawn carriages passing through. Most of the villages I passed through were stuffed to the rafters with refugees from East Prussia. Some decided to stay, too tired and despondent to move on. The farther west I get, the more unwelcoming people seem to be. In some villages, the treks aren't even allowed to stay and rest for a night. I have heard of treks that turned around to go back because of rumors the Russians had broken through the front on the west. If that's true, if the Russian army is heading toward us from both east and west, we don't have anywhere to go other than the sea, although I suspect that won't do us much good either."

"Oh." Peter thinks of the refugees walking down the road toward Stolp. He no longer knows whether those sad throngs of people were in his own time or in Lioba's grey world.

"There is a stable. That might be good for the night." Lioba points at a brick building with a pitched roof. Peter follows her inside.

Lioba sits down on a hay bale. "I'm sorry I yelled at you."

"It is nothing," Peter said quickly.

"I hate feeling helpless. Those men were going to get me. You distracted them."

"I am sorry they killed your dog."

"It was bound to happen. I haven't been able to find food for her for the past two days." Tears run down her smudged face. "It's just she made me feel less alone."

"Food … that reminds me," Peter says, digging his hand into his pocket. He had grabbed a piece of bread from the pantry when Mistress Nowak was out. "Here. I wish I had more."

"Oh, thank you," she says in a distracted voice, holding the bread in one hand and poking at the hay with the other. "You know what the worst was?"

"No."

"Those were Germans. I came close to shooting at my own people."

"What difference does it make?" Peter shakes his head. "People have been shooting each other for years—Swedes, Imperialists, Danes, whatever. I know of families where sons ended up in opposing armies. You had to defend yourself."

"Yes. Still, I hate it."

"Tell me about your home," Peter says, trying to distract her.

"Home?" Lioba's eyes are red and swollen. "You mean my parents' house in Stolp? Or Muttrin? Maybe they are both gone. I have a feeling it's all gone."

"You do not know that."

"You should see what villages look like farther east. People take what they can carry or fit onto a horse-drawn carriage and get on the road." Lioba rubs her eyes as if trying not to cry. "The Russians have already reached Elbing. The army is still fighting and trying to hold them back, but I think it's just a question of weeks."

Peter shakes his head. "Eat your bread. You will feel better."

Obediently Lioba takes a bite and starts chewing. "Oh, this

is good," she mumbles between swallows. "Reminds me of home."

"Home?"

"Well, my grandparents' place in Muttrin. I was born in Stolp, but Muttrin is also home. When I visited there during summer vacation, my cousins and I got terribly hungry during the day—and trust me, we had lots to eat, but we always were hungry—and would sneak off to the kitchen. The cook would give us fresh bread, and in the dairy, we got huge glasses of milk."

"You drink milk? That sounds revolting."

"It's not revolting. It's good. What do you drink?"

"Water—if it is clean," Peter says. "Beer mostly. My master has his own brewery. Only when you are sick, you get to drink tea—like chamomile tea. Now that is revolting."

Lioba smiles. "True. We get the same when we are sick." She takes another big bite and chews energetically. A little color has come into her face. Swallowing, she begins to grin. "This puts a new spin on the idea of day-old bread."

"What do you mean? Clare just baked this."

"I'm eating three-hundred-year-old bread."

Peter laughs. At the same time, he feels a sense of dislocation. His own world is blurry in his mind. It is as if he has known Lioba all his life even though most of what she says doesn't make any sense. He can smell and touch and see everything in this dream world.

To distract himself, he says, "Tell me more about Muttrin." In his mind, he has an image of a manor house in disrepair, burnt farmhouses, an abandoned watermill, and a few peasants trying to hold on.

"Oh, Muttrin." Lioba gazes at Peter with raised eyebrows. "It just occurred to me—there is a tree on a hill that one of my ancestors planted in 1555—it's still there. It's a linden tree."

Peter gapes at her in disbelief. She is talking about a tree planted almost one hundred years before he was born, and it would still be there three hundred years later.

"According to the story that's passed down, one of my ancestors used to light a bonfire next to the tree during stormy nights, a fire that could be seen from far away, even from the Baltic Sea, and the fishermen would send him salt and herrings in thanks.

"Anyway, you wanted to know about Muttrin. It's a big place; most of my cousins and aunts and uncles come there and often bring friends. My grandfather died nine years ago. I still miss him. Now my uncle is in charge." Lioba swallows the last piece of bread and begins to pick the breadcrumbs from her lap. "The main crop is potatoes, and there are woods and fisheries as well, a pond where we went swimming, and ponies and horses. I loved it as a child. I still love it. My grandfather was terribly strict with us and actually pretty strict with everybody around him. My brother and I always got in trouble. Of course, usually, I was the one who got blamed. My brother was my grandfather's favorite and could do no wrong in his eyes."

"Where is your brother?"

"Oh, he's dead—he was a soldier. He is buried somewhere in the east. Actually, you remind me of him—you don't look anything alike, but I can talk to you just like I used to talk to him."

"My brother is dead too."

Peter listened, mesmerized by her intensity almost more than by the stories she told. Much of it he could not understand—for instance, a casual reference to something called the railroad from Budow via Muttrin and Jamrin to Stolp—the names of those villages were familiar, but a railroad? Potato fields—what would that look like? However, after a while, he lost the sense of strangeness.

"You'd think with all the potatoes we grew, we could eat new potatoes at harvest time. But no, new potatoes have to go into storage." She rubs her arms and tugs on her collar, loosening it.

"Every day at the midday meal, my grandfather would put

my grandmother through an inquisition—had she remembered
to send food to this aunt or that uncle, had she taken care of the
peasant at the mill, had she remembered to set aside something
for the workers, on and on and on. Sometimes she pleaded with
him, saying that she still had to take care of everyone in the
house—and there were always many people staying there. Of
course, pretty much everything one needs is made right there—
in the dairy, the leather workshop and the cobbler, the mill, the
spinning works, and of course, everything to do with potatoes."

"You make it sound like a kingdom."

"Well, it was a bit like that—if your idea of a kingdom is
one where everyone is taken care of, and everyone works very
hard, including the king. My grandfather certainly worked hard.
When he first took over the estate, it was run down and in debt,
like many other places around here in Pomerania. He was very
young at that time, and at first, people thought they could do as
they pleased. They soon found out how wrong they were."

Lioba smiles as she goes on. "Once, a foreman in the dairy
came to him to complain that he needed more workers to get
everything done. My grandfather agreed and promised that help
would be there sooner than expected. And there he was, bright
and early, at 3:30 the very next morning, introducing himself as
the new farmhand. Shocked by the presence of this 'new farmhand', they got to work. They mucked out the cowshed, pitched
straw, and took care of the milking, feeding, and all other
chores, with plenty of breaks in between. After two days of this
drudgery," Lioba says, laughing, "when everything got done
much faster than ever before, the foreman came to my grandfather and said, using his military title 'Captain' from his days in
the cavalry, '*Herr Rittmeister*, I am glad to inform you, we can
manage alone.'"

Lioba is intense and animated in the retelling, seemingly
reliving every moment. Peter feels as if he is sinking into another
dream, this one even more vivid and tangible than the other.

"There is a saying we were taught. In fact, we had to memorize it." Lioba glances at him as if to make sure he is paying attention. *"Whatever you have inherited from your forebears, you have to earn for yourself all over again to claim it as your own.* It's something Goethe wrote."

"Who?" Peter asks.

"Never mind—after your time." Lioba laughs. "I keep forgetting. Anyway, they made sure we learned this lesson. We had a pony with a pony cart for driving all over the estate. If we didn't brush and feed the pony before we went inside to eat our lunch, it disappeared for a long time." She falls silent.

"My father never allowed us to have a dog," Peter says. Lorenz pleaded for a dog when he was a boy. It was rare for his parents not to give in to one of Lorenz's wishes. "Dogs eat too much," his father had said bluntly. "This is not the time for taking on another charge."

Then Peter realizes Lioba is not paying attention. She frowns, looking puzzled and amused at the same time.

"What is it?"

"I just thought of something. There are some things in the house—silver, brass candelabra, and other things, that were buried in the ground for safekeeping during the Thirty Years' War."

"Which war?"

"Yours," Lioba says. "Isn't it comforting to know that even your war will come to an end?"

That means it will be over soon. Peter shakes his head. It seems wrong to know something about the future of his own world. And yet, how wonderful.

Peter glances around at the walls of the barn, the hay bales, the tools leaning against the wall, and the girl sitting in front of him. He is overcome with a feeling of disorientation, trapped in a dream within a dream within a dream. He pinches himself, relieved to find that it hurts.

For an instant, the flat grey, black, and white tones seem to lift like a veil, and the colors of Lioba's world emerge—the red brick of the wall, the soft grey-green of the hay bales, the golden shimmer of Lioba's hair, her rosy skin, and her blue eyes.

He rubs his eyes. Everything has gotten blurry.

Her voice sounds distant. "I am glad you were with me today."

The world fades.

13

BÖNHASE

IT WAS PERFECT.

Peter contemplated the finished piece of amber on the palm of his hand. Everything about it was right. Polishing had brought out the warm golden color. Heart-shaped, with a little crease from one full curve pointing downward at the bubble just right of center, trapped there thousands of years ago. Warm, soft, and silky, the little heart seemed alive.

The final task was to drill the hole for the metal hook to hold the thin leather strip Peter had gotten from the cobbler. One day perhaps he could buy a silver chain, but for now, this would do. Besides, the supple leather would feel comfortable on the skin.

It was late. Peter stretched his back, suddenly feeling bone-tired. Quickly, he cleaned up the workroom. In the dark, he made his way up the stairs to the attic, taking care not to step on the creaking portions of the steps.

Just before he reached the top landing, he heard someone walk around below and froze.

Master Nowak.

Carefully, Peter peered around the banister and spotted a glimmer of light.

He was sure he had hidden all traces of his work and closed the door to the workshop, but the odors of someone having worked there just minutes before might permeate through the doorframe.

After a few moments, Peter heard the kitchen door shut followed by the sound of footsteps through the hallway, the living area, and into the back room where Master Nowak and Mistress Nowak slept.

Peter let out his breath. He did not want to imagine what would happen if Master Nowak had caught him. At the least, he would be dismissed from his apprenticeship.

Still shaken, he crept into the attic room.

"What are you doing up so late?" Cune's voice was muffled underneath his blanket.

"Nothing." Peter pulled off his breeches and jacket and got into bed.

"You never tell me anything," Cune grumbled. "I know you have been in the workshop again. You should not be doing that. You will get us both in trouble."

"Go back to sleep, Cune."

In the morning, the house smelled of fresh baking. In the kitchen, Mistress Nowak was trimming large fir branches and arranging them in an old butter churn that usually held walking sticks. Anne was attaching pinecones to a wreath of holly branches with red berries.

"Oh, that looks nice." Cune wrinkled his nose appreciatively as he gazed around.

"When are you boys going to your families?"

"This morning," Cune said.

Peter was silent. He had completely forgotten it was the day of Christmas Eve and he would have to go home.

"Here, this is for you." Mistress Nowak handed a small cloth bag to Peter and Cune each. "Some cookies for you to take home."

"Thank you so much." Cune sniffed at the bag. "Cinnamon stars? My favorite."

"Thank you," Peter echoed.

"I have something for both of you," Anne said proudly, pulling out two dark blue woolen scarves from behind her back. "I hope you like them. They came out a bit too thin and too long, but they should keep you warm."

Cune had carved a little bunny out of wood for Anne and a spinning top for Inga. The master gave Cune and Peter each a silver piece.

Peter was flustered and embarrassed. Last year, he and Cune had worked together on making a rocking horse for Inga and had sanded the wood and painted it. Now he had nothing at all for any of them.

His new scarf wrapped around his neck and holding the bundle with cookies, he set out for his father's house. It was a grey day, and the wind pushed rain and sleet into his face as he walked. By the time he reached his father's house, Peter was chilled to the bone.

Clare had tied fir and pine branches above the door to his father's study and placed a bowl with chestnuts and walnuts on the chest of drawers. A large pot of stew sat on the stove, and she had put a fresh loaf of bread on the table, with a note: "I will stay at my sister's house overnight. Take a tray up to Effie's room."

Peter's father was in his study, bent over his accounts. "Ah, Peter, you are home."

"I will check on Effie, and then I will bring out our dinner. Clare left everything all ready for us."

His father had already turned back to his work. With a sigh, Peter made his way up the stairs.

When Peter pushed Effie's door open, he felt rather than saw her scurrying quickly over to her bed. Papers were spread out on her desk. Perhaps she had been scribbling again. That had to be an improvement. Then he dismissed that thought when he saw several sheets crumpled up on the floor and others ripped to shreds. It seemed so unlike his sister, always neat and meticulous. All of a sudden, Peter remembered gripping his father's hand when they walked past a refugee woman sitting on the ground at the edge of town. Oblivious to the world around her, she picked at bleeding and festering scabs on her arms as if trying to dig them out. Why was this image so vivid in his mind? It was not as if his sister was scratching her own face bloody.

Effie hunkered on her bed, with her legs pulled up and her arms folded defensively over her chest. The tense posture and the slight movement from side to side usually preceded her violent rocking. At least she was clean and neatly dressed, her dark hair brushed until it was glossy, and the bruises on her face now faded.

He had never really looked at her before—her large brown eyes, the thick curls on her shoulders, her long limbs. No longer his little sister—she was growing up.

"Effie, I brought you something," he said. "Can I show you?" He lowered himself onto the bed, careful not to sit too close.

She blinked but did not shrink away from him.

"This is for you." He took the heart out of his pocket. "It will make you feel better." He held it up by the string. "You should wear it under your shirt right on your skin. That's how it will help."

Effie took the heart in her hands, sniffed at it, and held it up to the light. She shook it gently as if to see whether the bubble would move. She reached out her hand and placed it on Peter's chest, gazing at him as if about to speak.

"Yes, it is a heart."

With her slender fingers, she beat a rhythm on his chest. Then she held the amber against her own chest, her eyes glowing and her eyebrows raised in a question.

"Yes, it is for you. But do not show it to anybody."

His sister looked down, cradling the heart in her hand.

"Please, Effie, promise me. You cannot show it to anyone, not even Clare. It is a secret." If only she could talk, Peter thought. She understood everything people said to her. He wished he could shake her. The words were there, he knew it. They were locked inside of her, trapped. "Please, promise me."

Effie pushed out her lips and nodded slowly, her fingers tracing the contours of the heart.

"Just wear it all the time. I think it might bring you luck."

Obediently she slipped the leather string over her head and tucked the heart inside her blouse. She smiled at Peter, the first smile he had seen in a long time.

Peter stood up. "Good. I will get Father's dinner now. Will you come downstairs?"

Effie tensed, shaking her head.

Peter sighed. "I will bring you a tray."

Dinner with his father was quiet. Eating his stew and dipping the bread into the sauce, Peter felt guilty for missing Master Nowak and his family.

His father said nothing beyond asking for the bread and offering Peter another ladle full of stew.

Finally, with a sigh, Peter got up to take the plates back to the scullery.

"Thank you," his father grunted. "Check on your sister, Peter. Clare thinks Effie will get better, but I am afraid. I fear for her future."

"She will get better," Peter said fiercely.

His father shrugged and waved his hand despondently.

That night, Peter stayed awake for a long time. The seam of the pocket was getting weak. Maybe he could ask Clare to fix it before he went back to Master Nowak's house. It was as if the amber had gotten heavier. He wished he could let it go. It was preying on his thoughts and calling to him.

He dreamed of walking across snow-covered fields, trudging along with hundreds of grey people, venturing out onto an endless sheet of ice, slipping and sliding. The ice crackled beneath his feet as if it would burst open any second. Nearly blinded by the drifting snow, he tried not to lose sight of the makeshift path marked with tree branches. He dreamed of horses screaming as they broke through the ice, their owners abandoning them and their carts in a scramble for safety. He dreamed of the sound of cannon fire and artillery shells hitting everything that moved, of huge craters opening up, carts sinking into the icy waters, horses groaning. He dreamed of silence—endless dark mounds of bodies, covered by steadily falling snow. He dreamed of Lioba, rushing through the forest and hiding out in village barns as she kept traveling west, staying by herself because it was safer that way.

In the morning, his head ached. Once he got back to his master's house, he felt better and then immediately ashamed of his relief to be away from his father's house.

Over the next week, Master Nowak and his wife and daughter spent time away from home, visiting other relatives, and Cune went home to his family in the evenings. Contentedly, the two apprentices worked on their rosary beads during the day, and in the evenings, Peter was free. Finally, he could work on the large amber piece without the worry that someone would walk in on him.

The first step was to make a proper sketch. Peter always found drawing a challenge. Ruefully, he thought of Effie's scribbles. However, this time, to his amazement, the young crane emerged on the paper as if by itself—with folded wings, beak raised into the air, and one long leg slightly angled.

Peter took his time with the preparation of the amber piece. Of course, the hardest part was the process of carving and cutting. As he worked, he forgot all about the danger involved if anyone caught him. The only precaution he took was to do the work at night when he was sure no one would come to the house. He did not want this time to end. He hummed as he worked, his thoughts traveling, lost in a world that belonged to him alone.

By the time the family returned, Peter had finished the more complicated parts of the crane.

"It is good to be home," Anne said when she came into the kitchen, her cheeks reddened from the cold. She pulled off her woolen wrap and her cap and mittens. "How are you? How is Effie?"

"I am fine." Peter smiled at Anne, happy to see her. "And I think Effie is a little bit better."

The last time he had gone home for a brief visit, three days after Christmas, he had heard her humming in her room. It was a familiar tune.

The golden sun
Brings life and warmth,
And darkness flees.
As the morning rises
With a rosy glow,
Darkness flees.

One of the treads on the staircase creaked, and the humming stopped. When Peter poked his head in, he noticed that her papers were neatly arranged on the table. She had retreated to her bed but did not appear as frightened. Perhaps she was getting better.

The urge to tell Anne everything was overwhelming. Maybe he would not feel so alone then.

"I will go see her soon." Anne studied him, her eyes wide with concern. "You look like you have not slept in days."

"I am fine, really." Peter tried to think of something to distract her.

Fortunately, just then Mistress Nowak walked into the kitchen. "Anne, I need you to run to the bakery and the butcher, and Peter, would you help Master Nowak with the wood delivery?"

And so, life resumed.

At first, Peter was happy that Anne was back and Cune had resumed sleeping in the attic.

But soon both of them began to get on his nerves.

Cune asked questions all the time.

"You have got to stop staring into space as if you were in another world. What are you thinking about, Peter?"

"Why do you look so tired?"

"I know you have been in the workshop at night."

So far Peter had managed to shake Cune off with vague answers and claiming he was worried about Effie.

And Anne—that was confusing. Ever since Proclamation Day, Peter felt uncomfortable around her. All the ease that they used to have was gone. It had been so pleasant before. She had just been Anne. The youngest of Master Nowak's apprentices, she was a quick learner. She never tried to exploit her position as her father's daughter by jockeying for special treatment in the workshop. Her hair braided and pinned up, a kerchief wrapped around her neck, her skirts tied back with a shawl to keep them out of the way, she worked hard, laughed at her own mistakes, and did not stint with praise for Cune's and Peter's efforts. She was easy to get along with, always cheerful and uncomplaining. She was simply there.

Now, Anne often seemed tense with him, even snapping at him for no reason.

But Master Nowak gave his three apprentices so much work that Peter had little time to brood.

The only break was Three Kings Day. Even during the worst years of the war, people in Stolpmünde marked the day with a feast. Mistress Nowak prepared a roasted chicken, spiced and stuffed with apples and onions. There also was a dish of lentils and a loaf of fresh bread.

"This is wonderful," Cune said, his hands dripping as he chewed on a chicken leg.

Peter grinned at him. "Slow down, Cune, before you choke."

He sobered when he remembered Lioba hungrily wolfing down her bread the last time he had seen her.

The puckered golden-brown skin on the chicken wing in front of him reminded him of the amber in his pocket. The crane was not finished, but Peter was reluctant to complete the work. What could he do with it, anyway? He could hardly put it on his blanket chest or display it in his father's house. Something else stopped him from completing the work. Once it was finished, he would have to let it go. He would never see Lioba again. It had all become tied up in his mind.

"What's going on with you?" Anne asked. "You just looked as if you were far away."

"Oh, sorry," Peter said hurriedly and pushed the bowl with lentils over to her. "I was just thinking."

Anne pursed her lips. In an undertone, she muttered something. Peter thought he heard her say, "Marthe."

Peter's cheeks burned.

Then Master Nowak started talking about the latest news, and the moment passed.

14

THREE KINGS DAY

TICK TOCK. TICK TOCK. TICK TOCK.

The gold fittings of a tall-case clock gleam in the dark at the end of what appears to be a long, dimly lit hallway.

Peter stands in front of a partially open door, staring at the number 12 painted at eye level on the white paneling. Perhaps this is a tavern.

He enters the room. The covers of the bed are thrown back. The window is open, and white gauzy fabric flutters in the cold air so that the light from the moon flickers and waves across the walls.

Mystified, Peter gazes at a metal structure of tubes all in a row underneath the window, with a knob on one side, and one pipe disappearing into the floor. On the wall above the bed, a woodcut print—a bunny, with dark grey and white fur and long silky ears folded back as if listening to something behind it. On the lower edge of the print, the letter D sheltered by an A stands out in the glare of the moonlight. It looks familiar. Then Peter realizes he had seen it in a book of tales from which his mother read to them when they were little. Albrecht Dürer, that's the name of the artist.

Next to a chest of drawers, in the corner, there is a pot-belly cast-iron stove, with a white pitcher and washbowl on top. His father wouldn't be impressed by this little thing compared to their stove at home, covered with blue and white ceramic tiles all the way up to the ceiling. Linked to a hearth in the kitchen through a tube, it can heat the whole downstairs.

Crashing sounds startle Peter out of his absorption. *Bum bum bum,* like an army marching into town, followed by lighter tones with fragments of a melody. It does not sound like a church organ or like anything he has ever heard. Where is it coming from? He leaves the room to continue exploring this strange house.

He passes through the hallway where all the doors are marked with numbers and down the stairs into a large hall. Stepping carefully, he walks across black and white flagstones like a giant chessboard. Antlers mounted alone or attached to entire deer heads with glinting black eyes line the white-washed walls.

Stunned, he stares at a large black wooden cabinet as broad as the entire wall of his father's house. "Facit anno 1756" is written in wooden letters across the front of the cabinet. "Made in 1756," Peter whispers. Seeing the number makes him feel dizzy.

Boxes, made out of a strange paper-like brown material, are stacked in a corner. The boxes seem to belong in a warehouse—not in this elegant hall.

Peter glances through an open door into a large room with tall windows and a set of double doors opening onto a winter landscape of large beeches and oaks, branches bent under their burden of snow and ice, silvery grey in the moonlight. A chandelier glows with lights that are not candles. Bronze wall sconces with heads and wings of eagles bear more of these strange lights.

Three fir trees block his view of the rest of the room. Who would put up a tree inside a house, much less three huge ones like these? Last year, the mayor of Stolp had placed a fir tree in the main hall of the town hall for Christmas. But here there are three trees. Fir needles and drops of wax litter the floor. Shiny silver balls and hundreds of silver stars stand out against the dark green branches, many with small metal candleholders perched on their tips and covered with wax.

The music comes from the other side of the trees. Peter tiptoes around and sees a black wooden box, a cross between a shaped boat and a coffin, with the cover folded up.

Lioba sits on a bench in front of it; he cannot see her hands. Below the box, her feet move in rhythm on pedals close to the floor. She raises her head briefly, taking in his presence in the room, and continues playing.

Peter is mesmerized. He has heard a harpsichord once in the town hall, but this sounded nothing like a harpsichord. The music fills the room—wistful, searching, slow, gentle sounds alternating with dark strong ones, slow beats matched with rapid ones. It seems almost simple—notes repeated over and over again, as if it was a child skipping up and down a staircase, followed by large, layered sounds like a chorus of many voices.

Lioba plays for a little bit longer. Then she stops, resting her hands on the black and white keys as if frozen. She straightens up and closes the cover over the keyboard. "I will never play on this piano again."

"Why not?"

"You think it will still be here if I ever come back?"

Peter shakes his head. How can he possibly respond to that? "What is this place?"

"Muttrin. My grandfather's house—well, now my uncle's. I missed them. I came all this way, and I missed them. They didn't even take down the Christmas trees."

"Why? Where would they go?"

"I don't know. My uncle has been gone for some time, apparently since the fall, but nobody could tell me why. Something must have happened. He'd never just leave here—he'd feel like a captain abandoning ship."

"Why would he have left?"

"Perhaps the government arrested him." Lioba glances

around as if to make sure there really is no one else in the room who might hear her. "Last summer, I heard from a cousin that my uncle was talking to other people who want to do something about the Nazis. But they have spies everywhere, and maybe someone told on him."

"Where are the others from your family?" Nazis? Spies? Peter cannot even begin to sort out what Lioba is talking about.

"The villagers told me that my aunt, with her daughters and others staying here, went into town a few days ago and gave the staff time off. Perhaps my aunt decided to try to get other family members away from here while there are still trains running. She promised she would return soon. She definitely wouldn't abandon the staff and the people in the village."

"So, you are all alone here?" Peter asks, choosing to ignore the mystery of a running train.

"Yes. There are refugees in the smithy and the distillery on the other side of the yard, but nobody in here. The villagers told me some officers had been quartered here, but they left again. Treks must have stayed here as well. It's a mess upstairs. It's as if a herd of elephants slept in the rooms."

"But you told me that refugees are not welcome in the villages."

"Not here. The people here are different. They help."

Peter thinks of how the townspeople in Stolpmünde grumble about having soldiers stay in their houses. Housing the troops is a burden. Soldiers often travel not only with a baggage train but also with their wives and servants, and of course, horrible things happen when soldiers go around collecting tribute from the residents. How can anyone blame them for complaining about having to deal with refugees on top of all that?

"Where will it end?" they say, shrugging their shoulders defensively. "We cannot take care of them all. We have barely enough for our own people." He remembers his father's expressionless face when he told Peter about the time in 1627 when cavalry troops had come to the town.

People watched from church towers all around the region, ready to ring the bells when the soldiers approached and tried to hide whatever they could. "It did no good," his father said, talking in a flat monotone. "People were hauled out of their beds with burning torches. They were beaten, and many were executed. Those who survived were robbed of all they owned."

"And when the Swedes came?" Peter asked.

"It was no different." His father sighed. "Supposedly they were our allies, but the only change was that the demands for money and for food increased."

Lioba's description of her village makes no sense to Peter. If they helped all those refugees, they soon would be left with nothing for themselves.

"Come, today you will be my guest," Lioba says. "Let's go to the kitchen."

"Why do you have these boxes here?" Peter points at the boxes.

"Would you believe this?" Lioba grimaces. "My other aunt and uncle who live in a town farther west from here sent these boxes to Muttrin for safekeeping—all sorts of things—linen, silver, you name it."

"Why would it not be safe here?"

"Didn't you hear anything I said? The Russians have already overrun most of East Prussia. Never mind what the German High Command says; they'll be here in another month, if not sooner."

"But you said there are still people here in the village. Why are they not leaving?"

"For one, because some of them still believe in the final victory the Nazis have been bragging about for years. Fools!" Lioba practically spits out these words. "Besides, the government considers anybody leaving without permission to be a traitor. Like sitting ducks, people have to wait for the evacuation order."

She shakes her head in frustration. "My uncle had expected something like this."

"How do you know?"

"Mr. Drew, my uncle's principal manager, told me that he and my uncle had secretly drawn up plans some time ago, preparing for a possible evacuation. Once the official permission comes, they'll be ready. I'm not surprised. My uncle wasn't one to leave anything to chance."

"What about you?"

"I'm not going to sit around. My parents must be waiting for me in Stolp, so that's where I'm going. I haven't heard from them for a while. But it's not as if I can get mail these days."

"And then?"

"We will go as far west as we can, but I have to find them first. With any luck, the war will be over soon."

Lioba opens the door into a large room, the walls lined with cabinets and a wooden table that could seat at least ten people.

"Let me turn on the stove first." She twists one of the knobs on a square white box standing against a wall. "There, it takes a few minutes for it to get hot." She points at four round black plate-like areas on top of the box.

"That is a stove?" Peter steps closer to get a better look. "How do you light the fire?"

"Light the fire?" Lioba laughs. "Actually, we used to have a coal-burning stove for most of my childhood. It also kept the kitchen warm."

"Coal? I have heard of that, but not for cooking. And how does this one work?"

"Electricity. My uncle bought this stove a few years ago, and he was very proud of it. Muttrin always was more advanced than other houses. Isn't it great? No messing around with coal. It's called a Lucullus, which is pretty funny."

"Lucullus?"

"You know—the ancient Roman politician who loved to give lavish dinner parties? Now, sit down, and let me cook."

"This is a big kitchen." Peter perches on one of the chairs, gazing all around the room.

"Well, perhaps, but lots of people stay here—they all have to be fed." She puts a bowl filled with large brown fruits on the table. They look like unappealing, misshapen apples.

"What kind of fruit is that?"

"Potatoes." Lioba grins at him. "They come from our fields. I'm going to make mashed potatoes for you. If it were summer, I'd serve it with buttermilk. When it's hot outside, that's absolutely the most delicious meal you can imagine."

With swift, practiced motions, she peels the potatoes, flicking the skins into a bucket.

"Why do you have those big trees inside the house?"

"Oh, the Christmas trees? You should see them when the candles are all lit on Christmas Eve. It's magical. When we were children, the salon was locked while it was being prepared for Christmas. We waited outside the doors until my grandmother rang the bell, and then we were finally allowed inside. In front of everyone—the family, the cook, servants, and people from the village—we had to recite verses we had memorized. My grandfather read the Christmas gospel, and we sang carols. But the best things about Christmas happened right before." Her face glows as she talks.

"The night before, we were allowed briefly into the dark ballroom. Our parents walked around the tables and described the gifts we would get in the most fascinating and enigmatic way, so it was impossible to guess what they could possibly be."

Peter listens to her voice, almost more fascinated by her telling the stories than the stories themselves. He cannot take his eyes off her face.

Gaunt, tired, pale, with its slightly hooked nose, high forehead, and pronounced cheekbones, it could be the features of a man, commanding an army. Then, in a shift of light, it is the face of a young woman, with soft skin, large eyes, full lips, and thick, long wavy hair, kept in a braid hanging over her shoulder, a face that changes when animated, spelling warmth and laughter and love of life, shifting like a piece of translucent amber in front of a candle.

"Anyway, I have to get some water."

Lioba takes a pot from a shelf, walks into a room off the kitchen, and sticks it under a spigot at the edge of an enormous basin.

At this point, Peter has begun to accept many things he cannot begin to comprehend—matches, the light, the mysterious knobs, the stove, and the sheer size of the rooms. But when Lioba twists a knob, and a stream of clear water flows out of the spigot, he gasps.

"That's a pump? This is wonderful," he exclaims. Clare would love this. She has to get water from the well every day.

"Yes, running water." Lioba laughs. "But let me tell you, the villagers weren't pleased when my grandfather installed water pipes and bathtubs in their houses. Too much change, they thought. One even said to him, 'You think we are so dirty that we need to wash?'"

Lioba rinses the potatoes and puts them back in the pot, covering them with water. Then she twists the knob again and the water stops flowing. "I loved this sink when I was a little girl, and I was convinced the cook kept ducklings in it."

She lifts the pot and puts it on the stove. "Now for the onions and the bacon." She begins to peel onions and cut them up into small pieces. Her eyes start to tear, and she rubs her wrists over them, but it doesn't seem to bother her as she continues talking.

"Before the war, in the morning of Christmas Eve, we always loaded the sleigh carriage with gifts for all the people who worked on my grandfather's land. Then we drove all over from village to village. At every house where we stopped, we were fed cookies and other treats, and the carriage driver got a drink. So, by the time we turned for home, we moved at quite a clip across the snow-covered roads."

On the stove, the pot with the potatoes begins to bubble. Lioba throws a pinch of salt into the water.

"One of my favorite times was New Year's Eve just before we got ready for dinner." Lioba glances at him, her cheeks flushed. "One of the young guys from the village got dressed up as the New Year's Grey, pretending to be a wild and misbehaving horse. Supported by other villagers acting out the roles of a bear, a woman, and a stork, the New Year's Grey chased the kitchen maids all over the house. Then they went rampaging all over the village. People believed this would bring good health, prosperity, and fertility for the coming year."

The scent of onions and bacon sizzling in the pan fills the warm kitchen. Peter has lost all sense of time and place as he takes in the images Lioba draws for him.

Lioba smiles, and yet, to Peter, it is as if she is saying goodbye to a world that is already in the past.

It all sounds impossible—a beautiful, imagined world, something out of a storybook, no more real than the magical bird weeping golden amber tears. Of course, his world might sound just as unreal to her. It is a new thought. It has never occurred to him to question the world he lives in. It just is, with all the good and the bad. It is not as if there is any way to change it. Now, confronted with images of worlds that do not even exist yet, it makes him think about possibilities. His own world can change.

Suddenly, the amber crane is vivid in his mind, as if it has come to life, restless, burrowing in his pocket, ready to take off. There is so much he could do with amber beyond those dreary rosary beads. He just has to find a way to do it.

Lioba pokes the potatoes with a fork. "Perfect." She pours the water off into the sink, puts the pot back on the stove, and adds a generous chunk of butter and some milk. Then she picks up a knobby rounded wooden tool. Pushing back her sleeves, she begins to mash the potatoes. The steam, redolent of butter and milk and this strange earthy fruit, makes Peter's mouth water.

With a flick of her wrist, Lioba throws the bacon and the onions into the pot and stirs everything vigorously. "Some salt," she says as if walking herself through all the steps. She dips her hand into a bowl and throws a few pinches into the pot. "And now, the finishing touch." She grabs a little jar from a cabinet and shakes it for a few seconds over the steaming mess. A pungent scent fills the air. "I love nutmeg."

She gets two plates and forks. "Here, we are going to eat properly, not sitting in a barn or in a hut somewhere or on a tree trunk," she says firmly as she arranges everything on the table. "Glasses, napkins, and a serving spoon. What else? Oh, yes, a jug of water. Now we are ready." She ladles generous helpings on each plate. Bending forward, she puts one in front of Peter.

Suddenly, there is a flickering in his eyes, everything around him turns hazy, and he falls off his chair.

15

TO MARKET

"PETER." SOMEONE PULLED ON HIS ARM. "WAKE UP."

He opened his eyes. "What?" He was on the floor next to his bed.

"You were thrashing around." Cune was staring at him. "Bad night?"

Peter sat up. His nightshirt was damp with sweat. "Sorry I woke you."

"I was already awake. It is time to get up. In fact, you are late again. Master Nowak already called twice from downstairs." Cune looked at him curiously. "Are you all right?"

"Yes, thanks." Peter stood up and began to pull on his clothes. "I will be downstairs in a moment." After Cune left the room, Peter sat down again. His thoughts raced as he remembered the Christmas trees, the music, and the water flowing in the kitchen. The images of Lioba's world swirled in his mind. It was not real. Her world did not even exist. It was all just a dream, and yet he could still smell the boiling potatoes and the bacon with onions.

He reached into his pocket and took out the amber crane. Most of the carving was done, and the crane's shape had emerged. Just the thin legs and the beak needed more work. He turned the amber over in his hands, rubbing it and tracing its contours. There was something about it that forced him into this other world. Maybe he would be trapped there, forced to keep fleeing west in the company of this strange girl. What if he threw the crane away and gave it back to the sea? Then he would never see Lioba again or listen to her talk. Her world had begun to dominate all his thoughts. Home and everything he knew, his family, his friends, his life as an apprentice felt blurred, fading into the background. Maybe he was losing his mind.

"Peter!" Master Nowak shouted from downstairs. He sounded impatient.

With a sigh, Peter put the amber piece back in his pocket and went downstairs.

"There you are." In the kitchen, Master Nowak sat at the table with a ledger in front of him, checking entries. With a sigh, he closed the ledger. "I need you to come with me to the harbor. We have to take delivery of our consignment of amber."

Mistress Nowak had left freshly baked slices of bread on the table. Peter's mouth watered, but he did not dare test Master Nowak's patience and pulled on his coat.

"I wish I could have gone with you to the market in Königsberg," he said wistfully.

Master Nowak ignored him as he walked ahead of him out onto the street.

Peter followed, his head bent. For amber craftsmen, Königsberg was the center of the amber trade where amber roads from all points east and south had intersected since time immemorial. This famous Hanse town also exported grain, wood, coal ash, tar, leather, furs, linen, wax, and tallow. Just to see the harbor had to be amazing.

Peter had studied the different types of amber until he could recite every detail in his sleep. The assortment stones were the largest and most expensive, none weighing less than 112 grams. Smaller pieces, so-called ton stones, were sold in bulk by the barrel. The varnish stones, small pieces of very hard and pure amber, were used for the production of varnish. Even smaller pieces known as "sandstone" were used for pipe mouthpieces and the like. Finally, there was fine gravel as well as the waste produced during work, mostly used for the production of mineral oil and succinic acid.

Stones were distinguished by their purity and color, and Peter liked to picture the different colors in his mind—brown, grey, green, honey, lemon, cognac, cherry, dark red, golden red, and buttery white.

Some amber had layered coloring, but the rarest and most intriguing pieces were those with inclusions.

Master Nowak had once jokingly said that according to an ancient Roman called Pliny, people paid more money for a beautiful amber stone than for a living human being. Supposedly there were chunks of amber that weighed more than a pound, but Peter had never seen one. Master Nowak had purchased a few larger pieces for special commissions, but none weighing more than two hundred grams.

He would never get to go to Königsberg, Peter thought. Master Nowak kept putting him off. This war was never going to end. It would be the same thing next year. He would have to continue to follow Master Nowak like a dog along the same roads he walked on every single day, keeping an eye on the carter with the consignment of amber for their workshop, and then go on making nothing but rosary beads day in and day out.

At the harbor, ships had unloaded their cargo. Barrels were lined up next to the dock, and two clerks supervised the distribution, checking off the shipments against names in big ledgers.

"Those ledgers are especially important when it comes to the sale of individual pieces," Master Nowak said. "Every single one has to be accounted for." He checked to make sure he had received everything he had purchased and made arrangements for delivery to his workshop.

Peter watched in silence with one hand gripping the amber

crane in his pocket. It felt heavy and bulky, and it preyed on his mind. Lately, he had managed to put the possible consequences of his actions out of his mind, but when Master Nowak described how clerks had to record every piece of amber down to the last gram in the ledgers, he was overwhelmed with guilt.

"That's done." Master Nowak put away his paperwork and looked at his apprentice. "Now, we will get the amber for your exam."

Peter was dumbfounded. The exam. This was finally going to happen. Then his face fell. "But I did not put my name forward at the quarterly guild meeting. And I do not have any money."

"I put your name in, and the money is taken care of."

"Master Nowak, I cannot accept this." Peter was embarrassed. Did Master Nowak know that his father was struggling to keep his business going? "You said I was not ready yet."

"Well, you are. As to the money, your father deposited the necessary amount with me last spring and even remembered the pieces of silver you need to present to each of the guild elders. He said he wanted to make sure you had the money when the time came."

"Truly?" Peter eyed him doubtfully.

"Truly. If you promise to stop wasting my time with this ridiculous discussion, I will provide the required barrel of beer," Master Nowak said sternly, but with a twinkle in his eyes. "I have already made the purchase of a pound of amber in your name when I was in Königsberg, but you can now choose a larger piece and pass on the equivalent in weight to me. Have you thought of what you want to do? Aside from the standard rosary beads?"

"I am permitted to make something else?"

"Indeed, you are. According to the rules, you have to work a pound of amber into something marketable. There is no rule that it has to be all rosary beads."

"I thought all the amber trading is done in Königsberg."

"Yes, however, this year, the guild decided on allowing a small amount of amber for discretionary buying, provided each guild member stays within the allotted total amount. I doubt they will do so again next year." He glanced around and added in a lower voice, "There is less amber to go around than there used to be. That drives up the price and makes the guilds in Königsberg and Stolp even more insistent on controlling who receives raw amber. I suspect there are changes ahead of us in the way in which amber is made available to guild members."

Peter followed Master Nowak to the other side of the harbor where clerks sat at tables. Awed, he gazed at the amber pieces of varying sizes and colors displayed on cloths of dark felt. Even in their raw state, they were striking.

"I can choose a piece from these?"

"Yes, remember, you have to produce a pound of marketable amber altogether. I suggest that you use about three quarters of a pound for rosary beads and the rest for something else. Take your time. It is only once in your life that you get to make your graduation piece."

"I know what I want." Peter pointed at one reddish-golden piece and at another much smaller warm yellow one. He could see it already: a jewelry box with a lid, inlaid with a glowing rosebud.

"That was quick," Master Nowak said with a smile.

The clerk weighed the two pieces on a scale. Together it came to 110 grams. The clerk recorded the purchase under Master Nowak's name, carefully noting the weight and color of each piece. He folded them into a scrap of felt and handed them to Peter. "Good luck, young man."

"Thank you." Peter took the little bundle and followed Master Nowak to catch up with the carter transporting the consignment of amber to the workshop.

"Thank you, Master Nowak," he said as they walked in the carter's wake.

"No need to thank me. It is your amber. You just have to work it into a marketable product."

Peter tried to picture his father's expression when he learned his son was finally about to take the exam.

He wondered what Cune and Anne would think. Cune might feel bad. Peter was surprised Cune hadn't been chosen instead of himself. He was such a reliable and steady worker. Anne would be pleased for him; she still would have to wait a few years in any event.

But perhaps his friends would not even be interested. He hadn't been able to talk to them properly for a long time now. Cune had stopped asking questions all the time and seemed more withdrawn and quiet than he had been before.

Anne sometimes stared at him as if she was trying to read his thoughts, and then she would glower and turn away. At other times, she nagged him about Effie. "You should go home more often," she said, frowning at him. "Your sister needs to see that you care."

To make matters worse, Peter did not trust them anymore. Several times he heard them whisper, stopping immediately when they saw him. They had been his best friends for years. How could he suspect them? He was angry and ashamed in turn. If only there were someone to whom he could talk about everything.

"Now, Peter, you need to get your papers together for the day of the exam," Master Nowak said as he was picking his way around the refuse littering the street.

"Papers?" Peter asked, jolted out of his daydreaming. "What papers?"

"A certificate of legitimate birth as a freeman and your baptism certificate. I will prepare the certificate of your completion of the apprenticeship. Of course, eventually, if you want to run your own workshop, you have to obtain a craftsman's citizenship document. But you need not worry about that for now."

"Who will be at the exam?"

"You have to do the work in front of an elder of the guild in his workshop. Of course, it cannot be in mine. All other guild masters have the right to attend."

"All of them?" Peter asked uncertainly.

"Not the entire guild. Maybe four or five of the masters will be there."

Peter did not say anything. There was no point in getting nervous now.

"And, then, when you are done, and you have been accepted into the guild, you are expected to present each of the guild masters with two marks of silver and to treat all to a feast."

"Oh," Peter said. He was beginning to feel intimidated.

"Do not worry too much about all that. Mistress Nowak will help you with the details. And the beer is taken care of." Master Nowak smiled.

"Thank you."

"Thank Duke Barnim. He was the one who granted amber guild masters the privilege to brew and sell beer in 1534."

"Can I go to my father's house? I want to tell him about this."

"Yes, of course. Send him my regards."

Peter walked quickly, not paying attention to anything around him.

As a journeyman, he would go to other towns like Gdansk and Königsberg, working for different masters. He might finally learn new techniques and get to work with large pieces of amber. He would become the best master at his craft. He could picture everything—gorgeous beakers, chess sets, religious figures, boxes, and jewelry. Then he chided himself. Master Nowak had been so kind to him, and now was not the time to gripe about his rigid approach.

He crossed the town square, lost in thought, when he stumbled over a cobblestone. He righted himself by holding on to the rim of the well in the center of the square.

"Hello, Peter."

He raised his head and looked directly into the shining blue eyes of Marthe, sitting on the other side of the rim and playing with the satin ribbon of her cap. Her cheeks dimpled as she smiled at him.

Peter hadn't thought about Marthe lately. The amber crane and Lioba's world had crowded out everything else. He had forgotten how beautiful she was.

"Where are you headed?" She lowered herself onto the ground. "I will walk with you for a bit."

"I am going to see my father. I just found out I will have my exam on the day before Shrovetide." Peter glanced at her to see if she was impressed.

"Congratulations." Marthe's voice sounded flat. "So, you are going to go away as a journeyman soon?"

"I believe so." Peter was disappointed with her reaction.

"I envy you." Carefully, she stepped around a refuse pile. "You can go everywhere. I am stuck here. Every day is the same. And my father keeps inviting fat merchants for me to marry."

Peter was silent. Marthe had everything. He thought of her father's house, in excellent trim and freshly painted, unscathed by the war and the big fire in 1638, when the Swedish Field Marshall Johan Banér and the entire Swedish army had spread out, covering Pomerania like a horde of locusts. He thought of her clothes, her governess, and her father's evident wealth and power, but he said nothing.

"How is your sister?"

"She is fine," Peter said, surprised. Why did Marthe ask this?

"I have not seen her in town for a long time. Maybe I will go visit her."

"Thank you," Peter said awkwardly. He could not picture Marthe with Effie.

"I would love to walk along the beach," she said. "I get so tired of the same old paths around the town square. Do you ever dream of finding something precious in the sand?"

"Marthe, I am sorry, but I have to hurry. I am already late,"

Peter said, trying to act as if he hadn't heard her questions. He sketched a bow and ran off.

When he was out of her sight, he slowed down. His thoughts were a jumble. A few months ago, he would have been flattered by Marthe's attention. Now, all his pleasure in her presence had evaporated. He could not delude himself any longer. She had seen him on the beach, and she was baiting him, like a cat playing with a mouse. But if she meant to tell anyone, would she not have done so already? Perhaps she planned to expose him after he had taken the exam. Of course, he could just deny it, but who would believe him over the word of the mayor's daughter? He should get rid of the amber right now. But he could not possibly take Effie's heart away from her; it would make her so sad. And he could never ever let anybody find out about the crane.

Then he chided himself. It was absurd to think that someone like Marthe would be bothered to hurt him. She was just teasing him. She had nothing to gain by exposing him. No, he would not let Marthe spoil this day for him. His thoughts turned back to the exam and his life as a journeyman.

"Watch where you are going." A gruff voice startled him out of his absorption.

Peter had almost careened into a woman walking in the opposite direction. In fact, there were at least fifteen men, women, and children trudging along, carrying bundles. Their clothes looked grimy and torn, and many of the children had rags wrapped around their feet instead of shoes.

"I am sorry," Peter muttered, averting his gaze and hurrying his pace.

They had to be refugees in search of food and shelter. There were so many. He almost hated them for taking away his happiness. He had just been dreaming of becoming a wealthy guild master, perhaps with his own beer brewery and several fields and meadows to his name. These people had lost everything.

Peter had reached the little wood near his father's house. He could not bear going home yet. He brushed the snow off a fallen tree trunk, sat down, and closed his eyes, trying to regain his earlier mood of excitement about the exam. Marthe with her sly questions had unsettled him.

16

KILLING MARCH

HIS PANT SEAT FEELS DAMP. HE REALLY HAS TO STOP sleeping outside in the middle of winter. His cheek stings from the rough bark of the tree trunk where he had been leaning. He rubs his face as he stares at the scene in front of him.

On the road beneath the steep embankment, a group of bedraggled men, with shaved heads, gaunt faces, striped breeches and tops, a few with coats or blankets draped over their shoulders, shuffle along, heads bent and silent. Men in grey uniforms shout at them, "Faster, faster." A guard cuffs one of the prisoners over his shoulder with a long-barreled musket. At least, it looks like a musket, albeit different from any Peter has ever seen.

Just then, two men sheer off and sprint toward a dip in the embankment close to where Peter is hidden.

"Halt," someone shouts, and shots ring out. Arms flailing, the men collapse about ten meters from Peter's hiding spot, one sprawling halfway across the other, with his arms reaching out to a pine tree as if praying.

One of the guards walks toward the prisoners and casually pokes them with his weapon.

"Don't waste a bullet. If they aren't dead yet, they will be soon," another says. "Two less to worry about."

The other prisoners shuffle along as if nothing happened, staring straight ahead or at the ground in front of them.

Peter is unable to take his eyes off the scene. He lifts himself up over the shrubs along the embankment to get a better look when firm hands grab him, one clapped over his mouth and the other pulling him back down.

Peter twists his head around, trying to shake off the hand over his mouth. It is Lioba, and she looks furious.

She shakes her head at him and holds a finger to her lips. Then she points behind her, beckoning him to follow her. They crawl into the woods, only standing up when they are both far enough from the road that they cannot be seen.

"Are you crazy?" she hisses. "Don't you realize you could have been shot if they had seen you?"

"Why? I have not done anything."

"It's lucky I saw you." Lioba rolls her eyes. "You really show up at the worst times. Come on, let's get away from here."

"Wait," Peter says. "What if one of them is still alive?"

"What are we supposed to do?"

"We cannot just walk away."

"Fine," Lioba snaps. "We'll take a look, but let's not take all day about it." She is already turning back, adjusting the straps on her pack at the same time.

"Let's make sure there is no one on the road," she whispers when they reach the edge of the woods.

Cautiously, they approach the embankment and stare at the two bodies on the side of the road, one sprawled on top of the other. Blood is pooling on the ground next to the slain men.

Lioba is right, Peter thinks. They are both dead, and he has placed her at risk.

"Go on then," she growls in his ear. "This is your idea."

The man on top is definitely dead. A rain of bullets had struck his back, neck, and head, which has been shaved so harshly the skull seems to press against the blue-veined skin. His stained striped breeches are too short for his long legs, exposing the bony ankles. His shoes are falling apart, with string wrapped around them to keep the sole in place.

Peter shrinks back, appalled and frightened. But then he remembers something Lorenz told him. *Dead men do not bleed.*

"Help me," he says, bending over the dead man.

Lioba joins him, and together they grab his arms and legs and lift him off the other man, lying face up, one arm clamped to the side, where blood is seeping out and mingling with slush and mud. His eyes are squeezed shut and his lips pinched in a rictus of fear. For an instant, Peter thinks of Effie, who tries to block out the world by rocking as violently as she can. He can see the man's chest move up and down convulsively.

"Don't be afraid. We won't hurt you," Lioba says. "But can you stand? We need to get you away from the road."

The man's eyes fly open. He gazes up at them with a mixture of fear and disbelief.

Peter holds out his hand to help him. The man pulls himself to a stand, trembling and still leaning on Peter's arm.

"Come on. Follow me." Lioba turns to begin making her way back up the embankment.

"Wait," the man whispers. He holds up his hand then he crouches next to the body. Gently, he turns the dead man's face to the sun, running his hand over the staring eyes and muttering something. Then he gets up.

"Can you walk?" Peter asks.

"I think so, just not very fast."

Peter helps the man climb up the embankment.

Lioba leads the way. They walk underneath tall pines with a thick layer of pine needles covering the ground. Peter, following in the back, watches the man wobble when the flapping soles of his shoes catch on roots and twigs.

Finally, they reach a clearing, and Lioba turns to the man. "Let me see where you got shot. Maybe I can help."

Getting a first proper look, Peter is shocked by how gaunt and pale the man is, with scabs on his cheeks, and his hands and ankles knobby and swollen, tinged with blue. He seems older than his father. Peter is almost embarrassed as he takes in the threadbare striped hose and shirt.

Wordlessly, the man leans against a tree and lifts up his shirt. It got stuck to the wound, and he grimaces as he tugs on the cloth, exposing an angry-looking gash near the rib cage. His rib bones stand out starkly.

"You got lucky." Lioba purses her lips as she inspects the wound. Blood has soaked the top of the man's breeches. "It bled a lot, but it's just a graze." She digs a hand into her bag and pulls out a little silver flask. "I hate to do this, but this will help to disinfect it," she says. Carefully, she dribbles a clear golden liquid onto the wound in the man's side.

The man flinches but does not shift away. "The last thing I expected was someone to pour cognac over me," he says, startling Peter with his deep voice.

"Nice flask," Peter says enviously.

"I found it in my uncle's desk. I figured I might as well take it with me." Lioba pulls out a rolled-up piece of yellowish cloth and starts to wrap it around the man's torso. "It's the best I can do. I don't exactly carry a first-aid kit around."

The man twists his head to see what Lioba is doing and smirks. "An ace bandage? I am impressed."

Lioba ignores him as she firmly tucks the last end into place and secures it with an odd pin shaped like a stunted butterfly.

Peter peers over her shoulder. The only ace he knows is the one in a deck of cards. But before he can get a closer look, Lioba lets the shirt drop down, so it covers the bandage.

"I stocked up on bread before I left yesterday." She reaches into her bag and pulls out something wrapped in glossy white paper. "You can have this."

"Bread?" the man says in a voice of wonder and reaches for it. Then his face turns blank, the little parcel forgotten in his hand. "It was supposed to be me," he mutters, his voice breaking. "We had agreed, but when the soldier shouted, he pushed me down and laid on top of me. I wasn't supposed to live."

Peter and Lioba glance at each other.

"I am glad you got away," Lioba says. "They were going to kill all of you. At least that's a rumor I heard."

"I am afraid you are right." The expression of utter devastation gives way to something else. His eyes focus on them as if taking on a new burden. "Can I have a sip of your uncle's cognac, or do you reserve it purely for medicinal purposes?"

"Here." Lioba hands him the flask.

He lets a small amount of the golden liquid flow into his mouth. "Great cognac." He takes another small sip and hands back the flask. "I never thought I would taste anything like that ever again."

"I am glad you like it. I'll be sure to tell my uncle if I get the chance." Lioba smiles at him. "My name is Lioba, and this is Peter."

The man half-bows in Lioba's direction. "Gustav." The courtesy seems incongruous given the state he is in. "Where are you from?" he asks politely, as if just having been introduced to Lioba at a formal gathering.

"Stolp," Lioba responds. "I was planning to attend university but worked as a land girl for the last six months. And you?"

"Well, I was studying history at the university in Königsberg." He sounds almost surprised, as if he doesn't recognize himself.

Peter rapidly revises his estimate of the man's age. If he is a student, he cannot be that old after all.

"That is, I already started with my dissertation before all this happened." Gustav waves vaguely at the forest behind them.

"Your dissertation?" Lioba exclaims. "On what, may I ask?"

"The Thirty Years' War."

Lioba raises her eyebrows, her eyes briefly flicking toward Peter.

He shivers. A war that lasted thirty years—that's his war.

"And you?" Gustav asks, glancing at Peter's jerkin, shirt, and knee-length hose curiously.

"He is a friend," Lioba intervenes. "He lives around here."

Peter wants to ask the man about the war but stops himself. He cannot even begin to explain his questions. "We should not stay here indefinitely," he says to change the subject. "It is too risky."

"You're right," Lioba says. Helplessly she looks at Gustav. "What are you going to do?"

"We had a plan to try to make it to the next harbor and blend in with other refugees. I guess I will stick to that." After an awkward silence, he adds, "Thank you for helping me."

"It was Peter's idea," Lioba says gruffly.

"Well, thank you, Peter. Thank you, both. I better get going." He sketches a curiously dignified half-bow toward both of them, then winces from the movement.

They watch Gustav in silence as he makes his way through the trees. He holds his arm close to his torso and is limping slightly. Peter thinks of the man's swollen ankles. His feet had to be sore and blistered.

"Wait," Peter shouts at the last minute and runs after Gustav.

Gustav stops and turns around. "Yes?"

Peter bends down and slips off his shoes. "Here, take them. Yours are falling apart."

"I can't do that." Gustav frowns at the pair in Peter's hands.

"No, take them. The soles are new, but the shoes are old." Peter almost starts to giggle when he thinks about what he just said. "Sorry, the buckles are a bit rusty."

"And you?" Gustav says, with a puzzled frown.

"I live close by." He pushes the shoes into Gustav's hands, turns around quickly, and heads back to where Lioba is standing, with her eyebrows raised.

"What are you?" she scoffs. "Some sort of latter-day St. Martin?"

"St. Martin?" He grins at her. "I did not give him my jacket. Anyway, it is just a ploy to convince my father I need new shoes." His father is going to be furious, Peter thinks, but then again it might stir him out of his apathy.

Peter has a hard time keeping up as she follows a snow-covered trail through the dense forest. Walking without shoes is more painful than he has anticipated despite the thick, springy layer of pine needles. Occasional cones and twigs push through his stockings against the thin skin on the arches of his feet.

Lioba hums as she walks, swinging her bag.

> *Wild geese are sweeping through the dark*
> *Northbound, with shrill wail into the morrow.*
> *Harsh and loud their cry, "Oh hark, hark, hark!*
> *The world is full of sorrow."*

"I always liked this song. But then my father told me it has become a favorite marching song of soldiers. It's hard to forget that little detail now. There is nothing the Nazis haven't touched." Her expression is bitter. Then she smiles at Peter. "I changed the lyrics. It's supposed to say 'the world is full of murder.'" Suddenly, Lioba stops so that Peter almost runs into her. "I have been hoping for one of these."

Following her pointing hand, Peter sees what looks like a tiny wooden house perched in the fork of an oak tree, with two long poles in the front supporting the structure and a wooden ladder hanging down on the side where there is a little opening. "What's that?"

"A high seat. Hunters use it."

"Oh," Peter says. This is far removed from his life as an apprentice. He has heard peasants who rented Master Nowak's meadows complain about hunters. "Master Nowak, can you not do something?" they pleaded with him. "You should see the damage the hunters caused, riding over the field before the harvest is finished. It is a disgrace." Master Nowak had nodded sympathetically, but was clearly reluctant to challenge the gentry on this issue. Lioba did not seem to think the hunters were so bad.

"It is safe, and it is dry," Lioba says. "We can rest there for a while." She begins to climb, moving deftly as if it were her own house.

Peter follows her, hesitating as he feels the ladder swing with his weight. When he reaches the top, he finds himself in a surprisingly spacious chamber with benches along the sides and small openings that let in light. "Amazing. I could live here."

"Yes, during hunting season you sometimes find bottles of wine and even food in the high seats. Anyway, it's safe and provides a shelter of sorts."

Peter puts his face close to one of the openings. It is like being adrift in a sea of green and silvery pines and oaks, shifting and waving in the wind. A hawk sails across the treetops in the distance, with a high-pitched, staccato-like screeching. He sits down on the bench across from Lioba, who is rummaging in her bag.

"Nothing left." She grimaces and then looks hopefully at Peter. "Do you have any food?"

"No, I am sorry." Regretfully, he shakes his head.

"Can't be helped. I'll find something tomorrow."

"Lioba, who were those people back there?"

"I don't know how to explain." She stares at the floorboards, her hands clenched in her lap. "I have heard rumors about this sort of thing, but I had a hard time believing it. I believe these prisoners are Jews."

"Jews?" Peter asks with a frown. "What did they do? Why so many of them? And what are Nazis?" Master Nowak sells amber pieces to a Jewish merchant who sometimes comes through Stolpmünde. Peter never thought about where he went or where he lived. He was just a merchant.

"They didn't do anything, but the Nazis …" She glances up at Peter's perplexed expression. "Sorry, the government …

anyway, I have heard they are trying to get rid of them all. People whispered to me incredible stories about camps where they keep prisoners and places where they are killed. I think these people we saw must be from one of those camps."

"Where are the guards taking them?"

"I don't know. A friend of my uncle, an officer in the army who came to Muttrin with his regiment, told me in secret the people who are responsible for all this are afraid of the end of the war and want to hide the evidence of what they have done. This officer took a big risk in telling me about this. The Nazis execute people who speak out against the government."

"Are those guards going to kill the prisoners?"

"I think so. But maybe they are just trying to hide them somewhere."

Peter looks away from Lioba's drawn face. It has begun to snow. Flakes drift into the opening, settling like wet stars on the wood and vanishing again. "Why did you not stay at your aunt's house?" he asks after a long silence.

"I need to find my parents. When my aunt came back to Muttrin, she told me she hasn't heard from them either. I'm getting worried about them. Besides, more treks had arrived, and the house was getting rather crowded. Army officers were also billeted in the house."

"Why were you in the forest?"

"I know the woods and fields. I feel safer this way. I'd been thinking of using the road, but it's too dangerous."

"What if you do not find your parents?"

"I don't know," Lioba says. "Maybe they have already left for the west. I suppose I would try to go west myself. We have relatives in Hamburg and Hannover."

Lioba sits straight-backed on her narrow bench, her hands holding on to her pack, with a determined, dogged expression, seemingly undaunted by her uncertain fate.

"Maybe you could go on a ship in Stolpmünde," Peter says

hesitantly. Ship travel cannot be that different, even if it is three hundred years from his time.

"True—then again, I suspect the ships will be quite crowded."

"So how would you go west, then?" Peter is amazed at Lioba's matter-of-fact attitude.

"I don't know. Walk, I suppose. I got this far, didn't I?"

"And later? What are you going to do?"

"You mean when the war is over?"

"Will you come back here?"

"I don't know. This is home. It's where I grew up, but I have to do more with my life than paddle around in the fish ponds of Muttrin."

Peter shakes his head. He has never heard a girl speak like that. "So, what will you do?"

"I want to go to university."

"Go to university? You can do that? How old are you anyway?"

"I am seventeen. What does that have to do with anything?"

So, Lioba is just two years older than he is. Sometimes she seems as old as Clare, serious and focused, and then like a little girl again in her delight with a piece of bread or the crumply skin of a sweet apple. He studies her eyes, so fierce and intent, and the hooknose making her appear stern.

Lioba frowns at Peter. "Come on, even in your day, some women must have gone to university."

"Perhaps. I wouldn't know. What would you study at university?"

"Architecture."

Peter laughs. "I definitely do not know any women architects."

"Hah," Lioba scoffs. "That's because you never bothered to find out. How about Katherine Briçonnet, who designed castles in the Loire valley in the 16th century, or Lady Wilbraham in Britain in the 17th century?"

"How would I know such a thing?" Peter retorts angrily. "You don't have to be so arrogant. I am just an apprentice. I do not know anything at all about architecture."

"Sorry," Lioba says, looking abashed. "I didn't mean to hurt your feelings. It's just something I really love."

"So, are there women architects in your time?" Peter asks.

"There aren't many now, but that's going to change if I have anything to do with it," Lioba says fiercely. The girl's intense expression makes her hooknose and high cheekbones stand out even more starkly. "Anyway, once this war is over, they'll need architects to rebuild all the houses that got bombed."

"Bombed?"

"Destroyed. Wiped out. Kaput." She waves her hands. "Pfft. Gone. Entire cities gone."

"I have seen buildings burnt down in Stolp. You mean like that?"

"Yes, like that. Only worse. Think of all of Stolp turned into blackened rubble in a few minutes."

"Oh," Peter says, unable to imagine anything like it. "So, you want to build palaces and castles?"

"Well, not palaces. Houses. Houses that belong in the land-scape, with soft lines and colors. Buildings with large windows, rooftop gardens, and courtyards full of light." Her eyes gleam, and the vertical line down her forehead has smoothed out. "I love to draw. I can't wait to do that again."

"My sister likes to draw," Peter says. "It is just scribbles, of course."

"Just scribbles?" Lioba raises her eyebrows. "I bet when you first started working with amber, you didn't get much farther than 'just pebbles.'"

Peter feels his cheeks reddening. "That is true," he says in a low voice.

A loud cawing of crows just outside their high seat is a welcome distraction. Peter moves his head closer to the opening on his side of the little shelter and peers out. Snowflakes land on his lips; they taste faintly metallic. He turns his face back to Lioba. "What color are your eyes?"

"Are you color blind?" Lioba stares at him. "They are blue."

"Everything in your world is grey and black. I cannot see any colors."

"That's funny," Lioba says, studying him intently. "You look like you just stepped out of a Bruegel painting. And he certainly used plenty of colors."

"A Bruegel painting?" Peter shakes his head. "I do not understand."

"You haven't heard of Bruegel, the famous Flemish painter? He died about a hundred years before your time, I think." Lioba raises her eyebrows expectantly. "Ah well, maybe one day you will get to see one of his paintings. You remind me of them." She falls silent, frowning in concentration, and then grins at him. "I just realized that for you, my world must look like a movie."

"A movie? What's that?"

"Black and white moving pictures." Lioba waves her hands. "Sort of like having thousands of pictures you flip through, so it's as if you see movement. Never mind. I don't know how to explain it any better. Anyway, when I watch you, it's like standing in front of a painting." Her dirt-streaked face is transformed by her laughter.

Just then, a loud bang in the distance startles them both.

Lioba leans over to get closer to the little opening next to Peter. "I hope that wasn't someone shooting at our new friend."

Peter notices the slim silver chain around her neck that had attracted the attention of the three men on the road. He opens his mouth to ask about it when there is the familiar roaring and buzzing in his ears, and he falls off his bench.

17

TOOLS OF THE TRADE

CLARE RAISED HER EYEBROWS WHEN PETER SHOWED UP AT home without shoes and his feet blue from the cold.

"I gave them to a refugee," he told her, figuring this actually had the benefit of being the truth. But he was relieved when Clare did not pursue the story.

Without any further comment, she helped him dig through an oak blanket chest containing various discarded clothing items.

"Here, maybe these might work." Clare held up a pair that had belonged to Lorenz. "Effie has been much more cheerful in the last weeks. Even your father noticed."

Peter was not convinced. When he had gone to his sister's room to check on her the last time he had been at home, she had immediately pushed all her papers out of sight and glared at him apprehensively, her arms folded over her chest. How long would she be afraid like that? He had been stupid to hope for a change.

In the town square, he saw Lars, Greg, and Urban playing a game of ninepins even though it was snowing. They had taken some floorboards from a scrap pile and created a lane with a board in the center for rolling the ball. For a moment, he thought of joining in when one ball sailed past his head, followed by laughter. He squared his shoulders and continued walking. His new shoes pinched, and he could feel a blister starting in his right heel.

Before heading to Master Nowak's house, he stopped at the cobbler's workshop to pick up a pair of shoes for Mistress Nowak.

"Is your sister ..." The shop girl hesitated, apparently searching for a word and blushing as she took the coins he held out to her.

"Effie is fine," Peter snapped. "There is nothing wrong with her." He snatched the shoes and ran out of the workshop.

Why had he gotten so angry? It was probably just an innocent question. Besides, something was wrong with her, just not anything he wanted to explain.

Perhaps he could ask Cune to play a game of mills that evening. Cune loved board games, and they used to play regularly. Anne sometimes sat with them, doing her needlework. However, when he entered the house, Cune and Anne were together in the kitchen, talking eagerly. As soon as they saw him, they fell silent.

It hurt. It was as if he had contracted the plague. Peter waved at them casually, trying to give the impression he had just wanted to say hello, and went upstairs.

He tossed and turned all night, repeatedly waking up in a cold sweat. Bleary-eyed, he went down into the kitchen in the morning.

"You lucky dog." Cune, already at the table, grinned at him. "You get to take your exam today."

Peter nodded awkwardly. He was lucky; he just hadn't appreciated it enough. Cune would have deserved this so much more, and yet he did not sound envious.

Peter crumbled the piece of bread Mistress Nowak had placed in front of him, barely able to swallow. He was going to fail the exam, he knew it.

Finally, Master Nowak pushed his plate away and stood up. "We need to leave," he said.

"Wait." Mistress Nowak took a brush and brusquely went over Peter's tunic. "There, that is better. Good luck."

"We need to go now," Master Nowak said impatiently.

Peter followed Master Nowak down the road, his heart beating fast.

"That is it?" Peter was shocked when they stood outside Master Hegemann's workshop. Lost in thought, he had not realized how quickly they had been walking.

"Ready?" Master Nowak looked at him with raised eyebrows.

"I do not know."

"Well, I hope you will know soon. Come on, we must not keep them waiting.

There were five masters in the room. They murmured a greeting when Master Nowak and Peter walked inside.

Nervously, Peter eyed the turning lathe, the stool, and the workbench, set with all the tools he would need, in the center of the room. A bowl filled with water held the amber pieces he had to turn into marketable products.

The senior guild master, Master Jan Hegemann, stated the rules. First, he asked Master Nowak to sit on a chair to the side so he could not influence his apprentice by looks or frowns or assist him in any way.

Then Master Hegemann focused his gaze on Peter. "You, Peter Glienke, come before us today to be tested as to your skills and expertise in the noble craft of working with amber. As tradition decrees, you must work a total of one pound of amber into a marketable product while we observe your work. You have chosen to make one item in addition to the traditional amber beads. That is permitted."

Master Hegemann looked at Peter sternly before continuing. "Meanwhile, I remind you that you must work without the use of a caliper, relying solely on your visual judgment, when fashioning perfectly round and evenly proportioned beads, and you must drill even and straight holes into each one. When you have completed this task, you may commence on the individual project you have chosen."

Peter found it hard to concentrate on the sonorous voice. His thoughts tumbled around in his head, from Lioba to Effie and back.

"Are you ready?" The guild master sounded puzzled. "You may begin."

Peter took a deep breath and approached the workbench.

All the tools of the trade were laid out in front of him—a bucket with water for rinsing and cooling the amber, a turning lathe with a stool in front of it, a caliper, a rasp, a smoothing plane, a drawknife, and a scraper. There were several gouges for drilling different sizes, a stylus, and a saw for working the amber, with shavings, pumice, triple, and spirits of wine for polishing. Peter's pound of raw amber had already been soaking in a bowl of water. From the corner of his eye, Peter could see Master Nowak's legs and his bent head, apparently absorbed in studying his feet.

Peter sat down on the stool and reached for the turning lathe. It was as if someone had tossed him a lifeline. He breathed in the faint scent of resin and amber dust permeating the workshop. These were his tools. This was his world and his time. With steady purpose and complete concentration, he worked, oblivious to the eyes watching him, his mind swept clean of all doubt and fear. The tools fit his hands like old friends who read every one of his thoughts. He lost all sense of time.

Once he had a small pile of shiny beads lying on the table, he turned to the next task, picking up the amber intended for the little casket. He worked deftly and without hesitation. He carved and rasped and polished, bringing to life the reddish-golden amber of the round container and shaping the lid to fit perfectly on the indented groove of the rim. The yellow sliver in the shape of a rosebud slid into its space on the top, where he fixed it with a minute amount of resin. He was done.

He cleaned up the table, aligned the tools the way Master Nowak had always taught him, and bowed to the masters.

Master Nowak gave him a tiny smile. The others gazed back at him, their expressions unreadable.

"Thank you," Master Hegemann said. "Would you and Master Nowak please step outside so we can confer?"

It was snowing lightly when they reached the street. Peter licked some of the flakes from his lips, surprised at how salty they tasted. He must have been sweating during the exam. Carters and people laden with baskets were already returning from the market. How long had he been in there? Several hours at least. He did not dare ask Master Nowak how he had done. Anyway, it was too late now. He had done the best he could. He felt drained. He was too tired to worry about what would happen if he failed.

Fortunately, the wait was short. Master Hegemann himself came to the door to call them back inside.

All the masters stood as they entered.

"We are pleased and delighted to tell you that you performed in accordance with the requirements of the guild and finished the assigned tasks to our satisfaction. Well done, Journeyman Glienke." Master Hegemann smiled at him. "The decision was unanimous." He went on to talk about Peter's journeyman time and advised him to consult Master Nowak for advice.

Peter heard it as a distant murmuring. He was too giddy with excitement to pay attention.

He followed Master Nowak onto the street. The sun had come out, it was mild for February, and the snow was melting. Everything glinted and sparkled. Peter thought he had not seen the town look so pretty in a long time.

"Have you thought about where you want to start as a journeyman?"

"Oh," Peter said and stopped walking. The reality was beginning to sink in. He would leave Stolpmünde soon. Upon the completion of his apprenticeship, he was supposed to go on the road, working for various masters all over the region. "Is it true I can just pick and choose where to begin?"

"Who else would choose?"

"Then I want to go to Königsberg."

"Königsberg is a good choice," Master Nowak said. "It should not be too difficult to get you a berth in the next trading ship. Anyway, I think you should go home and tell your father. He will be pleased."

Peter was in a daze as he trudged along the road. His steps got lighter and quicker. He had passed. He was now Journeyman Glienke.

The house was quiet when he opened the front door. He went to his father's office and slowly opened the door. It occurred to him that he had never done this without trepidation. Would his father be lost in his gloom or sitting over a bottle of ale, oblivious to the world around him? Would he be harried and tired, making Peter hesitate to tell him anything about his own life?

"Did you take your exam?" His father looked up from his papers.

"Yes. I passed."

"I'm not surprised. Master Nowak told me you would do well."

Peter was lost for words. They had talked about him, and Master Nowak had praised his work.

"You know how much I miss your brother." His father gave him a sad smile. "But I knew I could always rely on you."

Peter looked down. It was always the same. Lorenz would forever be the beloved son, the golden one who made everyone smile. Peter was the steady one, the one whom nobody noticed. His father's backhanded praise hurt almost more than not getting any praise at all. Then, he was ashamed. How could he fault his father for his grief?

"I miss Lorenz too," he said. "I will always miss him."

When he sat down on his bed that night, his happiness over passing the exam faded as he thought about all that could go wrong. Marthe was still out there, like a cat waiting to pounce. His father would not be around forever. Peter would have to take care of Effie. And there was Lioba. It was as if his thoughts and emotions had split in two. He had enough problems. Why did he have to worry about someone who did not even exist yet?

Not bothered to pull off his clothes, he laid back and closed his eyes.

18

STAMPEDE

IT IS SNOWING.

Peter shivers in his thin jacket. He squints against the onslaught of unceasing swaths of sleet and snow blowing almost parallel to the ground. Hundreds of people push past, all grey and dark, carrying bundles and bags and dragging children by their hands. Peter shuffles along, dazed and bewildered. In the distance, he can see lights flickering. It must be a big town.

There is something Peter has to do. It is urgent. He doesn't know what it is, but it propels him forward. But he is hemmed in on all sides and cannot walk any faster in the crowd.

"I heard there aren't many trains running anymore," a woman says.

"If we don't get there soon, it won't really matter," another mutters.

"I want Lisl," a little girl cries. "Why didn't you let me take her?"

"There was no time," a weary voice responds. "Stop crying, it's just a doll."

An old man drags a handcart with a woman perched on top. He moves slowly, while the crowd flows around them with hisses and curses to get them to shift out of the way.

"I told you, we should never have gone," the woman grumbles. "But of course, you never believe me."

"Stop harping on it. Anyway, we have come this far. Let's at least try to get to Stolp. We can decide what to do once we get there."

"Didn't you see the trek back there? They turned around as well. And they have come from much farther east." The woman's voice cracks with exhaustion. "I want to go back to Allenstein."

"We can't go back home. Don't you realize that?" The man continues pulling the cart along. "I don't think we can ever go home again," he adds in a low voice, as if talking to himself.

Allenstein? That was somewhere south of Königsberg, far away from Stolp.

Peter has often dreamed of leaving and getting out into the world. But not being able to go home ever again?

Two men elbow him out of the way. Skidding on a patch of ice, he glances at their profiles. He knows them; they were two of the men who had threatened Lioba and injured the dog. They shuffle along with the crowd as if trying to blend in.

Where is Lioba? She has to be close by. He has to get to her. She is in danger. He can feel it. He wipes the sleet off his face and eyelashes. He cranes his neck, standing on his toes for a moment to look across the heads in front of him. Then he catches sight of her tall, slim figure, the satchel slung over her shoulder and the long thick braid down her back. She is walking with her head bent and apparently oblivious to the people around her. The two men have moved closer to her, nudging each other and pointing at the girl.

"Lioba," Peter shouts, trying to get her attention.

She turns her head, scanning the crowd behind, then shrugs and continues.

"Let me through," Peter pleads with the women blocking his way. "That is my sister."

Reluctantly, the women shift aside.

"His 'sister'. Hah, that's what they all say," one grumbles.

"Just wants to get on a train," says another. "Can't blame him."

The two men are now right behind Lioba. Peter reaches them just as one tries to grab her by the shoulders, fumbling for her silver chain.

The other one holds on to her arms, jeering. "No faithful retainer to help you out today. You still have that dainty little thing with you, don't you?"

The crowd flows past them, oblivious to the byplay.

Peter kicks at the men from behind as hard as he can and pulls on their jackets to throw them off balance. One falls down, while the other turns and starts swinging punches at him.

Lioba stumbles and almost falls, but she is free.

"Go," Peter screams. "Go."

Stupefied, she stares at him, her necklace swinging free on her chest. For an instant, Peter can see a hint of color, a dark golden glow.

A fist connects with his jaw. It feels as if his head is exploding. Then the world turns dark, and he feels nothing at all.

19

MEMENTO MORI

PETER'S HEAD ACHED WHEN HE WOKE UP. HIS THROAT hurt as if he had been screaming for hours. Lioba was out there somewhere in a crowd of desperate people.

Then he sat up, glancing around the attic room. It was just a dream. His life was right here, and today was Shrovetide Tuesday.

It was a day of feasting and celebration before the start of Lent, and most townspeople came out to see the Shrovetide play on the town square. Peter always looked forward to it, and now that he had passed the exam, it should be a wonderful day. But he was torn inside. It was as if part of him was still in that crowd on the road to Stolp, worrying about Lioba.

He pulled on his clothes and made his way downstairs.

"Would you like to join the mistress and me when we leave for the play?" Master Nowak asked Peter when he entered the kitchen. "It is fortunate the town elders decided to go ahead despite the hard times. I suppose they figured it would cheer everybody up."

"What about Anne and Cune?" Peter asked, surprised that they wouldn't all go together.

"We will join you there," Anne said. "I have to help Cune

with something, and we will be a little bit late." Pulling on her cloak, she followed Cune out the door.

Puzzled and hurt, Peter looked after them. Silently, he helped Master Nowak clean up the workshop before they set out together.

"It is lucky we Protestants do not hold with confession," Master Nowak said with a smirk as they walked out the door. "Otherwise, we would have had to go to church right before Lent. I do not know where I would have found the time. We have been so busy these last few days."

Peter's cheeks burned. He would have had a lot to confess. As he glanced at Master Nowak from the side, he wondered whether there was a hidden message there. He hunched his shoulders. There was nothing he could do about it right now.

Maybe he should just lose the crane somewhere far away from home so it could not be traced back to him or to Master Nowak's workshop. He reached for the amber in his pocket, but stopped himself, clenching his hand into a fist. It repelled and attracted him at the same time. He hated its power over him, ripping him from one world into another without any warning. And he was afraid of what would happen if someone found him with it. And yet, it was his link to Lioba and her strange world that filled him with wonder even as it terrified him. Her fate had become important to him. He could not give it up yet.

Peter could not help but feel a thrill when they reached the town square. Torches had been set up all around the edge of the square and flanking the stage. The platform in front was raised high enough so people in the back of the audience could also get a glimpse of the performance.

In the grey winter afternoon, the haze of the snow flurries blurred the contours of buildings and turned the people attending the event into clumps of greys and browns. The crowd seemed sparser than in other years, and there were some unfamiliar faces. Thin, weary, and drawn, men and women with children in threadbare clothes huddled close together.

Nonetheless, sounds of laughter, shouting, and excited talking echoed around the square. Town elders dressed in their finery wandered around, greeting friends and neighbors with jovial handshakes and claps on the shoulders.

"Fresh beer! Come and try it! Fresh beer!" Brewers presided at tables with barrels next to them.

The scents of spilled beer, roasted meats, smoked eel, pickled herring, and baked pasties from the food stalls made Peter's mouth water in anticipation.

He craned his head, looking all around. To his surprise, there was Effie, neatly dressed, her dark shiny locks sticking out underneath her cap and her face flushed with excitement. Clare and her sister's family stood next to her.

Clare waved and gave Peter a reassuring nod. She would watch out for Effie.

"Where are Anne and Cune?" Peter pulled on Mistress Nowak's sleeve. "They are going to miss everything."

"Do not worry," Mistress Nowak said, smiling at him. "I am sure they will be here soon." She pointed at the stage. "Look, they are starting."

Indeed, the Death Dance was about to begin. The customary twenty-four couples made their way onto the stage, moving ponderously. There were actors dressed as a bishop, a king, a lord, town elders, lawyers, wealthy burghers, merchants, artisans, peasants, beggars, and children. They were followed by three figures representing Death—actors in black robes with skeletons painted onto their limbs, torso, and hood. The skeletons danced around, weaving in and out of the row of dancers, leering at them, tugging on their robes, sniffing at their collars, and allowing long, black-gloved fingers to linger affectionately on their cheeks.

The actors representing the good citizens of the town swayed arm in arm. They were seemingly oblivious to the fact that every now and then the skeleton figures would choose one from their ranks, gently leading them off the stage one by one, while the others continued to dance as if nothing had happened.

Peter shook his head. He could not imagine anyone needing a reminder that Death came for everyone and knew no differences of wealth or rank or hierarchy.

The three supporting members of the cast, men in dark robes who stood off to the side, accompanied the dancers with their monotonous chant, intoning the words of the *Vita Brevis*.

> *Life is short, and shortly it will end.*
> *Death comes quickly and respects no one,*
> *Death destroys everything and takes pity on no one.*
> *To death we are hastening, let us refrain from sinning.*
> *If you do not turn back and become like a child,*
> *And change your life for the better,*
> *You will not be able to enter, blessed, the Kingdom of God.*
> *To death we are hastening, let us refrain from sinning.*

Peter's thoughts wandered. Again and again, they circled back to the amber crane, growing larger in his mind's eye. He could not shake images of Lioba, alone, rushing from tree to tree as she tried to evade pursuers. He pictured her making her way west and north across a desolate waste of snow and ice, littered with bodies, carriages sunk into the mire, and horses screaming in agony.

One of the skeletons fell off the stage.

Peter jerked awake.

The skeleton tumbled into the arms of the people standing in the front row. Suppressed laughter ran through the crowd. Peter stood on his tiptoes to get a better view.

People in the audience pulled the actor to his feet, although not all the outstretched arms and hands were helpful. They pummeled and cuffed him, before unceremoniously pushing him back up onto the platform, where he tried to resume his role after quickly adjusting his robe.

Peter turned to Master Nowak and his wife, grinning. Then he realized Anne and Cune had still not joined them. "Where are the others?" he whispered.

Mistress Nowak shook her head, pointing her chin at the stage as if to reprimand Peter for not showing the appropriate somber demeanor required of the occasion.

There was just one lonely figure left on the stage, an actor dressed as a young maiden, in a white flowing robe, with a veil and a headdress of white flowers laced into her hair. One of the skeletons wooed the maiden, going down on a knee, fondling her, trying to entice her into a dance, and pulling on her veil. Finally, the skeleton tired of this game. Firmly holding on to the maiden's arm, Death led her off the stage.

"Go with God, but go," Master Nowak said with a chuckle.

Some people turned around, eyeing him with disapproval. Mistress Nowak jabbed him in the side with her elbow, scowling and pursing her lips.

A sigh of relief went through the crowd at the end of the performance. People shifted and murmured to each other as they gazed at the stage in anticipation of the next act. Acrobats jumped up onto the stage, followed by three musicians in brightly colored tunics over tight hoses with tassels hanging off their sleeves and hems.

Peter found the high-pitched flute grating. The tambour player at least made an effort to follow the movements of the acrobats.

The hurdy-gurdy player had brought his own stool. Perched on it, he held the boxy object with its short neck on his lap. It looked more like a mechanical contraption than a musical instrument. He turned a wheel on one side of the instrument while manipulating various keys on its body with his other hand. Long, drawn-out, mournful sounds emerged akin to those produced by a bow scraping across the strings of a viola.

"This always makes me think of cats being slowly strangled," muttered Master Nowak. "Ouch."

Mistress Nowak had stepped on his foot.

Finally, the tambour player went into a crescendo of drumming while the acrobats somersaulted off the stage, followed by the three musicians.

Now the town crier made his way onto the stage. For the occasion, he had brushed his tunic and fixed new feathers onto his hat. This did not disguise the fact that he appeared frail and shaky on his legs and that his voice quavered as he called for attention.

"I thought his apprentice was going to take over this year," Mistress Nowak whispered.

Master Nowak shook his head. "He is dead."

His wife raised her eyebrows.

"He had gone home to visit his family," Master Nowak spoke in an undertone. "Swedish soldiers were looting, and he intervened to keep them from taking his mother's last cow. Now no cow and no son."

Another one gone. Peter wondered whether any of this could even surprise him. It was as if they all had hardened callouses over their souls.

The town crier banged his cane onto the wooden boards until the crowd quieted down.

"Mr. Mayor, town elders, esteemed guild masters, and citizens of the proud town of Stolpmünde," he shouted over the whispering and coughing from the audience.

"Keep it short, Karl!" someone yelled from the back.

The little man blinked at the crowd as if he had lost his train of thought, but after a moment continued. "We are honored to present to you a one-act play authored by Hans Sachs, the Sad Tale of the Stolen Shrovetide Hen."

The audience broke into cheers, clapped, and stamped their feet. In the back of the stage, the tambour player banged on his drum. Then, the first actors appeared, a burly peasant pursued by his equally burly wife, brandishing a long hard sausage and trying to hit her spouse wherever she could reach. She ran after him, her skirts flying and her clogs falling off as she wobbled in her fury.

Peter laughed. But in the next instant, he tensed and stared. The wife was Anne, with a generous complement of pillows and bolsters under her clothes, her usually neat hair unbraided and in a wild tangle slipping out of a grimy-looking lace cap. The skirt was hitched up in an indecorous fashion, exposing part of her legs. Anne. She was funny and completely convincing as the shrewish, slatternly peasant wife.

Peter could feel Mistress Nowak glancing at him from the side. She was beaming and her eyes glowed. He smiled at her.

Then a servant, wearing a jaunty cap on his head, a shirt with the sleeves rolled up, and slim hose that showed off his legs, appeared on the stage.

Peter blinked. It was Cune. Cune? Peter's mouth fell open in disbelief. Quiet, plodding, with never a mean word about anyone or anything, always cheerful, and painfully shy, Cune was up there on the stage for all to see, impersonating a brash young man with a roving eye, quick hands, and a smart mouth, and he did so perfectly.

Peter took a deep breath. It stung. They had not told him about any of this. Of course, he admitted to himself, he had hardly been paying attention in the last months. He settled down to watch.

What followed was a wild romp. It involved the peasant and his wife, his servant and the girl of his dreams, and a hen. The hen only made a brief appearance, accompanied by loud squawking, while clutched under the girl's arms as she ran off. To the audience's delight, the sausage appeared repeatedly. In the final scene, the wife used it to chase the servant out of the yard.

Peter was so absorbed he forgot about everything else. Together with the people in the audience, he laughed and stamped his feet and shouted when it was over, and the actors took their bow. Jugglers reappeared on the stage for a final act. Meanwhile, the crowd around him began pushing and shoving on their way to the food stalls. Bemused, Peter kept his eyes on the jugglers, while his thoughts wandered. *Where is Lioba? Did she get away from those men?*

"There you are," a breathless voice came from behind him.

Peter turned, startled, his heart pounding.

"Did you fall asleep again? Was it that boring?"

Anne had changed back to her regular clothes, but her hair was still unbound underneath her cap, and her cheeks glowed. Cune was next to her. He wore his habitual shy smile as if he had never acted the sharp-spoken young man on the stage.

"You were both great," Peter said. "Why did you not tell me?"

"You never bothered to ask," Anne retorted.

"I thought ..." Peter stammered. How could he say he had been suspecting her and Cune of gossiping about Effie? And he could not tell Anne about the amber crane. He could not tell anyone.

"I think I will check out the food," Cune said in his soft voice, but neither Peter nor Anne paid any attention. Cune shrugged and wandered off.

After an awkward silence, Peter said, "I am sorry."

"You never see me," Anne snapped. "You live in some sort of dream world. That is all that matters to you."

Taken aback by her vehemence, Peter wanted to retort angrily. Then he looked down, biting his lip. She was right. He had not been paying attention.

"Have you noticed what is going on with your sister?"

"Effie?" Peter asked, astonished at this question.

"Yes, Effie. Remember? Your sister? Have you bothered to look at her drawings?"

"Oh, that. How can I? She always hides them. What do her scribbles have to do with anything?"

"See? That is what I mean." Anne sniffed. "You do not even realize she has been doing better, and you are so dismissive of her 'scribbles'. Have you actually asked her to show them to you? You should take a look. You might be surprised."

Peter opened his mouth to protest and then stopped himself. He had heard this from someone else not so long ago.

"You never notice anyone around you." Anne pushed her hands into her hips, for a moment appearing as fierce as the character she had impersonated on the stage. "All you see is Marthe."

"That is not true," Peter said quickly.

"Yes, it is," Anne said heatedly. "And you do not really know anything about her." She shook her head and walked off, flicking her hair back over her shoulder.

Peter watched Anne until she disappeared in a throng of people moving toward the food stalls. Why was she attacking him like this? He did see her, he kept saying to himself. He just did not recognize her anymore. Lately, he had repeatedly caught himself watching her move around the house with her swift and confident step, slight, neat, and trim, with a faint scent of amber and resin. Her thick blond braids framed the face of a stranger, with dark golden eyes, with green flecks, and high cheek bones with a slight flush of pink. She had changed.

Someone jostled Peter as people pushed past him on their way to the beer stalls. On the other side of the marketplace, Effie stood in front of a table covered with *memento mori* rings and other trinkets. But he could not see Clare anywhere. Other people crowded around the display. Peter grimaced. How absurd. He hardly needed to buy a ring to remember Lorenz or his mother.

Then his eyes narrowed. Marthe, resplendent in a blue velvet cape and a broad-rimmed hat adorned with bobbing pheasant feathers, walked across the square, with Lars next to her, his hand under her arm. The two of them moved toward the table until they were directly behind Effie.

Marthe leaned over to Lars and whispered in his ear. He

laughed out loud while he reached out and slid his arm around Effie's waist.

Effie reared her head like a frightened horse and flung herself sideways, away from Lars. The table fell over. She lost her balance and sat on the ground. Her arms flailed all about her as if to ward off a swarm of wasps.

Peter was already running, pushing people out of the way. There was a roaring in his ears and a bitter, sour taste in the back of his mouth.

Lars. It had been Lars all along, with his beefy face, his lumbering gait, and his greasy hair. He had taunted Peter at the All Hallows' Eve bonfire, confident Effie could never tell anyone who had attacked her. Now Effie had shown Peter more clearly than any words could have. Lars had raped her.

Lars was still chuckling when Peter reached him. Peter slammed him with his fists, hitting him in the stomach and on his jaw. Stunned at first, Lars began to fight back. Peter did not hear anything other than the roaring in his ears. He kicked and screamed at Lars, oblivious to the blows he received from him.

A firm hand pulled Peter away and wrestled him to the ground. "We cannot have brawling in town, young man," a voice boomed in his ear.

Half leaning and half sitting, his shirt torn, and his cheekbone numb, Peter blinked. His eye smarted. He tried to turn his head to see what was happening.

Lars was on the ground as well, holding his head in his hands. "He attacked me," he moaned. "You all saw him attack me."

Peter tried to stand, but someone pushed him back down.

Effie sat next to the overturned table, her skirt tangled beneath her legs, rocking back and forth. The top of her gown had split open, and her amber heart swung out in synchrony with her motions.

People had formed a circle around her, watching in fascination as if this was the third presentation of the carnival plays, their faces blank with astonishment at her high-pitched keening.

"She is a witch," one woman muttered.

"Look at her odd motions."

"She is probably cursing us right now."

"What is this?" A man bent forward and grabbed Effie's pendant, yanking on it until the string came undone. "Now, how does a girl like you get hold of such a fine trinket?" He held it up high. "Look, a piece of amber. In fact, it is a heart."

Peter could not move. Someone had pinned his arms back and the pain was excruciating. Something dripped from his head into his eyes, and he blinked again, but everything was blurry. He could hear the people talking.

"She must have stolen it."

"I have always said so."

"She got her lover to get her that amber heart."

"Definitely a witch."

"I have heard such rumors about that family."

"I always wondered where that uncle gets all his supplies from."

"Yes, and the father spends all his time drinking."

"And there is her brother, drunk no doubt. Brawling in broad daylight."

How could they talk like this about Effie or everyone else in his family? For years, these people had been in and out of his father's house, trading and buying merchandise from him, and many had received help from his uncle over the years. Now they trashed his family with their words. Peter blinked again and his eyes cleared.

Marthe had stepped back, her face blanched. Her shawl had fallen down. Momentarily distracted from his worry about Effie, Peter was stunned by her expression. She was covering her mouth with her hands, visibly shaken and appalled.

Peter felt himself go cold inside. He had been blind. Flattered by her attention, he had chosen to ignore every warning sign. Clare had warned him. He remembered Master Nowak's skeptical comments. Even Anne had warned him, and he had thought it was just jealousy. Marthe must have started the rumors. That would explain why she had been so curious about Effie and had been watching him all these weeks. But why had she done something so malicious?

Peter tried to shake off the hands holding him down. Someone had to help Effie.

To his relief, he saw Clare and Anne pushing their way through the crowd to get close to Effie.

"So, what happened here?" The town watchman, followed by several guards, had arrived.

Several voices began to talk all at once.

Peter closed his eyes. Everything hurt. Then he found himself being dragged upright.

"Off to the town jail with you, young man," the town watchman said.

"What about my sister?"

"That is not for me to say. She will be taken in for questioning."

"She did not do anything wrong." Peter began to tremble with shock. "She is not well. Please, just let her go."

"Stop struggling, young man. You are just making it worse for yourself."

Craning his head around, Peter saw Anne, crouching on the ground next to Effie. "Anne, please, stay with her," he shouted.

Anne glanced at Peter, her face pale but calm. She nodded.

A guard lifted Effie from behind, pulling her to her feet and pinning her arms to stop her from flailing.

"What are they doing to her?" Peter asked as he stumbled along in the firm hold of two guards.

"You have other things to worry about now. I am sure they will put her somewhere safe where she cannot hurt anybody." One of the men started to chuckle. "In fact, they might have just the right place for her."

"I told you, she did not do anything." Peter tried to stop walking. "She just got frightened. Can you not see that?"

"Come on, hurry up." The guards continued dragging him along. "We do not have all day."

To Peter's surprise, they took him to the town hall, past various offices and large meeting rooms, all the way to the back of the building.

"There you go." One of the guards bent down and picked up a heavy grate in the corner of the room.

"You want me to get into that?" Peter asked, staring at the dark hole. Dampness rose up like a cloud mixed with the cloying stench of something decaying.

"Did you expect a palace?" the man jeered. He raised his arm and shoved Peter so that he pitched forward into the hole.

At the last instant, Peter managed to twist, bracing his arms and landing on his side. "Hey," he yelled, almost grateful for the pain of his fall since it kept away the dread that threatened to overwhelm him.

Above his head, he heard the jailer lower the grating. Bits of rust from the grating fell onto his exposed neck. The floorboards creaked as the jailer walked away. Then it was quiet. Peter was alone in the dark. He groped around on the cold flagstones and encountered crumbly bits. Mouse droppings. Poor mouse. It probably had died down here, which accounted for the smell. He tried to stand up to get a sense of how large this cell was but bumped against the grating with his head. Awkwardly he sat back down, wincing in discomfort. His ribcage hurt. Lars must have hit him there, and he hadn't even noticed in his fury.

What is happening to Effie? It is my fault. I should have protected her better. I should never have given her the amber heart. He felt his stomach heave, and he threw up in the dark, trying to aim away from his shoes. He wiped his sleeve over his mouth, but he could not do anything about the sour taste in his mouth. He closed his eyes.

20

BEAR OF HAPPINESS

HIS HEAD HURTS. TENTATIVELY HE TRIES TO OPEN HIS EYES. Everything is blurry. With his fingers, he explores his face. The skin around his left eye feels puffy. There is something sticky and encrusted on his cheek, and his entire body is sore and bruised.

A low-pitched moan.

Startled, Peter sits up. He is not alone in his cell.

"Effie?"

No response. All his feelings of guilt come crashing back. Puzzled, he moves his hand back and forth on the ground and touches something soft and woolen. Did they put a rug in his cell while he slept? Where does the light come from? It had been dark when he fell asleep.

Peter notices an odd-looking lamp next to him on top of a table, with a round metal foot and topped by something in the shape of an upside down barrel made of silk. Behind it on the wall, four large etchings show horses performing in an arena. A piece of furniture with a backrest and pillows on each side is probably a bed. A long low table in front of it is covered with books, and bookshelves line the walls.

No, he says to himself. *Not Lioba's world. I cannot deal with that now.*

Someone draws a shuddering breath. Peter sighs and stands up to look around.

Lioba sits on a large chair, covered in dark red fabric and with wing-like protrusions, in the corner. She stares at the table in front of her, her eyes vacant and her face splotchy and swollen.

"Lioba?" What happened to her? "What place is this?" he asks awkwardly.

Lioba focuses her eyes on him. "Oh, it's you again," she says dully, gets up, and starts walking around the room aimlessly, picking up a book from the table and putting it down again, adjusting the angle of one of the pictures on the wall, and fiddling with a set of scissors and a letter opener on the desk. Then she sits back down, pulling her legs up and wrapping her arms around them. Her long braid has come undone.

"What place is this?" she repeats Peter's question. "This is my parents' house in Stolp, where I was born."

"I was hoping you made it to Stolp," Peter says, looking at her doubtfully. "Did you find your parents?"

"My parents?" She stares at him, her eyes red. "They killed themselves. They didn't even wait for me."

Peter blinks. "How do you know that?"

"The neighbors told me."

"I am so sorry," he says slowly, but the words feel like wisps of air in his mouth, blowing back at him, meaningless, pointless.

Lioba begins pacing again, back and forth, past the bookshelves, to the window, around the table, stopping in front of him, staring at him without seeing anything at all, and starting all over. "They left me a note. Very thoughtful."

With one hand, she sweeps a stack of books from the bookshelf in passing. "Everywhere, people have been talking about this for some time. Really, a charming topic for conversation over coffee and cake. 'What would you advise, Herr Prof. Dr. Schmidt, a bullet or poison, or do you think I should exchange my ration cards for poison?' The pharmacists have been handing out little poison pills like candy. I heard people talk about this in the villages I passed through."

Another stack of books flies to the floor. "I heard of a mother who shot her children and then herself. Old people sat down in their kitchen and shared a glass of whiskey with their pills."

Lioba stops moving and stares out the window. "I just never thought my parents would do this. I suppose I have to be grateful they didn't do it here. They went to the woods outside the city with others from the town." She rubs her hands over her face. "I can understand why some old people chose this route. They might have thought they were too old to flee. But my parents weren't too old, and they had to know I was going to come here." She resumes her restless pacing.

Peter looks at her helplessly.

Then, it is as if she collapses inward, like a house crushed by the wind, and throws herself onto the chair. "I don't know what to do anymore." Tears are running down her face. "I failed them. The last time we spoke, my mother pleaded with me to come home. I didn't listen. I was so tired of her whining and complaining. I couldn't bear it. It's my fault." She rocks back and forth, hitting the armrests with her fists.

"It is not your fault," Peter protests.

"It is my fault. I should have come here sooner." She keeps hitting the armrests and moaning as she weaves back and forth.

It is like watching Effie. Peter has to do something. He thinks of Lorenz sitting on the floor next to his sister, singing to her until she calms down. He misses Lorenz so much it hurts.

Peter glances around. Then he notices a glass sculpture on a shelf. It looks like a bear, albeit with stubs for legs and arms, a disproportionately large head, and a foreshortened snout. The ears are distinctive for being so detailed. The nostrils echo its two perfectly round eyes. The creature looks pleased, as if about to smile. He picks it up, running his fingers over its stout body and tiny ears. It could be a bear. It could also be a fat rat or a vole or something else entirely, but no matter, he can use it.

"Have you ever heard of the amber bear?" Peter asks, speaking in a soft voice, and then continues without waiting for a response. "People say that thousands of years ago, magical spirits gave amber the power to heal and to make people happy." He holds the little glass creature on the palm of his hand, so its eyes face Lioba. She has stopped fidgeting, her hands wrapped around her knees and her head bent.

"A long, long time ago, a hunter caught a wild bear." Peter keeps his voice low, as if telling a story to a child in the middle of the night. "After his successful hunt, he carved a tiny bear amulet out of amber. As long as the hunter carried his little bear with him, he never lost heart or feared anything when encountering trials on his journey. People believe bears have magical powers that allow them to do great things and to find happiness if only they look for it. Bears are powerful, clever, and resilient. Anyone owning a bear amulet would be able to draw on the bear's powers."

Lioba has raised her head.

Peter pretends not to notice, keeping his eyes on the figurine in his hand.

"Eventually, the hunter lost his precious amulet, and his long and fruitful life came to an end. The amber bear vanished forever, but people still believe in its power. I heard stories about the amber bear all my life. Of course, I never saw it. I do not know whether it even existed, but I always loved the thought of it."

"But it does exist." Lioba sits up.

"Truly?" Peter stares at her.

"Archeologists found it buried in a peat bog near Stolp. It's ancient—I think something like two thousand years. Whatever the exact age, it is definitely the oldest item ever discovered in Pomerania. I don't know where it is right now, probably in a museum."

"What does it look like?"

"Like that." Lioba points at the glass figurine. "It's just a copy. You can buy it anywhere. Sort of like a cross between a pig and a seal and something else. It doesn't work as a pendant. If it were suspended by the little hole in the back, it would hang upside down—hardly a decorative piece of jewelry. It can't even stand on its stubby little legs by itself, but if you hold it in your hand, facing you, it seems alive. That's why archaeologists are convinced it had magical significance."

Peter runs his fingers over the figurine. His heart is pounding. The amber bear is real. It exists, and it has magical powers. It is just like his crane, his amber crane, which transports him into this strange, distant future.

Taking his silence for disbelief, Lioba says, "Honestly, I am not making this up. I have seen photographs of it. It looks just like this, sort of pig-like with short stubby legs and a round body, and it's translucent. When I was a kid, I was convinced it was the model for a candy we used to get, the gummy bear. They called it the 'Bear of Happiness'." Lioba smiles. "It was pretty much the only candy anybody could afford. It cost one penny each. Once a year, my grandfather would bring a little bag back from town and hand them out one by one, blue and red and yellow and green. We all loved it. We even made up stupid rhymes." She stands up and waves her arms, hopping up and down. "Oh, gummy bear, oh, gummy bear, you're a funny, runny gummy bear! You're a sticky strappy happy gummy bear."

Lioba's voice falters, and she sits down as if someone has pushed her. "How can I be so silly? My parents are dead."

"I think your parents wanted you to live," Peter says. "That is why they did not wait for you. They did not want you to have to choose."

"Fine choice they left me. What am I supposed to do now?"

"You keep going."

"How? Where?"

"You said you wanted to go west. So, do that."

"Yes, me and hundreds and thousands of others." Lioba shakes her head.

"So? How are they going to get away?"

"I have no idea. Try to get on a ship or by train, perhaps."

"Train?" A group of pack animals or people? What sort of train could Lioba be talking about?

"Never mind. Trains move fast, but I don't know if any are running, at least not from here, or if there are any, the army probably has requisitioned them. I thought I would see if I could get on a ship, but I heard the *Wilhelm Gustloff* was torpedoed."

"The what?"

"A big ship full of refugees." Lioba frowns at him.

Peter gives up trying to figure out what a running train would look like and latches onto the next word that mystified him. "Torpedoed?"

"Stop asking silly questions. Yes, torpedoed. Shot out of the water. Sunk in the middle of the ocean. Thousands of people are said to have died."

Peter shakes his head. A ship with more than a thousand passengers. He cannot imagine anything like that. "You cannot keep wandering around in the woods. You have to do something. Maybe another ship?"

"You don't understand. I have heard that in Königsberg, people stood at the harbor by the thousands, trying to get onto anything that floats. The army sent as many ships as they could find for the evacuation—minesweepers, torpedo boats, cruisers, even icebreakers, fishing trawlers, colliers, you name it. And it still wasn't enough. It's not going to be any better there."

Peter is bewildered by the rush of incomprehensible words but refrains from asking more questions, shaken by Lioba's face —raw, desolate, and without hope.

"I'm afraid," Lioba says in a small voice after a long silence. "I keep thinking of all those people who drowned when that ship went down."

"There must be something you can do," Peter insists.

"I don't know. The only thing that's keeping me from giving up is this." She reaches for the silver chain around her neck and pulls it out. "I have carried it with me all this time. It's all I have left."

Peter makes out the shape of the pendant. It is a bird. Shocked, he stares at the exquisitely curved neck and slender beak. Then, everything becomes blurry, and the room vanishes.

21

THE WITCHES' BASTION

"Phew, you stink."

It had been a long night, with nothing but a chamber pot to keep Peter company in the dark hole.

He had been awake for hours, thinking of Lioba's pendant and struggling against the temptation to root around in his pocket where his amber crane rested. It was as if he could feel it tremble and flutter, trying to get to Lioba's world. He did not understand it, but he had no doubt that his amber crane was the key. Perhaps there was a law of time that dictated that something from the past could not meet itself in the future. That would explain why he was sent back to his own time whenever he caught a glimpse of Lioba's pendant. *Just imagine meeting myself, perhaps with a long beard and a cane.* Peter's mouth curled into a grin. *That surely would be enough to send me spinning back into my own time before I could even blink.* Then he sobered again when he remembered where he was.

But why was this happening to him? Perhaps there was something he was supposed to do in that other strange time. He had to help Lioba. *But what can I possibly do to help her?*

He must have dozed off after all. A familiar voice boomed in his ears and jarred him awake.

Dazed, Peter looked through the grille above his head into the frowning face of Master Nowak.

A key scraped in a lock, and with a squeal, the grille was lifted.

"Well, are you going to make me wait all day? Come on. Let's get you out of here so you can clean up."

"How ..." he tried to ask, but his voice cracked. It was hard to stand up. Peter was stiff from sitting hunched over for so long. Holding onto the edge of the opening, he pulled himself out of the hole. He coughed and swallowed. "How did you get me out?"

"I paid the fine for disorderly behavior."

"Oh." Peter stumbled in his master's wake out onto the square in front of the town hall. "Thank you." He blinked in the bright sunshine. "What about Effie? Is she at home?"

"That is more complicated," Master Nowak said. "There will be a hearing. We are both supposed to attend."

Peter swayed, trying to fight a wave of nausea rising up in his throat.

"Hey," Master Nowak barked at him and grabbed his arm.

"Where is she?" Peter asked, his voice shaking.

"Let us go home first."

Anne rushed into the hallway when they entered the house, her work apron askew and her hair tangled. There were shadows under her eyes, but she greeted Peter with a smile. "I am so glad you are home," she said. "Thank you, Father. I knew you would get him out."

"I will be in my office. Anne will tell you about your sister. Peter, you better get yourself cleaned up and sorted out, so you will be ready for the hearing tomorrow morning."

Peter blinked. "Tomorrow morning?"

"At least you will not have to wait around all day." Shaking his head, Master Nowak turned and went to his office, closing the door behind him with a thud.

"Anne, where is Effie?" Peter pleaded.

"Right now, she is in a holding chamber in the town hall," Anne said carefully. She talked to him as if he were sick.

"Why? I thought they would let her go. In a holding chamber? Like the one where they kept me? She will be so frightened."

"She is in an attic chamber in the town hall, with several other women awaiting sentencing."

"But she did not do anything wrong. Why are they holding her at all?"

"Do you remember what people were saying on the square?"

"I heard them, but they cannot have been serious. Everybody in town knows Effie. They have to know she is harmless." Peter's voice quavered and rose higher.

"Several people talked about her. One woman kept going on and on. She claimed she had seen Effie moaning and cursing many times. Others said they always thought Effie was a witch, and Lars yelled that you attacked him and that your sister put a curse on him."

"That is ridiculous."

"People have always gossiped about her, you must know that. Only, lately, someone had been spreading far more than just gossip. These days, when there is so much trouble and sickness everywhere, people are afraid and suspicious, and they start to believe malicious rumors like that. Also, you know that …" Anne hesitated.

"Know what?"

"She had an amber heart on a chain. She was waving it around and moaning when she was on the ground. That made them more suspicious. Where did she get that?"

Peter avoided meeting Anne's eyes and pretended to be absorbed by the sight of his hose and shoes, covered with dust from the cellar jail. He shook his head as if to imply that he had no idea what Anne was talking about without lying directly.

"They took it away," Anne said when Peter stayed silent. "I heard that the guild elders are questioning all the members and apprentices to determine whether anyone fashioned the amber heart."

"Did you see her?" Peter tried to change the topic.

"I brought her some clothes. The other women are a little bit afraid of her, so they are leaving her alone."

"What is supposed to happen now? They cannot keep her there indefinitely."

"Father thinks there is nothing we can do right now. We must wait for the hearing." Anne paused, her brown eyes full of concern. "But there is something else. The guard told me the town elders are working on a new prison in the big tower in the Stolp town wall. They are calling it the Witches' Bastion."

"So that is what the jailer meant." Peter sat down on the wooden bench in the hallway. He felt close to tears.

"Meant what?" Anne asked.

"He said the town is getting a special place ready for the likes of her. I did not understand. Effie must be so scared."

"They let me talk to her, and I explained everything," Anne said. "She was calm. She took my hand and stroked it."

"I have to do something. I have to help her."

"Right now, you better get cleaned up." Anne glanced at his hose and shoes. "We will eat soon."

Peter rose to go upstairs.

"Remember, Father has lots friends among the elders," Anne said. "They listen to him." In the attic, Peter sat down on his bed. He was glad Cune was downstairs. It gave him time to collect himself.

The bedspread, the wooden cross on the wall above Cune's bed, his old boots at the wall, the washbowl and pitcher filled with water on the table—everything was dear and comfortable and familiar. Tears welled up in his eyes. The momentary sense of solace was drowned out by a persistent clamor of thoughts. *They think Effie is a witch. I am a thief and a Bönhase. I betrayed Master Nowak. I betrayed everyone. Father will be devastated. I will never be allowed to work in the amber guild.*

Peter wanted to reach into his pocket for the amber crane. It was perfect in every way except for one unfinished wing, still rough and unpolished. Again, he felt a sense of urgency. It called to him. There was something he needed to do. Then he quickly pulled his hand out of his pocket. *It is not as if I can steer with that piece of amber as if it were a row boat.* So far, he had not had any control over when it would transport him from one time to another. It happened when his thoughts wandered or when he was sleeping. Perhaps there was a way to focus on the amber to make it work for him.

This is not the time. He had to think about how to help Effie.

His thoughts went round and round. He should tell Master Nowak the truth. But if he did that, it would put Master Nowak in an impossible position. Peter had worked on the amber pieces in Master Nowak's workshop. Perhaps he should go directly to the town elders and plead for Effie. Of course, he could not admit everything and could never tell anybody about the amber crane. Besides, nobody would believe him anyway. Would he be put in jail? When the truth came out, he would not be allowed to work as a journeyman. Maybe the town elders would just make him leave the town. He could try to serve as a mate on one of his uncle's ships.

Peter's stomach hurt. There was no guarantee the town elders would release Effie, even if he explained about the amber heart.

There was one thing he could do. He had to try.

He stood up, rinsed his face over the washbowl, and brushed his hair back with his hands.

When he entered the kitchen, the smell of Mistress Nowak's cooking and the sight of her round arms placing bowls on the table made him realize how hungry he was. The blue and white tiles on the stove gave off a cheerful warmth. A spray of witch hazel in a copper vase glowed amid the pewter plates and mugs on top of the mantelpiece.

Peter's eyes started to burn. He would lose all of this. Once he confessed, he could no longer come back here.

Master Nowak came out of his office, rubbing his hands. "I finally finished the ledgers for the month," he said, sitting down. "It has not been a good month. Actually, the market has gotten worse for a long time now," he added with a sigh. "It almost makes you wish for more Catholics in the area buying rosary beads." He pulled the large soup terrine toward him. "Ah, lentil soup, wonderful."

Mistress Nowak smiled at him. "Yes, and apple dumplings."

Any other day that would have been Peter's favorite meal. He never got tired of lentil soup. Sometimes, Mistress Nowak added bacon bits to spice it up, and he loved apple dumplings with hot browned butter, especially when it was cold outside. Today, he barely looked up from his plate, and the one dumpling he managed to get down, after poking it hesitantly with his fork, sat in his stomach like a rock.

Anne and Cune kept up a steady stream of chatter, talking about work, Cune's family, and even ideas for another Shrovetide play. A few times, Anne's eyes drifted in his direction, but nobody asked him any questions. Whenever he glanced at his friends, he cringed inside. Anne would never have started any rumors, nor would Cune. How could he have suspected them? He had been blind.

"I want to go to my father's house," Peter said at the end of the meal, glancing at his plate so Master Nowak would not be able to read his expression. "May I be excused? I will be back soon."

Master Nowak nodded. "Very well, but do not be too late."

Peter walked quickly toward the central part of town to the row of patrician houses near the town hall. The mayor lived in a well-maintained three-story building, with pale blue paintwork and tall, shiny windows. Peter ran his hand through his hair and tried to straighten his tunic. Then he shook his head. None of this would matter now. Pressing his lips together, he raised the heavy bronze knocker and let it fall against the metal plate.

The door opened. A servant eyed him disapprovingly. "Do you have a delivery?"

"I need to see Mistress Marthe Neuhof," Peter said, pulling back his shoulders and raising his chin.

The girl sniffed and looked as if she was about to close the door in his face.

"Please, it is urgent."

"Wait here." She disappeared.

After a long time, the door opened again and Marthe appeared, dressed as if she had been planning to go out, wearing a dark blue cape and a shawl draped over her hair.

Peter caught a whiff of her rich musky scent and for a moment was overcome by doubt. Then he felt nauseous and angry at himself.

"Why are you here?" Marthe hissed.

"I need to talk to you."

"I do not want you inside."

Peter bit his lip. After months of her waylaying him everywhere, he was not good enough to step across the threshold of her house. However, such thoughts were pointless now. "I do not care where," he snapped. "I need to talk to you. Do you want me to force my way inside?"

"Fine." Marthe glanced over her shoulder and stepped outside, pulling the door shut. "I will walk with you."

Silently, they headed toward the open area in front of the church at the end of the big square and stopped underneath the elm tree. It was a quiet afternoon, and there was no one near them.

"I do not have all day." Marthe glowered at him. "What do you want from me?"

"You have to help Effie," Peter said firmly.

"Me? Why me?"

"You know perfectly well why. You started the rumors."

"I have better things to do than to gossip." Marthe raised her chin. "Why would I do such a thing?"

"I do not know why you did what you did. But if you had not started the rumors, things would not have gotten so bad for Effie. Now you have to undo the damage."

"Why would I bother?"

"Because you were fond of Lorenz. Because Effie never hurt you. She never hurt anyone in her entire life."

"Why should I care about any of that?" Marthe hissed, her cheeks flushed. "And your precious brother? He led me on, and then he laughed at me. He told me he liked his girls to be smart. I hated him."

Peter stared at her. Now things fell into place. He had gotten it all wrong. It was not Lorenz who had pursued Marthe. It had been the other way around. She had been fascinated by Lorenz, with his shock of golden locks, his uproarious laughter, and his wit. He might not even have realized how she felt about him. Yes, Peter could picture his brother mocking Marthe. Lorenz hadn't always been kind. He had mocked everyone, and the only person who had escaped his sharp tongue was Effie.

For an instant, Peter felt almost sorry for Marthe. He had been at the receiving end of Lorenz's laughter and disdain often enough.

"But what did Effie ever do to you?"

"Everybody has always been so protective of her. It annoyed me."

"You started the rumors out of revenge?"

"Well, not at first. It was fun. And I was playing with you just like your brother played with me. You were so flattered. It just got out of hand."

"Are you telling me this was just a game for you?"

Marthe twirled her scarf. "I never meant Effie to be accused of being a witch."

"It is one thing to tease me. But how could you spread rumors about Effie? How could you do something like this?" Peter raised his voice. "Do you not realize what might happen to her and to my whole family?"

"You do not understand what it is like for someone like me."
Marthe shifted restlessly. Her face looked pinched, with blotches
of red standing out like stains. Everything about her appeared
deflated all of a sudden. "My father did not want me to learn a
trade. He told me I am not smart enough for learning. He wants
me to marry well. It is as if he has forgotten there are hardly any
young men left alive."

Peter was silent, gazing at the gap along the trunk of the tree.
In 1637, when the Imperialist had fought with the Swedes for
control of the town, a cannonball had hit the tree during a brief
pitched battle. Since then, the bark had partially closed over the
gap, but the deep scar remained.

So many people were scarred. Clare. His father. Lorenz.
Marthe. Different scars, but all part of the same war.

"You have a trade." Marthe tugged and twisted a strand of
hair that had slipped out from underneath her cap. "I do not
have anything like that. You are good at something. Even your
sister is good at something. Anne told me. All I am supposed to
care about is what I wear and how I appear."

What did Marthe mean by that? What about Effie? But
Peter dismissed that thought. It was not going to help right now.
Anyway, he could not afford to feel sorry for Marthe.

"Look, perhaps you did not realize what you had started,"
Peter said. "But you did it. Now you need to fix this."

"You cannot make me."

"You are not the only one who can start a rumor."

"You would not dare." Marthe flushed. "I cannot believe you
would do that."

"Trust me, I would. How would your father like it if he
heard his only daughter has been meeting people at the beach in
the evening and is consorting with lowly apprentices?"

"But what can I do?"

"I have no doubt you can think of something. I do not care
what you tell your father. You might even consider telling him
the truth. But please help her."

"What about you? You will be in so much trouble when it comes out that you were on the beach."

"That is my problem. I just want to make sure Effie gets to go home."

There were steps behind them. People were crossing the square and coming toward the church.

"I need to go," Marthe snapped, adjusting the scarf over her head, and walked off.

Peter trudged back to Master Nowak's house. Fortunately, Anne and Cune did not ask him any questions at supper. He tried to eat a piece of bread with smoked herring, but gave up after a few bites.

"Go to sleep," Master Nowak said finally, a faint note of exasperation in his voice.

22

SNOWMEN

"Ouch."

A snowball hits Peter in the face. Its fragments trickle down his neck. He is standing on a street without his coat, facing a row of houses, with walls of white or yellow stucco and red-slate roof tiles, each fronted by fenced-in yards. A blanket of fresh snow covers everything. In the yard on the other side of the street, three boys toss snowballs at each other, squealing and laughing. Two girls are patting the rounded belly of a headless snowman.

"This is insane."

Peter turns to the familiar voice behind him. "Lioba."

She seems unchanged, still in her hose and jacket, her satchel over her shoulder, and a cap hiding her hair. However, her face has gotten greyer and sadder since Peter last saw her.

"Can you believe this?" Lioba scowls. "They are making a snowman."

"It looks like fun." Bemused and wistful, Peter gazed at the children. He remembered Lorenz helping Effie and him to build a snowman. "What is wrong with that?"

"Did you forget what's happening?" Lioba stares at him. "They should be helping their mother pack. For that matter, they should be gone already. All hell will break loose when the Russians get here. If they waste more time, there will be bloody snowmen soon."

Peter shakes his head. He picks up a few pebbles and walks across the street. "Here, you could use these for the eyes." He holds them out to one of the little girls. He bends down and rolls a small round mess of snow into a larger ball. "Do you want any help to lift the head on top?"

"Please." The girl beams at him. "I don't have a carrot."

"Use a stick."

Suddenly, Lioba is next to him. She is rolling a snowball until it is large enough for the base of a second snowman. The two girls giggle and rush around, making more balls for the body and the head.

"Hey," Peter shouts. A snowball has landed on his back. He bends down to scoop up a handful of snow.

A volley reaches him, hitting his arms, chest, and legs.

Peter returns the favor, hurling several snowballs at the boys and then, for good measure, at Lioba.

Snowballs start flying in all directions. The children and Lioba gang up and throw all their ammunition at Peter.

"Stop." Peter laughs as he tries to catch his breath.

"Are you asking for mercy? Then you have to say it," Lioba instructs him sternly.

"Really?" Peter ducks to avoid another volley, but too late. One clips him on the nose. "Fine, 'mercy'," he shouts.

Still smiling, Lioba and Peter brush the snow off their clothes, wave to the children, and walk off.

"You were right." Lioba's face is flushed, and her hair sticks out from under her cap.

"How was I right?"

"Those kids might never get to build another snowman. At least they are happy right now."

"Where are we?" Peter asks, rubbing his hands to warm them up. He grins at Lioba. Maybe they are in Danzig or in

Gotenhafen right now. It is fascinating, sort of like reading a book. This jumping back and forth from one century to another does not feel so disorienting anymore. Maybe it just takes practice.

"In a neighborhood of Stolp. I was looking for friends of my parents, but their house is shuttered."

"And now?" Peter sobers when he remembers Lioba's predicament.

"What's the point?" Lioba asks wearily, her feet kicking up snow as she walks.

"You cannot give up," Peter says, pulling Lioba to a halt underneath the shelter of a row of tall pine trees at the edge of a little park. "I want to say something to you, but first I want to ask you about that thing you are wearing underneath your tunic. I know it is precious to you."

"My tunic?" Her weariness apparently forgotten, Lioba grins at him. "Right, that's what we call a sweater." Then she reaches for the silver chain. "You mean this? Let me show you."

"No," Peter shouts, holding on to her arm.

Lioba raises her eyebrows. "Why not?"

"Please, just keep it hidden, away from view." This is awkward. "It is safer that way." He cannot begin to explain the link between his own amber crane and Lioba's pendant. But he wants to know more about it before being catapulted back to his own time. "I am just curious. Where did you get it?"

"It was handed down through the women in my family." Lioba leans against the tree trunk. A look of concentration has replaced the sadness in her eyes. "My great-grandmother was the one who found it. She had some sort of second sight. For instance, she foretold that six men of her family would be killed in the war. It came true."

"Which war?"

"The one before this one. It's called the Great War." Lioba frowns at him. "Don't interrupt. Do you want to know about my pendant or not?"

"Yes, sorry. Please tell me."

"When I was a child, her stories about our family and the story about the ghost of the evil reeve got all mixed up in my dreams. You know, the reeve who decreed that anyone who collected amber without permission from the Order ..." Lioba stops and looks at Peter inquiringly. "You know what that is?"

Peter rolls his eyes at her and recites as if reading from a book, "The Order of Teutonic Knights that controlled the amber trade in the Baltic since the 13th century—and pretty much everything else in the Baltic. We do learn some things, you know."

"Well, you never heard about Bruegel," Lioba retorts.

"When you are done bragging, please go on with your story."

"Well," Lioba continues, grinning at him, "anyone who collected amber without permission would be punished by hanging. But when the evil reeve died, he regretted his actions, and his restless soul was condemned to ride along the beach at night for all eternity, screaming 'Amber Free, Amber Free' in punishment for having executed so many people. At night, I was afraid the reeve would come into our house."

"Brother Anselmus," Peter exclaims. "They use his story to scare little children."

"Hah," Lioba says with a bark of a laugh. "They still do. But by the mid-19th century, the laws about picking up amber on the beach had been relaxed, and people who found pieces no longer had to surrender them. Anyway, my great-grandmother liked to ride alone on the beach, something unheard of for women in her time, the late 1840s. One day in the fall, on a stormy, windy day, she took her favorite horse and rode out along the trails all the way to the beach near Stolpmünde. Once she reached the beach, she let the horse run, galloping in and out of the waves. Finally, she stopped for a rest. She tied the horse to a pine tree and sat down in its shade, watching the incoming tide. Suddenly, she saw a golden glimmer in the waves. She stripped off her boots and socks, rolled up her pants, and went into the water. There it was, floating on the waves, a large piece of amber, roughened from years of exposure to salt water, but recognizable. It had been carved into the shape of a bird, with its wings folded and its beak raised in the air as if about to lift off. You know what was really strange?" Lioba looks perplexed. "It was perfectly crafted, except for one unfinished wing."

Peter is silent, his hand clenched in his pocket.

"My great-grandmother left it like that. She just had it polished a bit. When she was old and tired, she gave it to her daughter and said, "One day, this will help someone in need, and there may come a time to let it go. For now, keep it safe and pass it on." And my mother gave it to me. But why don't you want to see it?"

"Please, just keep it hidden," Peter says quickly. "Anyway, I think it is like a lucky charm. If someone else sees it, the charm might not work."

"You are making that up," Lioba says. "Seriously, why not?"

"I cannot explain it. Not right now. Perhaps another time."

Lioba shrugs and moves away from the tree. "There might not be another time." Her face has resumed its hopeless expression.

"Listen to me." Peter reaches out and puts both his hands on her shoulders as if to shake her. "You have your own amber bear. Never mind that it is a crane. It is a magical piece of amber. It will give you strength. Remember? You told me so yourself. Do not give up now. You said you wanted to go west. You want to find your relatives. You want to go to university. So, go west."

"Fine, I'll try." Lioba gazes at him doubtfully. "But I have to be realistic. I heard people who tried to reach the harbor in Elbing were cut off and forced back by the Russians. The same thing is going to happen here soon. And the ships in Stolp-münde are going to be packed."

"There must be other ways of getting to the west."

"How?"

"What are those trains you talked about?"

"I told you, as far as I know, the army has requisitioned them all."

"Did you try?" Peter asks. He is itching to see what a train could possibly look like. "How does it move, anyway?"

"Steam."

"Steam?"

"Yes, don't ask me to explain."

"Where would you find a train?"

"At the train station. It's in the center of town."

"So, that is where we should go."

Within minutes of walking through quiet streets, they emerge onto a tree-lined avenue flooded with a steady stream of people, most of them carrying bags and sacks. At one building front, there is a commotion. People are shouting as they crowd into an open door, pushing and shoving each other out of the way.

"Come, let's keep moving." Lioba plucks on Peter's sleeve.

"What is happening?"

"It's a bakery." She points at the sign above the door. "They are trying to get bread."

"At the church, they stacked the dead outside in the church-yard." A woman ahead of Peter and Lioba talks to another in a low voice—flat, devoid of emotion. "I guess they ran out of room in the morgue."

The other woman doesn't respond, just keeps moving forward.

Peter sees several wheeled metal carriages sitting along the side of the road, but none that move about. Then his eyes grow round. An old man, holding a basket in front of him, sits on a two-wheeled metal contraption and makes the wheels move by pumping his legs up and down.

"What is that?" Peter whispers.

"What?" Lioba turns her head to look at where he is pointing. "That's just a bicycle."

"Oh, a bicycle." Peter tastes the strange word. Perhaps he could make something like that.

After crossing several more streets and moving along with the steady stream of people, they reach a square with a large red brick building on one side.

"See, I told you," Lioba mutters, pointing at a group of men in grey uniforms in front of the entrance. "The army is unlikely to make room for civilians."

"You do not know that," Peter says stubbornly. "You should at least try."

Lioba shakes her head but follows him as they move with the crowd through the doors. Inside the large hall, shouted commands mingle with the noise of the crowd, echoing in the cavernous space, interspersed with occasional hissing as if from a gigantic snake.

On the other side of the large hall, Peter can see an elevated platform that appears to extend out of the back of the building into the open air. People are moving along this platform. But that is not what caught his attention. Right next to it, there is a black and brown metal behemoth. He cannot think of any other word for it. Like the body of a monstrous worm, it has many segments, all in a row, with doors that open into cavernous interiors. At the front end, large pipes stick out like battering rams, with big glass eyes above. On the platform, soldiers holding muskets in their arms, shout at the people and wave them on.

"That is a train?" he exclaims.

Lioba nods.

Jostled and buffeted from all sides, Peter pulls her along the platform. Soldiers crowd the openings of the metal worm.

A man lifts a funnel-shaped device to his mouth. Suddenly, his voice booms over the platform. People in the crowd stop moving to listen.

"The army has requisitioned this train. However, the two last wagons still have room."

The voice is drowned out by the renewed roar of hundreds of

people desperately pushing and shoving to get to the end of the worm. Children are crying, some falling down in the melee. Relentlessly, the crowd moves forward.

Peter tries to block out all the sounds while he urges Lioba toward the end of the platform where people are already trying to climb up the steep metal steps.

A young woman with a baby wrapped in a shawl on her arm stands next to Peter, her face pinched and pale. Her thin grey coat smells of sweat and sour milk.

"There is no more room," angry voices grumble.

A loud whistle cuts through the noise like a whip.

"The train is about to move," a soldier shouts. "Stand back."

"Grab that bar," Peter says, his hands on Lioba's back to push her up.

"I can't do this." Lioba shakes him off and steps away from the opening. "Here, you go," she says to the woman with the baby in her arms. "Peter, help her."

Shaking his head in frustration, Peter struggles to push the woman up the metal steps. One man reaches out and pulls her inside. It smells of pigs, manure, and other unidentifiable substances. People inside the container shift back, creating a small space where the woman can stand. Holding onto a metal bar on the edge of the opening, she glances back at Lioba and mouths "*Thank you.*"

At that moment, the behemoth starts groaning and huffing and begins to roll out of the station.

Another shrill whistle. Peter covers his ears, appalled and mesmerized in turn. He cannot take his eyes off the huge wheels with their metal bars that move up and down and forward and back in rhythm with the huffing noises. Black smoke pours out of one of the stacks, and steam emerges from the bottom.

So that is a train. It is almost as if it were alive, even though it appears to be made entirely of metal. *I will never forget that.*

Just then, someone behind them pushes through the crowd, knocking Lioba over, trying to reach one of the openings. He fails, slips, and falls onto the narrow space between the train and the platform. Hands reach out to pull him back, but it is too late. His scream is drowned by the thundering noise as the wagon rolls past.

Shaken, Peter turns to Lioba to help her up. There is a buzzing in his ears, and dizziness washes over him.

"Lioba, go to Stolpmünde," he shouts. "I will look for you at the harbor."

He catches a glimpse of her pale face and distended eyes.

Then everything goes dark.

✣ 23 ✣

TANGLED WEBS

PETER WOKE UP, TREMBLING WITH COLD UNDER HIS blanket. Sunlight flowed into the attic from the small window. He felt disoriented, split in half. He had to go back. He had to help Lioba.

Then he took in his surroundings, and he closed his eyes in despair. Today was the hearing, and Effie was in jail.

He clutched his blanket to pull himself up when he saw Cune's empty bed on the other side of the room. He had overslept again. Quickly, he pulled on his clothes and went downstairs.

Master Nowak was already at the door. "We need to go."

"Sorry," Peter mumbled as he followed him onto the street. "Where is the hearing?"

"In the house next to the church where the guild elders usually meet." Master Nowak glanced at Peter as if to see whether he is paying attention. "The town elders decided to hold the hearing there."

Peter shook his head. "What difference does it make where they do this?"

"It could mean they want to keep the matter at the level of an infraction against the guild. I know the town elders do not like involving any members of the church or the council of patricians unless they have to. They do not like having the patricians or any outsiders tell them what to do. This might be a good thing. I am hoping they do not want this to escalate to the point of questioning your sister."

"Good luck with that," Peter interjected angrily. "How is that supposed to work when she doesn't speak?"

"Where have you been all these years?" Master Nowak stopped in his tracks. "Once the questioning starts, nobody cares about the answer. Guilt or innocence is not even a question anymore. It is totally irrelevant in what state your sister is going to be at that point."

Peter winced.

Master Nowak started walking again. "Then again, they might not even bother questioning her and instead decide to put her through a trial by ordeal."

"They will not do this to Effie, right?" Peter's voice trembled. He had heard of these trials. How could people think that they could determine the guilt or innocence of a person by whether or not they floated when thrown into a body of water?

"I hope not." Master Nowak had regained his customary composure. "Of course, it all depends on the mayor."

"About the amber heart," Peter began, stumbling over the words. "It is my fault. I used your workshop. I am so sorry."

"I do not want to hear another word." Master Nowak glared at him.

"But I want to tell you—" Peter tried again.

"Not now," Master Nowak snapped. "We are wasting time here." He walked so quickly Peter had to run to keep up.

Peter gave up trying to say anything else to Master Nowak. He had every right to be angry at his apprentice, and it was hardly surprising he did not want to listen to Peter.

When they reached the meeting house, Master Nowak led the way through the main doors and down a hallway. Then he put his hand out and gripped Peter's shoulder. He looked as if he was about to say something else, but then dropped his hand and pushed open the door.

Peter followed him with his head bent. It all depended on Marthe.

Inside the large room, Peter glanced around quickly. Seated at a long table in the center were three elders from the amber guild. One was Master Roth, who today appeared remarkably clean and trim. He pursed his lips, his eyes resting on Master Nowak with a speculative glance.

The other men in the room had to be town elders and members of the town council. At the head of the table sat a middle-aged man, small and slight in build, with thinning hair and a face with an unhealthy yellow tinge. A leather folder lay in front of him. He sat with his hands folded as if in prayer, his expression grim.

That was Marthe's father, Mayor Neuhof. Peter recognized him from the Proclamation. He had never been interested in the mayor. Now, he could hardly keep from staring at him.

"Master Nowak, please, take a seat," the mayor said, pointing to a chair in front of the table. He glanced briefly at Peter as if he could not bear his sight. "And you sit there." He pointed at another chair next to Master Nowak.

Gingerly, Peter lowered himself, taking comfort from the wooden seat and straight back, solid, sturdy, and reassuring in its familiarity. He braced his legs and tried to keep his hands still by folding them on his lap.

"Now, let me state the purpose of this hearing." Mayor Neuhof shuffled some papers in front of him, peering at them through a magnifying glass. He cleared his throat repeatedly and raised his eyes. For a moment, he scrutinized Peter, before he continued speaking in a nasal tone. "Gentlemen, we have in front of us an accusation of battery by one Peter Glienke and an accusation of witchcraft leveled against one Euphemia Glienke. Second, Mistress Glienke is charged with theft—an expensive item of amber, in particular, one with an inclusion, was found in the hands of the accused. And finally, there is the question of the origin of the amber and where it was crafted. Needless to say, these are grave accusations and must be addressed."

Peter pressed his hands down on his thighs to keep his legs from trembling. He could not take his eyes away from the mayor's yellow-grey sagging jowls and pale lips.

"However, before we refer the matter to outside authorities," Mayor Neuhof cleared his throat again and shifted in his seat, "we first need to examine the facts at hand."

Outside authorities. Peter shivered. At least they hadn't done that yet.

"Several witnesses have come forward."

Peter tried to stand up when he felt a hand grip his own under the table. Master Nowak shook his head slightly and mouthed "*Wait.*" Reluctantly, Peter obeyed. He kept his eyes on the table in front of him.

Mayor Neuhof rapped on the table.

Everyone quieted down.

The mayor lifted a little bell and shook it.

A clerk entered the room. "Yes, Mayor?"

"Please ask our first witness to step inside."

A woman entered the room.

Peter recognized her. Mistress Wollenhaver lived near the harbor with her family. Her husband was a fisherman who had sometimes dealt with his uncle. She had donned a lace cap for the occasion, although her gown was worn and threadbare. She held her hands folded as if in prayer. Her eyes darted quickly back and forth until they settled on the mayor.

"Mistress Wollenhaver," the mayor said sternly, "would you relate to these gentlemen what you have told us?"

"Yes, Mayor Neuhof," she responded, licking her lips nervously. For a moment, her eyes met Peter's, and her face took on a pinched expression. "I have known that family for many years. The mother was strange. The son, Mistress Glienke's brother, disappeared. And nobody can understand why her uncle continues to do so well when others have suffered."

"Mistress Wollenhaver," Mayor Neuhof snapped, coughing and adjusting the papers in front of him. "We have no desire to sit here all day. I suggest you address the matter at hand."

Peter clenched his hands. He could hardly sit still. His uncle had done so much for the town over the years. Now, he was being slandered. And this woman slandered Peter's entire family.

"Mistress Glienke has always been odd." Mistress Wollenhaver fumbled and twisted her bony hands. "I have often seen her with my own eyes sit on the ground with foam coming out of her mouth, making strange noises. Other people told me she meets strangers at night, while honest, hardworking citizens are sleeping in their beds. I have had my suspicions for a long time. On Shrovetide Tuesday, I saw her sway as if getting ready to dance and stare at the people around her. She saw me, and her eyes rolled. Then she sat on the ground and swung the amulet back and forth, muttering incantations. She went on faster and faster until the guards stopped her."

Peter wanted to scream. *How could anyone believe any of this?* Then he remembered what Master Nowak had said. *Nobody cares about the answers.* The mayor and the town elders probably already decided what was going to happen. His legs started shaking, and he shifted position so they were once again firmly on the ground.

Mayor Neuhof gazed at Mistress Wollenhaver with pursed lips, his fingers gently drumming on the table.

"But that's not all," she said quickly. "The shed next to our house burned down the very next day. She must have placed a curse on it."

"Thank you, Mistress Wollenhaver. The town council will take your comments into consideration."

The woman looked dissatisfied. She opened her mouth to start speaking again, but the clerk already stood next to her and began to shepherd her toward the door.

The council members muttered and whispered to each other. One nudged Mayor Neuhof, and Peter could just make out his words, "... a miracle that rotten old shed did not burn down a long time ago."

The next witness stepped inside the room, and Peter jerked in his seat. Master Nowak gripped his shoulder in warning. Peter subsided.

It was Lars, looking grave and troubled as if fulfilling an onerous duty, with his greasy hair brushed back, exposing a black eye and a bruise on his cheek, his boots polished, and a new tunic, a bit too tight for his beefy build. For an instant, he glanced at Peter, his lips curled into a smile. Then he resumed his expression of concern and sadness.

"Lars Steiner, an apprentice mason in good standing, you have told us that you are a witness to the events on Shrovetide Tuesday. Now, share with us what you have to say."

"Yes, Mayor." Lars bowed politely. "Along with everyone else, I watched the play. Afterward, I walked around the food stalls in the marketplace. I noticed Mistress Glienke, standing alone at one of the stalls behaving strangely. I felt sorry for her. I thought perhaps she was lost. When I approached her, thinking to offer her my help, she flung herself against me and then sat on the ground, muttering curses and chanting and waving something that looked like a charm back and forth. And then I was vilely attacked by him." He pointed at Peter. "Fortunately, the town guards came quickly. I am afraid to think what would have happened otherwise."

Peter fingered the worn fabric of his hose to calm himself, hardly able to contain his fury at this fabrication. He did not dare to glance at Lars's smug face. He would give anything to administer a bruise on the other side of Lars's face. But he could not allow Lars to provoke him. That definitely would not help Effie.

Meanwhile, Lars was not done. "I have also become aware of strange doings at night at the workshop of Master Nowak.

Repeatedly, I saw mysterious lights flickering and heard strange sounds emanate forth into the street. It looked like someone was performing mysterious rites." His eyes flickered, and he hunched his shoulders and appeared to tremble. "I was frightened."

The town elders listened attentively, their faces grave.

Peter could hardly stop himself from leaping across the table and charging Lars. Suddenly, his thoughts cleared. He stood up. "Mayor Neuhof, would you allow me to speak?"

"Very well," the mayor said curtly.

"I cannot deny what I did. I attacked Lars in the town square. I thought he had frightened my sister. However, I would like to ask Lars a question if I may."

Mayor Neuhof raised his eyebrows and nodded.

"Lars, what was your reason for repeatedly lurking outside Master Nowak's house in the middle of the night?" Peter paused and glanced at the other faces. "He has a young daughter. Maybe he needs to be concerned about her safety." He sat back down.

Master Nowak frowned.

Lars turned red. "I was just getting concerned and wanted to ..." he began, sounding flustered.

"Really?" Master Nowak snapped, two red spots appearing on his normally sallow cheeks. "So, you have admitted to hanging around my house in the middle of the night, hardly an activity that inspires confidence." He faced the other masters and town elders. "I might add I have personally witnessed several incidences where this same young man chose to attack my apprentice. Forgive me if I question his motives in coming forward now."

The town elders began speaking to each other in low voices.

Lars stood with his head bent as if mesmerized by the pattern of the floor planks.

Master Nowak leaned back in his chair, watching Lars. He looked stern and forbidding.

"Lars Maler," Mayor Neuhof said, "do you have anything to add?"

"No, sir," Lars mumbled.

"We have made a note of your testimony and will take it into consideration. Meanwhile, I advise you, young man, to be careful when lodging charges in the future. See to your own actions."

Lars shifted, clutching his hands behind his back. "May I leave?"

"Yes, you are dismissed."

Lars bowed his head and lumbered out, no longer cocky and self-assured. Peter could not help grinning at his obvious discomfort.

"Mayor Neuhof." Master Nowak stood up. "May I address the hearing?"

The mayor inclined his head. He appeared distracted and kept his eyes on the papers in front of him.

"To impugn that my workshop may have been used for any improper work as if I was harboring a Bönhase under my roof is an insult to me, a long-time member of the guild in good standing." Master Nowak coughed. "Occasionally, I have my apprentices work at night when we are behind schedule. I absolutely reject any other inferences the council may draw from this witness's statements." Master Nowak's expression was stern and forbidding. "As to ..."

Peter got up, knocking the chair over in his hurry. He had to stop Master Nowak from saying anything else. None of this was Master Nowak's fault.

"I found the amber on the beach," Peter shouted. Then he lowered his voice. "I told no one. No one knew, certainly not Master Nowak."

Peter could see every detail of the faces staring back at him.

Mayor Neuhof raised his head.

"Master Nowak did not know I used his workshop," Peter repeated. "I beg his forgiveness. None of it is his fault." His legs had stopped trembling. "My sister is entirely innocent. Effie did not steal the amber heart, and it is not an evil charm. It is just a piece of amber. I carved the heart for her in the hope it would help her feel better. I never intended to profit from it." Peter had to catch his breath before continuing.

The town elders gazed at him, their faces blank. Meanwhile, Mayor Neuhof, with his lips pursed and eyes narrowed, looked as if Peter was nothing more than something that had stuck to the bottom of his shoe.

"Effie is sweet and gentle. She never harmed anybody in her entire life. That day on the market, she was badly frightened when someone accosted her from behind. Please do not punish her for something that is not her fault."

Nobody made a sound.

Finally, Mayor Neuhof rapped on the table. "We now have the facts of the case before us, and we have listened to relevant witness testimony. We will consider the matter and arrive at a decision. Master Nowak and Master Glienke, you may go for now. You will return here in three hours, at which point we will announce the sentence. Fail to appear at your peril."

Outside on the market square, Master Nowak placed his hand briefly on Peter's shoulder.

"I was proud of you in there. You did the right thing."

"I am so sorry for everything," Peter said.

"What is done is done. By the way, you realize you have an enemy for life?"

"Lars?" Peter asked. He was getting angry all over again.

"He has been sent back into his corner, but no doubt he will resurface eventually. You have to learn to handle this."

"Lars raped my sister," Peter blurted out.

"I thought it was something like that." Master Nowak nodded, his expression grim. "Can you prove it?"

Mutely, Peter shook his head.

"I did not think so. This is the best we can do for now. At least we taught him not to hang around underneath our window. Anyway, I will go back to the workshop for a while. What about you?"

This question hurt. It was as if Peter was already no longer a member of the workshop. Well, most likely he would not even be a member of the guild in a few hours.

"I want to walk around for a bit if I may."

"Of course."

Peter pulled his coat tighter around himself as he made his way toward the pond on the outskirts of town. Fragments of ice drifted along the shore and pushed up onto the ground, clanking and groaning like a piteous beast in chains.

On the field beyond the pond, several crows had surrounded a small bird, pecking at it and making hissing and screeching sounds. The bird cowered, its beak almost level with the ground.

There was one more thing he had to do before the sentence. It could not wait. He gripped the amber crane in his pocket and tried to cast his mind toward Lioba's world as firmly as he could.

Buffeted by the harsh wind, Peter's eyes blurred. When his sight cleared, the pond was gone. The field was gone.

24

FLAMES ON THE WATER

SNOW WHIPS INTO HIS FACE.

Lights pierce the dark, flickering and swaying as if floating on water. Next to Peter, an impossibly tall flagpole reaches into the sky, the incessant clanking and clattering from a metal chain hitting the pole like a song of mourning. People walk past him, all in the same direction, clutching bags and boxy-looking leather cases.

Squinting to shield his eyes from the snow, he tries to get his bearings. He notices long jetties reaching into the ocean and a canal that narrows at the upper end. The shape of the harbor seems familiar, but he recognizes none of the buildings. As his eyes adjust to the dark and the unfamiliar scene, he begins to make out small vessels and fishing boats that appear to be ferrying people to ships farther out in the water. Squealing sounds make him think of powerful winches. They come from a vessel moored directly along the harbor wall. A dense crush of people is inching forward on a ramp leading up to its deck. Officers on board close to the ramp are shouting orders. Holding their muskets like a barrier, they force some of the people to back up while pulling others onto the deck.

"Would you move?" A hoarse voice behind him startles Peter

out of his absorption, and he steps to the side. A woman, dragging a little boy by the hand and holding a leather box in the other, passes him.

"Let the children through," someone yells.

The crowd parts reluctantly. An older woman leads a troupe of small children, all holding on to a long rope. The children do not make a sound as they trudge past, woolen caps and coat hoods dusted with snow, only partially obscuring their pinched, pale faces.

Incessant loud booms punctuate the roaring, but mostly everybody seems to ignore the noise, just cowering or hunching shoulders in response. Those who cannot move forward because of the mass of people in front of them stamp their feet to ward off the biting cold.

Peter backs up to get away from the crowd. A muffled groan behind him makes him turn around.

A woman falters, sliding on a patch of ice, and lurches forward onto her knees. A large bundle rolls onto the ground, and her bag bursts open. Others walk past her, oblivious to her plight. Peter extends his hand to pull her up.

"Get your hands off me," the woman snarls as she struggles back onto her feet. Her face looks bruised, and her eyes are bloodshot.

"Sorry," Peter mumbles and drops his hands. "I just wanted to help." He cannot tell how old she is. All he can see is the face of someone half-crazed, driven beyond desperation. It makes him think of Effie. He bends down to pick up the bundle. It is a baby wrapped in a blanket, oddly heavy in his arms.

"I hope the baby isn't hurt," he tries to say, but his voice falters. He can see the tiny face, still and pale, eyes closed, lashes tipped with snow, and with a bluish tinge around the lips. The baby is dead.

"Give her to me," the woman snaps, grabbing the bundle and pulling the blanket around the lifeless body protectively.

Avoiding her eyes, Peter bends down to gather the things that spilled out of her bag. "Where are you going?" he asks.

For a moment, she stares at him blankly as if unaware of her surroundings, with her hand stroking the bundle with the baby in it. "There." Lifting her chin, she points toward the harbor, where people trudge up a gangway, amidst shouts and yelling from men on the ship. "They said the women and children get taken first."

Nodding helplessly, Peter hands the woman her bag. His throat hurts. Trying to get away from the crush of people struggling to reach the gangway, he moves closer to the water on the other side of the pier.

In the distance, at the mouth of the harbor, a ship is in flames. Dark specks fall into the water, flailing about and sinking, lit up by the shimmer from the fire.

Several dogs run along the pier, barking. One, in particular, catches Peter's attention. A small dog with short legs and a stubby body, fluffy, grey, with floppy ears, darts back and forth on the pavement, its toes making clicking sounds. It sits down, tongue hanging out, and gazes up at the ship next to the pier, making high-pitched squealing sounds.

"Mirko!" A little girl leans over the railing, her long braids dangling down, crying and holding out her arms to the dog. Someone behind the girl tries to pull her away, but she struggles, clutching the railing with her hands. "Mirko," she screams again. "Mirko."

Peter moves forward and grabs the little dog by the scruff of its neck. It scratches and growls, trying to bite him and to twist out of his grip, but he doesn't let go. He steps close to the edge of the pier and hurls the beast across the water over the railing of the ship. Just as the little girl's arms reach out and catch the grey mass of fur, Peter loses his footing.

He flings out his arm, reaching for a wooden piling, but his hand slips on the slick surface, icy and coated with algae. He scrabbles for purchase along the edge of the pier, barely holding on. *I am going to be caught between the ship wall and the dock, and the damn dog bit me for all my trouble.* The water slaps the pilings with sucking noises. Glancing past his arm, he can see it just below his dangling feet, a dark greasy sheen covering its surface, lit up by the flickering lights from the burning ship. Something floats along, bumping against the pier with a thud. Unblinking eyes stare up at the sky. A hot sour taste wells up in Peter's throat.

"Why do I always find you in these impossible positions?" A hand has clamped onto his wrist.

He looks up into Lioba's scowling face.

"You know that dog will probably end up as ship ration?"

Holding on to her hand and with the other wrapped around the piling, Peter manages to pull himself back onto the pier. His arms tremble from the exertion.

"Lioba," he gasps. "Why are you not on a ship?"

"I gave up." With a brusque motion, Lioba pushes her hair back under her cap. With her jacket and hose, she appears like a slim young man. She still carries her bag over her shoulder. "I just couldn't do it. There were so many kids with their mothers."

"You cannot keep doing this." Peter shakes his head in frustration.

"Many of these people had less than a day to pack up and leave," Lioba shouts as if it is Peter's fault. "At least I had weeks to accept all this."

"But why?"

"Why what?"

"Why did they not leave sooner?"

"Because they would have been shot as traitors if they had," Lioba says bitterly. "The army gave civilians in the area permission to leave only on March 6. So now they have to compete with all the refugees from further east." She shifts her pack. "You know the saddest thing about this? Until just a few days ago, many people still were convinced the army would be victorious and would protect them. I tried to tell them. Every single village

I passed through, I tried to tell them to get ready, but they didn't believe me."

Peter stands next to Lioba as they watch the crowd beginning to thin out. People left on the dock wander around aimlessly. The square is littered with abandoned bags and bundles.

"And you know something else?" Lioba glances at Peter. "That train in Stolp—it was going east to Danzig because the route west was already cut off by the Russians. There is literally no place to go now."

The ship at the end of the pier is drawing up the gangway.

One of the smaller barges has begun to move out of the harbor. People crowd along its guardrails like desperate seagulls. The wind and drifting snow blur the ship's outlines, but Peter can see it lurching and swaying in the rough seas on the edge of the harbor mouth.

Then he gasps in shock.

Like a hollow walnut shell in a stream, the vessel tips onto its side, tossing people into the sea. It sinks within seconds.

The people on the shore watch silently. The other vessels, dimly lit, their decks packed with dark shapes, sit in the harbor like massive paralyzed beasts. The fire from the burning ship has disappeared.

Hunching her shoulders, Lioba stares at the vague outlines of shapes floating in the water where there had been a ship a few moments earlier.

There is nothing Peter can say about what they just witnessed.

"Lioba." A tall, slim man suddenly stands before them.

"Gustav," Lioba exclaims, shaken out of her apathy.

Somehow, Gustav has managed to exchange his striped clothes for an ill-fitting jacket with a split seam along one shoulder and dark breeches. He looks oddly cheerful. "Look, Peter, I still have your shoes," he says proudly. "But Lioba, I thought you'd be on a ship by now."

"I came too late." Lioba shrugs. "Anyway, the officers took women and children first, and there was no room left for any others."

Gustav blinks, and the corners of his mouth twist up in a strange smirk as if he hadn't smiled in years and had forgotten how. "Forgive me, but aren't you a woman?"

"I hardly remember." Lioba chuckles, but then she is serious again. "Anyway, those ships are packed. They can't take on anybody else." She waves an arm across the disconsolate huddle of people left on the dock, amidst a bewildering litter of abandoned bags.

"So, what are you going to do?" Gustav asks.

"I don't really know. Admittedly, being on a ship isn't all that appealing. Those ships are probably just waiting for first light to pull out of the harbor, straight into the arms of the Soviet navy." Her voice sounds flat as if she did not care anymore. "East or west, by sea or by land, what difference is it going to make?"

"You cannot quit," Peter says firmly, stubbornly disregarding the words he doesn't understand. He can feel the weight of the amber crane in his pocket. It brought him here for a reason. An idea takes hold of his thoughts. "You should try to find someone with a boat."

"I think anything that floats is already out there," Lioba says dismissively.

"What about going away from the harbor, further up the river? Somebody might still have a boat there."

Booms roll across the night sky, followed by a *rat-tat-tat*.

"That's the Russian army getting closer," Gustav says flatly. "We can't keep standing around here."

"Exactly," Peter agrees. "Come on, I have an idea." He knows now where he is—at the western bank of the Stolpe. He leads the way along the upper edge of the harbor and up the canal. "Here, just beyond where the canal turns into the river, there used to be shelters where fishermen kept boats, safe and secure from winter storms."

"What do you mean, 'used to'?" Gustav looks at him curiously.

"Never mind that now," Lioba says.

Peter gazes around. Some of the houses hugging the riverbank are familiar. "There," he exclaims, trembling with excitement. It has to be his uncle's ice cellar.

Puzzled, Lioba and Gustav glance at the thick brambles and shrubs, growing wild on a raised mound above the riverbank.

Peter has no doubt whatsoever. Only there is more shrubbery on top, obscuring it from view. He almost falls as he makes his way down the riverbank onto the little beachfront and turns back to the mound at the waters' edge. With shaking hands, he pushes the brambles and vines aside. They tear at his skin, but he hardly notices. Gasping to catch his breath, he stands in the opening hidden by the shrubbery. "There," he says, pointing at the door to the ice cellar, trying to disguise the tremor in his voice.

"What is this?" Gustav runs his hands over the dark oak panels and cast-iron fittings. "How did you know this was here?"

"It is an ice cellar. People used it to hide things." Peter almost tells them how his uncle hid things from the Swedes and the Imperialists. "Sometimes they widened openings of cellars like this for easier access and to store boats." He scrutinizes the field stones framing the door. The opening appears wider than he remembers it. Someone must have worked on it since his uncle's time. Perhaps it was a relative. Peter shivers.

Gustav glances at him with raised eyebrows. "Fine, let's look."

They pull on the door until they are able to wedge it partially open. The pale light from the moon flowing through the gap allows them to make out a surprisingly large space inside.

"What do you know? There is a boat there." Gustav sounds angry. "See that tarp? He's been hoarding it just when the need is greatest." He points at the bulky shape underneath a dark covering. "I wonder where the owner is."

"Hah, maybe he is on one of those ships." Lioba stands next to them. "Or hiding out inside his house. He ought to be ashamed of himself. It's amazing it wasn't requisitioned."

"Never mind the owner. We are going to take this boat."

"You mean steal it?" Peter asks.

"Well, yes, not to put too fine a point on it. To be honest, I already tried a bit of stealing in empty villages on the way here. I figured I needed the stuff, and why should the Russians get it all? I have been putting together a cache to help us when we get underway."

"Who is 'we'?" Peter is intrigued by the man's changed attitude. He is no longer lost and defeated; instead, he is full of energy, even optimism.

"Family," Gustav says abruptly.

Lioba glances at him and stays silent.

"Sorry to bark at you like that," Gustav adds. "I thought they were dead. I'm still getting used to the fact that I found them again."

"Where are they now?"

"They have been hiding in the basement of their house for the last three years. I told them to stay put until I figured out what to do."

"They hid in a basement?" Peter asks, bewildered. *What is a basement?* He would ask Lioba later.

"Never mind that now." Lioba frowns at him. "Gustav, run back and get them."

"I think you should stay together," Peter says, thinking of the thieves they had encountered. "You should get your family right now." Perhaps Lioba would not have to travel west all by herself.

"What do you mean *you*?" Gustav asks. "Aren't you coming with us?"

"I will explain later," Peter says quickly. "This is not the time."

"Fine, let's go," Gustav says. "They are just a few blocks southwest from here."

They hurry through the dark streets. Only a few houses have dim lights.

Peter walks gingerly, puzzled by the smoothness of the street's surface. He cannot imagine what sort of material this is. It reminds him of hardened tar he has seen on his father's ships, but that seems impossible. It would take mountains and mountains of the stuff to create surfaces like this. He quickens his pace to keep up while he stares at the houses along the street, strangely familiar, with red brick, timber beams, and white-painted window frames. Perhaps descendants of people he knows live there.

"Why did Gustav's people have to hide?" Peter asks Lioba in an undertone.

"I guess because they are Jews." Her face is drawn and pale.

"It sounds like the Spanish Inquisition," Peter mutters, shaking his head.

"Yes, like that, only worse," Lioba says softly.

Gustav stops in front of a small brick house, set back behind a snow-covered front yard. He pulls open the front door and touches something on the wall. A light comes on.

"No need for secrecy anymore," he says with a twisted grin. "Nobody left in town who would denounce us."

Inside, it looks as if the Swedes together with the Imperialists had descended on the house repeatedly, smashing everything in sight, slashing up mattresses, tearing down wall hangings, ripping the stuffing out of chairs, and gouging walls.

Silently, Peter and Lioba follow Gustav through to the back of the house into what appeared to be a kitchen. Here as well, chaos rules, pots and pans tipped out of cabinets, smashed crockery littering the floor, and drawers gaping open.

Gustav kneels in the middle of the room and raps three times slowly and then three times with a rapid beat on a floorboard. "We arranged a signal so they would know it was me," he explains.

"They lived down there?" Lioba whispers, her eyes distended.

"Well, when I helped my cousin build this, we didn't think they would need it for so long, but yes, they spent a lot of the time right there in hiding. A neighbor brought them food until a few days ago, but then it stopped, and they didn't dare to come out. They don't know what happened to the neighbor." He moves his hand gently across the floorboards and presses on one. A small gap appears, and several floorboards shift to the side.

Peering over Gustav's shoulder, Peter can see pale faces staring up from a dark space underneath the kitchen floor. They shrink back when they notice Lioba and Peter.

"It's all right," Gustav says, reaching down to help the woman. "They are friends."

One by one, four people climb out: a woman, an elderly man, and two children, all gaunt, pale, and moving stiffly.

"Sophie, we found a boat. We are going to get out of here."

The woman stares at Gustav, speechless.

"A ship?" the little boy asks excitedly. "Will you be the captain?"

"Uncle Gustav is not a captain, Simon," the girl says chidingly.

The boy looks like he is about five and the girl a bit older. It is hard to tell because they are so thin and pale.

"We should go quickly. Sophie, do you have any coats?"

"I'll see what I can find," the woman says. "Most of it got destroyed during the searches. They kept coming back looking for us, but not so much in the last year." She rushes out of the kitchen and goes upstairs.

"I can't believe this," the old man says to Gustav, his voice quavering. "First, you come back after we thought you were already d—" He stops in mid-sentence, glancing down at Simon, who leans against his leg, with his thumb in his mouth. "And now, you are taking us out of here."

Sophie returns, carrying a small pile. "There isn't much left that we can use." She stuffs the little boy's arms into a jacket with a hood.

"Wait," Gustav says abruptly, kneeling in front of the boy. "You won't need that anymore." With a pocketknife, he rips off a yellow star, sewn onto the front of the jacket.

"Let me hang on to it." The old man reaches out and takes it from Gustav's hand. "I want to explain it to them later."

"Uncle Leopold, how can you bear it?" Gustav whispers. "Do you have any idea what has been happening?"

"I know." Uncle Leopold places his hand on Gustav's arm gently as if he did not want to startle him.

Gustav's face is like a colorless mask. For a moment, Peter has the curious sense the mask is about to crack open down the middle, releasing a torrent of something unspeakable. Then Gustav closes his eyes and hunches his shoulders as if trying to shoulder an impossible weight.

"We have to bear it so we can remember and tell others," Leopold says softly.

Lioba coughs. "Listen, we really should get going if we want to have any hope of getting out of here. What can we carry?"

"Oh, I almost forgot." Sophie lowers herself into the compartment underneath the kitchen floor.

Peter bends forward to look. There are four cots, a few bags, buckets, some crockery. That's it. That's where they spent most of their time for the past years.

"Here," Sophie says with an uncertain smile. "Would you hold this for a moment?" She hands him a bag and climbs up, clutching a bronze candelabrum with seven arms, two silver candlesticks, a doll with long braids, and a stuffed bunny rabbit with ears almost bald and one glass eye missing. "Simon, you carry Bunny."

The girl snatches the doll and tucks it under her arm, patting it and smoothing down the embroidered skirt.

"You still have that doll, Dorthe." Gustav smiled at the little girl. "I gave it to you years ago."

"That's Margret," she says proudly.

"Nice name." Gustav glances at the candlesticks. "Sophie, don't tell me you lit Shabbes candles in the basement."

The slender woman scowls at him. Without responding, she wraps the bronze candelabra in a towel and sticks it into a bag. "That's it. We are ready."

"Fine, let's go," Gustav says. "Peter, would you take that?" He points at a bag and grabs two others. Sophie carries a leather case and gives a small one to Dorthe. Lioba hoists Simon onto her back, and they begin to walk toward the river.

Peter glances at Gustav's feet, firmly encased in Peter's shoes, remembering how swollen and rubbed raw they had looked in the forest. The stiff leather has to hurt, but Gustav moves along swiftly as he leads them through the dark streets.

When they reach the river, Gustav makes a sign to the others to stop. "Come, Peter, time to break into the cellar."

The latch opens with a loud squeal. Quickly, Gustav and Peter pull off the tarp. Grunting and heaving, they begin to push the boat out of the cellar and over the ramp.

"Hey," a voice shouts. "What do you think you are doing?" A small man, with bushy hair and a pointy nose, comes around the shrubbery, dressed in a dark purple robe, belted at the waist, striped hose flopping above his ankles, and leather slippers.

Peter almost begins to laugh. The man makes him think of an aggravated squirrel, baring his teeth and literally spitting with anger. Then he sobers as he tries to see whether there is any family resemblance.

Gustav straightens up, breathing heavily. "We are taking your boat," he says.

"No, you are not. That's theft." The man glares at him, his hands on his hips. "I'll call the police right now."

"Have you been asleep over the last days? Don't you know what's happening?" Lioba asks angrily.

"Hard not to," the man says. "That doesn't give you the right to take my property. How did you know about this hiding place, anyway?" The man looks at Gustav and Peter accusingly. "You aren't from around here. I bought this house twenty years ago, but I know pretty much everyone in the neighborhood."

"I remember others like this," Peter says vaguely, secretly relieved. At least he is not a relative. It would be like meeting a part of himself.

"Why aren't you leaving? Aren't you afraid?" Lioba asks.

"What's to be afraid of?" The man shrugs. "I already lost all that matters. My wife is upstairs." His face crumbles. "She took a cyanide pill."

"I am sorry," Lioba says, her eyes welling up.

"What's a cyanide pill?" Peter asks in a whisper.

Lioba glances at him blindly. "Something that kills you quickly."

"Oh." Peter steps closer.

"My parents did the same," Lioba says to the man. "They went somewhere else to do this. They just left me a note."

"My wife didn't leave me a note. She just waited until I went out."

"Lioba, let me talk to him," Peter whispers. He turns to the man. "Is there anyone to help you bury her?"

The man shakes his head. "She looks quite peaceful, up there in her bed."

"Are you alone?"

"Isn't it obvious? My son died in Stalingrad. I got a postcard from one of his mates. So, you see, there is nothing to be afraid of anymore."

Lioba has taken a step back and covered her face with her hands.

Peter puts a hand on the man's arm. "I am sorry."

The man flinches, but he seems less hostile.

"Would you please help these people? It is a mother with her children and their grandfather." Peter points at Sophie, holding Simon in her arms, and Leopold, his back hunched and his clothes hanging loosely on his thin frame, with Dorthe standing close to him. "They need to get away from here while there is time. Please, help them."

"I am alone too." Lioba has regained her composure. "My parents and my brother are gone. So, I understand how hard this is for you." She glances at Gustav as if asking for his approval. He nods and smiles at her. Lioba returns the smile and then focuses on the man. "Why don't you come with us?"

"No, I am going to stay here," the man says. "This is my home. I won't have any other."

"Please, let us take the boat. If you keep it, the Russians will be sure to take it," Gustav says.

"That's my son's boat. It's all I have left of him."

Peter can see Gustav's anxiety increasing with every boom in the distance. He would probably force this man to give up the boat.

But it should not happen like that. The poor man has lost so much already.

Peter plucks on Lioba's sleeve and pulls her away. "You should give him something in return," he whispers. He glances significantly at her tunic, pointing toward the pendant hidden underneath.

Her hand clutches at her chest. Momentarily lightheaded, Peter tries to focus on her face to shake the sense of the world sinking away beneath his feet. He grabs her hands. "Listen to me," he says. "Remember what your grandmother told you. *There may come a time when you have to let it go.*"

"It's the last thing I have." She gazes at him with despair. "I can't."

"Yes, you can," Peter says firmly. "That's why you have it." He hesitates, trying to find the right words. How can he explain something he can hardly understand himself? Over Lioba's shoulder he can see the others watching curiously. "I need to tell you something about your amber crane," he says, speaking quickly and urgently. "It has magic attached to it. It brought me here. Think of who may have carved this hundreds of years ago, maybe in secret, at risk to himself and the people he loved. He also had to let it go, hoping the right person would find it long after he was gone." Lioba stares at him and opens her mouth to speak. Peter shakes his head, still clutching her hands. "I do not know how this will go on. I do not even know if any of this is just in my dream. I do not think I am supposed to know. But I am sure of one thing. Sometimes you have to be willing to leave something behind."

Lioba's eyes fill with tears. She nods. "You are right."

"But do not hand it over right away. Just let the man have a peek at it. Give it to him only once you are all safely on the boat. I doubt he is going to fight you at this point, but it is better to be prepared."

"That makes sense."

"Wait," Peter says quickly. "There is something else. Please do not ask me to explain, but just before you hand it over, would you let me see it?"

Lioba frowns as if about to ask what he means but stops herself. "Fine, I'll do that." She turns away, steps up to the man, and tugs on the silver chain until it hangs free on top of her jacket. "Would you give us your boat in return for this?"

"That's beautiful," the man exclaims "Where did you get that? My wife loved amber."

"Would you let us take the boat if I give this to you?"

The man is silent.

"It's all I have," Lioba says, a note of desperation in her voice.

"Fine." The man shrugs. "Give it to me."

"You can have it when we are on the boat."

"Very well. Then let me get some things you'll need." He enters the cellar and roots around in the back, returning after a few moments with several blankets and an odd-looking jug.

The jug gives off a pungent scent, sort of sweet, sour, and biting. Hopefully, that was not supposed to be drinking water.

"Here, that should keep you going for a while. I've kept the boat in good shape, and she doesn't need too much fuel."

"Thank you." Gustav hefts the jug onto the deck. He looks at the blankets doubtfully. "We can't take your blankets."

"It's cold out there. Just take them."

Gustav nods. With the man's help, they push the boat out onto the water. White lettering gleams on the blue hull.

"Look, the ship is called *Margret*." Dorthe holds up her doll. "Just like her. That's Margret."

The man glances at the little girl and gives her a pained smile.

Peter and Gustav heft the bags onto the deck and help Sophie, Leopold, and the children up the ladder. The children immediately enter the little cabin.

"You might want to hug the coastline as you are heading west," the man mutters. "Less chance of getting blown out of the water that way."

"I'll keep it in mind," Gustav says. "Are you sure you won't come with us?"

"No, I'd rather take my chances here."

"And you, Peter?" Gustav asks.

"Do not worry about me." Peter shakes his head. "I will be fine."

Lioba gives Peter a hug.

"It's getting light. We must go." Gustav does something at the front of the boat, and it begins to make a *put-put-put* noise, humming and rattling softly in the dark. "Come on," he says urgently.

"I'm coming." Lioba turns to the man. "Thank you for your help."

He no longer looks like an aggravated squirrel, just a small, thin man, with windblown hair, and a face filled with sadness.

It has begun to snow.

Gustav holds out his hand and helps Lioba onto the deck. For a moment, they stand there, gazing back at Peter. Gustav's arm encircles her shoulders. She pulls the silver chain over her head and holds up the pendant.

Snowflakes cling to Peter's eyebrows and eyelids, melting and running down his cheeks. He blinks away the drops, and for an instant, he sees the questing beak, reaching toward the sky, and the folded wings, tensed and ready to burst into flight—a magical firebird.

Then Lioba pulls back her arm and tosses the amber crane in a wide arc through the glittering flakes.

25

TEARS OF THE GODS

"Wake up."

Peter opened his eyes to Master Nowak's face hovering above him. He was on the ground, one foot perilously close to the edge of the pond. Peter rubbed his eyes and his hands came away wet. He had been weeping and hadn't known it.

"Fine time to go to sleep, never mind sitting out here in the cold."

"How did you find me?" Peter stood up, brushing off his coat.

"I got worried and decided to walk in the direction I had seen you take earlier." Master Nowak scrutinized Peter. "You looked like you were sleepwalking. You were muttering and moving around."

Peter felt his face burn. Without answering, he followed Master Nowak back toward the town square.

Inside the room, the guild masters and town elders were quiet when Peter and Master Nowak walked in. They sat down in the same chairs as before.

Mayor Neuhof shuffled the papers in front of him, rubbing his eyes. He glared at Peter. "Master Glienke, stand up."

Peter rose. He pulled back his shoulders and raised his chin.

"Master Glienke, you have been charged with disrupting the peace by brawling on the town square. You admitted that you have walked on the beach and picked up amber in contravention of the rules, and you also admitted to working on the same piece illegally. In addition, there is the accusation of witchcraft leveled against your sister.

"First there is the charge of battery. I understand a fine has been paid on your behalf." The mayor glared at Peter as if this was a bad thing.

The masters murmured and whispered to each other. Two knew his father well and had had many business dealings with him and his uncle over the years. Sometimes they had brought presents for Lorenz, Effie, and Peter when they were younger.

"We declare ourselves satisfied on that count. The charge of witchcraft raised against your sister is a grave one, but we accept there are mitigating circumstances. I have also received several character testimonies about the young woman I must take into account." Mayor Neuhof paused, glancing at Peter with evident dislike.

Marthe must have said something to her father. It clearly had helped Effie, but it was unlikely to help him.

"We needn't go into that in any detail. In any event, based on these testimonies and my own knowledge of the young woman, the council has decided to dismiss the charges against Mistress Glienke. Meanwhile, that leaves your own actions. We are concerned about the increase in irregularities regarding amber production. The duke takes a close look at any such irregularities, and that affects the entire guild as well as the town."

They did not care about the witchcraft accusation, Peter thought. But they did care about the possibility a Bönhase might have been working in their midst.

"We accept that you did not intend to profit from your actions. Also, we have had several people speak for your character, and we have noted your honesty and ready admission of guilt. However, your actions cannot be ignored. Hence, we

impose the following penalty. You will leave the town of Stolpmünde by the end of this month and will be banned from
returning for five years."

Peter blinked. Five years. The words boomed in his head.

Mayor Neuhof raised his hand to indicate he was not
finished. "We also impose a fine in the form of three times the
apprenticeship dues your family paid to Master Nowak, payable
to the guild upon your return to Stolpmünde.

"Meanwhile, the council believes Master Nowak is not
entirely without blame. Different suggestions have been put
forth." He glanced around at the other guild masters.

Master Roth leaned forward, his tongue flicking over his
lips.

"In light of Master Nowak's standing and heretofore
unblemished reputation, the senior guild masters have pleaded
for leniency. However, we cannot ignore any irregularities.
Hence, for one year, Master Nowak shall surrender all beer
produced in his brewery and distribute it in equal proportions
among all amber guild masters, not including the beer for
Master Nowak's household and a certain amount set aside for
the town council. Master Roth will see to it that this distribution
is handled properly."

Peter almost burst out laughing. Master Roth appeared
surprised, disappointed, and annoyed all at once. Then the urge
to laugh vanished. How could he ever compensate Master
Nowak for his losses?

"I understand," Master Nowak said. "I will draw up the
requisite paperwork to help Master Roth in his task. Meanwhile,
I would like to make a request. For the sake of preventing any
perhaps overly eager citizens' actions, I would ask you to post a
public notice announcing that Mistress Effie Glienke and Master
Peter Glienke have been dismissed without a stain on their
character."

"Overly eager" seemed a tactful way of describing the strong
possibility of people running around with pitchforks and

burning torches to seek out a suspected witch, Peter thought. Perhaps, now she would be safe.

Mayor Neuhof scowled at Master Nowak and Peter, drawing down the corners of his mouth, but nodded and made a note on the paper in front of him.

Outside the town hall, Peter pulled on Master Nowak's sleeve. "I do not know how to thank you. I am sorry about the beer. I will pay you back as soon as I can."

"You will have plenty of opportunities to do so." Master Nowak chuckled. "Actually, I expected I would lose the brewery altogether. Master Roth has been after my brewery for years."

"What do you mean?"

"I'm sure he had tried to convince Mayor Neuhof before the meeting to award it to him, and you heard all that whispering at the end. I do not need to tell you the amber heart was just an excuse. It is all about continued control of the amber trade. It is a good thing that their greed won out."

"But accusing Effie of witchcraft? What did that have to do with beer or greed?"

"Well, that was the result of hysteria, which can be very dangerous. There are always people who like to exploit something like that for their own benefit. Fortunately, most of those men back there know perfectly well the last thing we need now in this town is the kind of hysteria induced by a witchcraft trial. They could not ignore it because too many people in the town square had heard it, but the masters were happy to settle it quietly. Still, I would advise your father to take Effie somewhere else for a while."

"This was all my fault."

"Well, I must admit your actions contributed to this. Incidentally, do you have any idea what happened in there? When the hearing began, I was convinced the mayor was going to go against you and Effie. He certainly looked that way. I wonder what changed his mind."

"I am glad he did." Peter did not want to reveal his conversation with Marthe. He had begun to feel sorry for her. She had done wrong, but perhaps she was just as trapped in her life as he was.

The reality of his sentence was sinking in. Banned for five years. He should be grateful he was not stripped of his status as a journeyman or expelled from the guild for life, but he could not imagine being away from home for that long. What was he going to do? What would happen to his family?

"I do not have much time—just a few weeks before I have to leave."

"Just start as you had planned already. Go to Königsberg. Everything else will follow."

Master Nowak chuckled. "It will be quite restful in the workshop without you to make trouble.

Now, you should go home. Your father will be relieved. Tomorrow you can start making your arrangements."

"Thank you, Master Nowak."

On the way to his father's house, Peter walked slowly, trying to sort out his thoughts. Profound relief, anxiety, grief, and anticipation swirled through his head.

Snow and ice had hidden the edges of the road, and the surface was slippery. At least it had stopped blowing. In the pale winter sunlight of the late afternoon, the stubble field to the right with stalks pushing through drifts of snow had turned into a shimmering golden sea. Its beauty hurt, he loved it so much.

A group of cranes sat in the middle of the field as if lost in a dream. Suddenly, following a secret call, they began to hop up and down. Making their rattling sounds, alternating with high-pitched screeches, they lifted off into the darkening sky.

Peter's eyes blurred. He brushed his hand over his face and it came away wet.

He was going home. For the first time in many months, he thought of his father's house as home. He now knew how precious it was. He had a home. Even though he was about to be sent into exile, he would be able to return—unlike Lioba and so many others who lost all they had.

It was dark by the time he reached the familiar white-washed front door framed by the scraggly vines of his mother's rambling rose.

"Where have you been?" Clare fussed as she brushed the snow off his coat. "We heard the news from the boy who brings the ale."

For a moment, Peter felt deflated. He had envisioned bringing the news himself and had pictured Clare's smile and his father's nod of approval. "Is Effie home already?"

"No, I'm fetching her tomorrow. It has been snowing hard for a while, and it seems better to wait. And your father is coming with me. He thought it might be safer that way."

Cautiously, Peter opened the door to his father's study.

"Peter, I'm glad you are home." His father stood by the window. Peter could see how thin he had become in the last months. "I heard about the five-year ban. It could have been a lot worse." In one of his rare gestures of affection, he reached out and patted Peter on the back.

"Clare told me she is getting Effie tomorrow morning."

"I want to show you something. You will not believe this." He pulled Peter over to the papers spread out on his desk, almost feverish in his intensity. "Look."

"What's this?" Peter gaped at the papers.

"Effie's drawings."

Speechless, Peter picked up one sheet after the other, gazing at images in charcoal red, grey, and black, with exquisite shading and detailed work. There were many drawings of plants, utterly familiar but astounding in their detail and beauty, the rambling rose at the front door with petals strewn on the ground, graceful sheaves of rye, standing tall in the field, young pinecone-like buds of hop vines, and dahlias with heavy flower heads bent after rain.

Peter marveled at a drawing of a dandelion head with its

seeds about to fly off, a miniature snowstorm so vivid it made him want to sneeze.

"Thistles," he said in disbelief, pointing at the prickly spines underneath the flower head like an exotic fruit or an animal from another age. He had never bothered to look more closely at thistles along the side of field paths, merely irritated when the spiny plants scratched his bare legs.

Peter glanced up at his father, who watched him in silence, with chagrin, pride, and grief chasing each other across his lined face.

Peter turned back to the drawings.

There was an entire series of birds. Effie had drawn birds in the field, nesting, and in full flight across the dunes, a crane in the marsh, watching and waiting, one foot carefully raised. Even a tiny barn owl in the tree across from the house, with its curious flat face and huge eyes looking lost and vulnerable.

The third stack made him want to weep. These were faces he knew—his mother reading, his father at his desk, Lorenz laughing with his head thrown back, Clare absorbed over a pile of vegetables at the table in the kitchen, and his own face, half-hidden, asleep at the kitchen table, and another from the side, his head resting on his hand.

"Your mother must have known," his father said. "After all, she bought Effie all that paper and charcoal. But I had no idea. Of course, your sister always hid everything whenever anyone else came into her room. Something happened over the last weeks—I do not really know. Anyway, she showed them to Clare and to me just a few days ago."

"They are amazing." Peter picked up one of the stacks, flipping through them again. "There is enough there for several books at least."

"That's exactly what I am thinking. I want to find a way to publish them."

"Master Nowak said it might be a good idea to take her away from here for a while."

"Yes, he might be right. Maybe we could visit some book printers in Augsburg."

"Father, I have been thinking. Could you do business with Uncle Frantz?" Peter almost stopped when he saw his father's raised eyebrows, but continued, speaking quickly. "I mean, he has sources for dried and smoked fish and other foodstuffs. You have connections to people selling timber. There is a great need for that, given all the buildings burnt down or falling apart. Remember, Uncle Frantz has that storage at the river, and he hasn't been using it fully. You could even have a boat there for ferrying timber. Maybe there's a way to enter into trade with that, and you wouldn't have to contend with the risk of losing ships at sea."

His father frowned.

"Perhaps it is not a good idea," Peter added, once again shy and uncertain.

"Actually, it is," his father said slowly. "It is just that I have always been a shipping merchant. You might have something there."

On his walk back to Master Nowak's house, Peter thought about all that had happened.

His hand twitched, and he wanted to reach for the crane, buried deep in his pocket. Before he left, he asked Clare for a thick piece of cloth. Raising her eyebrows, she searched in various drawers, came up with a square of green felt, and handed it to him silently. He could see she wanted to ask him what it was for, but he avoided her eyes. When he was alone, he wrapped the amber crane into the felt to keep himself from looking at it, but it was hard. He kept thinking of the boat, with its little cabin, doggedly making its way down the river and into the open sea, driven by the wind, with the rattling of artillery fire haunting its journey as it chugged along the coast toward the west.

Effie's scribbles. He was ashamed of having been so dismissive. Anne was right. He had never really bothered to look.

Perhaps the amber heart had helped Effie. Peter would never know for sure. His father said something had changed over the last weeks, and Anne also noticed that. It was his fault she had been in jail. And yet, there were Effie's remarkable drawings and his father's smile and renewed vigor.

The next few days left him giddy with tiredness and excitement. First, there was the celebration of his new status, and then he had to get ready for his departure. Afterward, Peter could not recall any of the work that went into preparing the celebration. Mistress Nowak gave him lists of things to get and to carry to the large hall used by the amber guild for such occasions. Her calm, commanding presence helped him to focus.

When he and Cune rolled two kegs of beer to the hall, he remembered Master Nowak's laughing comment. "Enjoy it while it lasts," he had said with a chuckle, adding, "Admittedly, I rather like the notion of Master Roth getting saddled with the responsibility of the distribution over the coming year."

Peter gathered everything he needed for his life as a journeyman and went to the harbor to arrange a berth in a trading ship on its way to Königsberg. Afterward, he visited his uncle.

"Father told me he is thinking about going into business with you."

"I understand I have you to thank for this." Uncle Frantz grinned at him. "I cannot imagine how you got through to him, but I am delighted."

Peter glanced at the shrubbery on the riverbank below the house. "Can I take another look at your ice cellar?"

"Why?"

"I will not be home for a long time." Peter fumbled for an explanation that would make sense. "I just want to see everything once more."

"Your brother did the same before he left." His uncle put an arm around his nephew's shoulders as they walked toward the riverbank. "Of course, you are coming back." The heavy door opened with a squeal. "I need to clean the hinges and oil them again."

"It is empty." Peter blinked, gazing at the cavernous space. It was as if he saw the shadow of a boat.

"I am waiting for a shipment. Anyway, I hope I live to see the end of this war. This would be perfect for storing fish."

"And for a boat."

"Yes, indeed," his uncle said. "It would be large enough for a boat. Actually, I thought I might widen the entrance even more."

After that, Peter became impatient to be gone. During a final visit home, he found Uncle Frantz and his father engaged in one of their usual arguments about trade, but his father no longer sounded weary and indifferent.

Clare searched through the old cabinets and blanket chests for things he might need. Later, sitting at the kitchen table with a needle and thread, she fixed a hole in his tunic.

Watching her work, Peter struggled for words. Clare had done so much for his father, Effie, and himself, never complaining. "Clare, I hope ..." he said and stopped himself. How selfish could he be to ask her to stay?

"Do not worry," she said. "I will look after your father and Effie. I might even go with them when they travel to Augsburg. It is time for you to get on with your life." She pulled the thread through the fabric and cut off the end. "Did you hear about the mayor's daughter? Rumor has it that she is going to visit relatives in Hamburg where the war hasn't done as much damage."

Peter avoided meeting her eyes. He did not know what to say.

"Perhaps she needs a new field to work her wiles." Clare's eyes twinkled. "She is quite subdued these days, almost soberly dressed and always in the company of that sour-faced aunt of hers."

"How is Effie doing?" Peter asked, trying to get her mind off Marthe.

"I have not seen her rocking for days, she eats her meals

downstairs, and a few times she has come with me to the market. Things will get better now."

When he walked back to Master Nowak's house, he had one of Effie's drawings in his bag. She gave it to him when he came to her room to say goodbye. He looked at it with a lump in his throat. It was of himself, bent over his tools. He could not remember Effie ever having seen the workshop. She smiled at him and pulled out the amber heart. To his surprise, the town councilman had seen to it that it was returned to her when she was released. Effie reached out her hand and patted him on his chest as one might pat a horse. Then she took his hand and briefly placed it on her chest, covering his hand with her own warm, long-fingered artist's hand. Her silence did not bother him. It was clear what she was saying to him. She was content, she knew he hadn't meant to hurt her, and she loved him.

The hardest part came last.

Anne, carrying a basket with food for his journey, which Mistress Nowak had prepared, walked Peter to the harbor where the ship that would take him to Königsberg was moored in its berth. It was still cold, but the late March sun cut through the gloom of winter like a sword, and all the ice had melted.

Peter had slung a canvas sack over his shoulder, stuffed with his clothes and his own set of tools, a present from Master Nowak upon the successful completion of his apprenticeship. He glanced at Anne, short and slight, but elegant in her dark green cape, a hood drawn over her head, the tips of the braids swinging on her shoulders. He could see her profile, the slightly upturned nose, the firm lips, and the broad forehead, accentuated by arched eyebrows. She was silent, her eyes turned steadfastly forward as they walked.

They stopped when they reached the edge of the harbor where Peter's ship was moored.

"Anne," Peter said. "I know what you meant when you were angry at me on Shrovetide Tuesday."

Anne did not say anything, her expression friendly but guarded.

"Really, I know now. I did not understand before." He spoke faster, stumbling over the words. "You were right. I did not notice many things. I did not pay enough attention to Effie or even to my father.." He hesitated before he continued. "But I do see you. I will miss you. You are the only one I will really miss."

Anne's cheeks turned pink. She looked down, and then her eyes focused on him again in her straightforward way. "I will miss you too."

"I made a lot of mistakes lately, not just about Effie," Peter said. Secretly, he touched the small felt bundle in his pocket.

Anne held up her hand as if to stop him. "Whatever you did, it was for your sister."

"I do not know anymore," he said doubtfully. "That hardly justifies placing your father at risk, now does it?"

"Perhaps not. But what you did for Effie matters, and you cared. Anyway, something has shifted for her. I noticed it right away when I visited her after Christmas, and later she showed me some of her drawings."

"You do not need to remind me." Peter sighed. "I know how wrong I was."

"You were not the only one. I think we all were."

Peter glanced at the water. The wind had turned, and he could taste the salty spray of the sea on his lips. Then he focused on Anne's face and her glowing eyes.

"Anne, I cannot say any of this well. I know now what I want to do more than I ever did before. I want to craft pieces of amber that will make people happy. They will not stop the war or bring back Lorenz. I know that. But they will be beautiful." Peter fell silent.

He could not describe the amber he saw before his mind's eye in colors that glowed butter yellow, blood red, shimmering brown, and golden—pieces that would be treasured hundreds of years later. He could not say that he wanted to learn new techniques because that might make Anne feel sad about her father. He wanted to say that each piece crafted by him would tell a story. Again, his hand touched the felt bundle. The amber crane was his secret, and it had to remain so. He could not say any of that. He just watched Anne's eyes, golden-brown and filled with warmth.

"I think you can see all the amber pieces in front of you." She smiled at him.

"Yes, I do." Peter tugged her braid, trying to hide his emotion. For months, he had felt alone, carrying a secret he could not share with anyone and trapped in a world of dreams. Now, even though he could never explain all of what had happened and what he had done, it seemed that he hadn't been alone at all. Anne, Master Nowak, Clare, Effie, and even his father had been there all along, walking beside him.

Sailors shouted and whistled. Carters moved up and down the gangway, rolling barrels of supplies on deck, where sailors received them and stored everything in the hold. The loading of the ship was almost finished. Merchants and other passengers started to make their way up the gangway. It was time.

Anne pushed back her hood and stepped close to him. Standing on her tiptoes, she reached up, kissed him on the lips, and whispered, "I will be here when you come back." She put the basket in his hand, pulled the hood up, and left before he could respond.

Glowing and trying to hold on to the feeling of Anne's lips, Peter hardly noticed how he got on board the ship. Anne was not a dream. She did not live in another time. She was as real and familiar to him as his room at home, the smells and sights of Master Nowak's workshop, or the sound of the waves breaking on the beach. Yet, lately, Peter had discovered how little he knew of her. She had become a mystery. But she would wait for him.

The Dutch-built ship was larger than any Peter had ever seen, with three masts that seemed to reach for the clouds.

"I want you to tell me all about it when you write," Uncle

Frantz had said, sounding wistful, even envious. "Our ships are getting a bit long in the tooth, and they are much smaller, with less cargo room."

Peter stood at the railing. The waves slapped the sides of the ship as it moved out into the ocean. His hand gripped the felt bundle. Now that the time had come, he hesitated. Ever since that night, when he watched Lioba on the boat waving to him, he felt a sense of loss. He would never see her again. His thoughts about Lioba and her world had become fuzzy, just like dreams that blow away in the light of day. The more he tried to hold on to what he had seen, the more everything became rigid in his mind, flat, without color, lifeless.

It reminded Peter of the times when he had held a chunk of amber in his hands. In its raw state, unpolished and unformed, it was full of potential, but then when he tried to work on it, he lost the vivid sense of what he had envisioned. And yet, after struggling with it for a while, it began to turn into something else, unexpected, solid, tangible, and just as marvelous. Maybe it had all been a dream. He would never know, but it was right that he did not.

The ship rose and fell with the swell of the sea beneath its bow. Above Peter's head, the rigging creaked, and the sails snapped, as the ship gained speed. He could just make out the shoreline to the south. Stolpmünde faded into the background.

It was time to let go. In another world and time, Lioba's great-grandmother would ride along the shoreline and come across a magical amber crane that had washed up after a storm.

The other passengers had gone into the hold. The sailors were busy and did not pay any attention to Peter standing at the railing. He took out the felt bundle and unfolded it.

The amber was warm and soft to the touch. With his fingers, Peter traced its outlines and gently rubbed the unpolished area. The dark golden bird looked delicate with its long legs and slender beak, yet sturdy, tensed, its wings about to unfurl. He held it up so it caught the light of the setting sun. For an instant, he thought he heard the repetitive boom of cannons or muskets and glimpsed the shadows of ships racing west. He drew back his arm and threw the amber as far as he could into the water.

A wave seized it and lifted it up. Triumphantly it rode on top of the foam, a magical firebird returning to its realm, and then it was gone.

On the dunes in the distance, a flock of cranes rose up into the air, rattling and screeching, followed by deep trumpet-like rolling cries. They flew parallel to the course of the ship, steadily beating east. Their incessant calling reached Peter like a dream, growing stronger and fainter with the shifting wind—loss, desolation, and hope—go on, go on, go on.

AUTHOR'S NOTE

Throughout the manuscript, I have retained the names of towns as they were used at the time in which the story takes places. Several of these names were changed after World War II, in particular: Allenstein (Olsztyn), Danzig (Gdansk), Elbing (Elblag), Gotenhafen (Gdynia), Königsberg (Kaliningrad), Lübzow (Lubuczewo), Muttrin (Motarzyno), Stolp (Slupsk), and Stolpmünde (Ustka). For additional information, see also "Pomerania" and "East Prussia" in the glossary below.

As far as details of the evacuation are concerned, I used a variety of sources, sticking to eyewitness accounts of those days as much as possible. One such eyewitness account, albeit from Königsberg during the evacuation, describes children building snowmen, their families apparently oblivious to the reality of the approaching army.

The manor house in Muttrin (Motarzyno) is still standing, as is the linden tree. Members of the Zitzewitz family appear in historical records as owners of Muttrin since the early 14th century. The last owner of the estate, Friedrich-Karl von Zitzewitz, was arrested by the government for involvement in plans to resist Hitler and only freed from prison when the Americans arrived in the spring of 1945. Lioba is pure invention, albeit inspired by the stories told by people who have lived through those perilous times. It is unlikely that the remaining members of the family would have left the house alone for a day in the months before the evacuation. However, I sent them away for the sake of the story. Meanwhile, officers and soldiers of the 7th Armored Division were quartered in Muttrin in early March 1945.

GLOSSARY

Amber – Fossilized tree resin. It is found all over the world, but especially in the Baltic, in a range of colors and degrees of transparency, sometimes with animal or plant materials trapped inside, known as inclusions. From prehistoric times to the present, amber has been valued as a gemstone as well as a healing agent in folk medicine. Unlike real gems, amber can be set on fire and burned, producing the aroma of pinewood. It is light and floats. Amber is harvested from the sea by various methods, including hand collection on shorelines after storms and the use of large nets, dragged through the water. Another harvesting method involves mining for it in marl pits.

Amber trade – Amber, light and easily transported, was one of the first items of long-distance trade. It linked the Baltic region with areas of the world as far away as India, from as early as 1500 B.C. In the Middle Ages, the Order of Teutonic Knights kept control of the amber trade in the Baltic. In 1533, they transferred control to a family of merchants in Gdansk in 1533, the Koehn von Jaskis. In 1642, Frederick William, the Great Elector of Prussia, bought the rights to the amber trade from the Jaskis, subsequently steadily tightening controls over the harvesting and distribution of amber. For instance, he decreed that individuals were prohibited from collecting amber on the beaches or even walking along the beaches. Penalties for infringing on any of the rules concerning amber ranged from fines and imprisonment to banishment or death.

Amber road – Dating back to antiquity, amber merchants traveled along five main routes, all running north-south. Some existed since prehistoric times, linking the high north of Europe and the Baltic sea with all of Europe. One such route began in today's St. Petersburg and traveled along the Baltic as far as Gdansk, where it shifted toward the south, leading all the way to Venice.

Anselmus von Losenberg – legendary 13th century reeve in Samland, East Prussia. When the Teutonic Order came to Samland (a peninsula in the Kaliningrad Oblast of Russia, on the southeastern shore of the Baltic Sea) in East Prussia in the 13th century, it claimed ownership of all amber. Brother Anselmus von Losenberg, the reeve, decreed that anyone who collected amber without permission from the Order would be punished by hanging. According to the legend, when Reeve Anselmus died, his soul was restless, and he regretted his harsh and merciless actions toward the people. During stormy nights, people would see his ghost rush along the beach, shouting: Oh, dear Lord! Amber free! Amber free! (see Ludwig Bechstein: *Deutsches Sagenbuch.* ed. Karl Martin Schiller, Leipzig: Georg Wigand, 1853; translation of excerpt by Malve von Hassell)

Banér, Johan (June 23, 1596 – May 10, 1641) – Swedish Field Marshall in the Thirty Years' War.

Bönhase – German word used to describe artisans who work illegally outside the limits imposed by the respective guild. The word literally means "hare in the attic", evoking the image of someone working secretly in a hidden space away from prying eyes. The image of the hare also is derived from the speed with which such rogue artisans made their escape, sometimes via interconnected roof attics of houses standing side by side along a street, hopping from attic to attic to evade pursuit.

Bruegel – Pieter Bruegel the Elder (c. 1525–30 – September 9, 1569), artist of Dutch and Flemish Renaissance painting, known for his colorful landscapes and peasant scenes.

Christina of Sweden (December 18, 1626 – April 19, 1689) – the only surviving legitimate child of King Gustaf II Adolph of Sweden and his wife Maria Eleonora of Brandenburg, Christina reigned as Queen of Sweden from 1632 until her abdication in 1654.

East Prussia – former German province along the Baltic Sea. After World War II, its territory was divided between the Soviet Union and Poland. The capital city Königsberg was renamed Kaliningrad in 1946.

Evacuation of East Prussia and Pomerania (1944–45) – Near the end of World War II, permission to evacuate was given only at the last minute, almost literally—in East Prussia on January 20, 1945, and in Pomerania on March 7, 1945. The Red Army reached Stolp (Slupsk) on March 8, 1945. Starting in mid-January 1945, hundreds of thousands of people in East Prussia tried to flee to the west despite the still standing decree that evacuation bordered on traitorous behavior. Many attempted to save their livestock, in particular their horses, and crossed the Vistula Lagoon in the icy winter of 1945. People fled from the oncoming Soviets on foot, by horse-drawn carriages, and improvised carts. Most motorized vehicles and fuel had been confiscated by the army at the beginning of the war. They tried to reach the harbors in Königsberg (Kaliningrad), Stolp (Slupsk),

Danzig (Gdansk), Gotenhafen (Gdynia), and Elbing (Elblag), in
the hopes of getting on board a cargo ship or a passenger ship.
Those who made it onto ships, mostly leaving all their belongings behind, faced a perilous ocean. As many as two hundred
ships encountered mines and were sunk by Soviet bombers or
submarines, with a loss of over 33,000 people. One ship, the
Deutschland, made seven trips, rescuing 70,000 refugees from
West and East Prussia. The last vessel to leave was a barge, pulled
by a rowboat with the name *Hoffnung* (in English "Hope").
Embarking during the night on May 9, 1945, from the island
Hela, the barge had 135 people on board, mostly injured
soldiers, women, and children, and traveled for six days and six
nights before it reached Denmark.

Evacuation of the village of Muttrin (Motarzyno) – On March 7,
1945, the villagers together with members of the Zitzewitz
family began to flee, traveling in the direction of Lanz (Leczyce)
where they suffered a Soviet air attack. Some members of the
trek met again in Gdynia, and a few managed to board a ship
bound for Denmark. However, most of them were overrun by
Soviet troops and forced to return home, only to be forcibly
expelled from Pomerania in subsequent years.

Frederick William of Brandenburg (1620–1688) – a descendant
of the house of Hohenzollern, Great Elector of Brandenburg and
Duke of Prussia, and thus ruler of Brandenburg-Prussia from
1640 until his death.

Gustaf II Adolph (December 9, 1594 – November 6, 1632) –
King of Sweden from 1611 to 1632.

Hanse (Hanseatic League) – a commercial and defensive confed-
eration of merchant guilds and market towns. Originating in the
12th century among several northern German towns, the league
grew in power and significance and dominated Baltic maritime

trade along the coast of Northern Europe for three centuries. After 1450, the league's power gradually declined.

Jaski – Koehn von Jaski, a merchant family from Gdansk (Danzig). From 1533 to 1642, the Jaskis controlled the harvesting and distribution of amber in the Baltic region. In 1533, the Grandmaster of the Order, Duke Albrecht of Prussia, granted an indefinite lease to the merchant Paul Koehn von Jaski. The Order was willing to relinquish its monopoly over the amber trade in part because the market had changed considerably as a result of the Reformation, reducing the demand for rosary beads, which used to represent the bulk of amber production. Meanwhile, in 1642, the Great Elector rescinded this arrangement with the Jaskis and took over control of Baltic amber.

Journeyman – Once an apprentice has completed his apprenticeship, he becomes a journeyman. As a journeyman, an apprentice is supposed to spend several years working for different masters in towns all over the region. Such a period is called "walking". Subsequently, a journeyman can qualify as a full master and start his own workshop. This custom exists in Germany to this day. While the majority of amber guild members were men, women could also qualify as journeymen and become masters of their trade.

Muttrin – Motarzyno, a village in the administrative district of Gmina Dębnica Kaszubska, within Słupsk County, Pomeranian Voivodeship, in northern Poland.

Muttrin linden tree – This tree was planted by Jacob von Zitzewitz, chancellor of Duke Philipp I. von Pommern-Wolgast, in 1555. Given its prominent position on a hill and visible from afar, even though located at a distance of more than 40 kilometers from the sea, the tree was recorded in nautical charts. In

1931, the tree was declared a natural landmark of the region. While a portion of it was destroyed during a storm after World War II, the tree still can be seen on top of its hill where it has stood for nearly five hundred years. The town of Slupsk sends an arbologist to Muttrin every year to check on the tree's wellbeing.

New Tower – also known as the "Witches' Tower" [*Hexenbastei*] (*Baszta Czarnownic* in Polish), in Stolp (Slupsk), formerly part of the town wall and built in the early 1400s. In the 17th century, it was used as a prison, housing those accused of witchcraft. As many as eighteen women were murdered there, and some were burned at the stake. Today, the tower has become an art gallery.

Pomerania – a historical region along the southern shore of the Baltic Sea that stretches roughly from the rivers Recknitz and Trebel in the west to the Vistula in the east. The name "Pomerania" comes from the Slavic *po more*, which means "Land at the Sea". From 1815 to 1945, Pomerania was a province of the Kingdom of Prussia and the Free State of Prussia. Afterward, its territory became part of Allied-occupied Germany and Poland.

Stoertebeker, Klaus – known as Germany's most famous pirate (c. 1360 – October 20, 1401). After a life of legendary exploits, he was caught, tried for piracy, and executed in Hamburg. His seventy-three companions suffered the same fate.

Stolp mass suicide – in the final months of World War II, an estimated 1,000 people committed suicide in the town of Stolp (Slupsk). In Germany as a whole, as many as 10,000 people took their own lives in that period.

Stutthof – a concentration camp with a vast system of subcamps, located about 34 kilometers east of Gdansk. More than 85,000 people died in Stutthof. Germans used prisoners as forced laborers. The SS guards sent many whom they judged too weak to work to the camp's gas chamber. Camp doctors killed sick or injured prisoners in the infirmary with lethal injections. In early January, there were approximately 50,000 prisoners left in Stutthof and its forty subcamps. The evacuation of prisoners began in January 1945. Divided into groups of 1,000 to 1,500, prisoners from the various subcamps were marched to the Baltic Sea coast, forced into the water, and machine-gunned. The rest of the prisoners were marched in the direction of Lauenburg in eastern Germany. Trying to evade the advancing Soviet forces, the SS guards forced the surviving prisoners back to Stutthof. Thousands died during the march, already severely malnourished, overwhelmed by severe winter conditions and brutal treatment by the guards.

Thirty Years' War – The Thirty Years' War (1618–48), one of the longest and most destructive conflicts in European history, resulted in eight million casualties, devastated towns and villages wherever the war raged, especially in German-speaking regions, and caused widespread poverty and hunger. Initially a war between Protestant and Catholic states in the fragmented Holy Roman Empire, it gradually developed into a more general conflict involving most of the great powers in Europe. In a very literal sense of the term "boots on the ground", there was hardly any strip of land untouched by the war. In addition to deaths as the direct result of battles, famine and disease decreased populations in many regions, in particular, in Brandenburg and Pomerania, by as much as 50 percent. Both mercenaries and soldiers in fighting armies were expected to fund themselves by looting or extorting tribute, which imposed severe hardships on the inhabitants of occupied territories. The war also bankrupted most of the combatant powers. The last years of the war were particularly devastating to Brandenburg and Pomerania.

Till Eulenspiegel – the lead character in a series of German folk tales, first published in 1515. He was a merry trickster whose practical jokes often poked fun at narrow-minded, condescending, or dishonest townsmen as well as the clergy and nobility.

Wilhelm Gustloff – a German military transport ship, sunk on January 30, 1945 by a Soviet submarine in the Baltic Sea while evacuating German civilians, a small number of officials, and military personnel from Gdynia (Gotenhafen). By one estimate, 9,400 people died, which makes it the largest loss of life in a single ship sinking in history.

Wullenwever, Jürgen (c. 1492 – September 29, 1537) – burgomaster of Lübeck from 1533 to 1535, a period of religious, political, and trade turmoil. Wullenwever took part in the uprisings of the inhabitants of Lübeck in 1530 and 1531. He joined the governing council of the city and become the leader of the democratic party, in sympathy with its ideas about religion and politics. Wullenwever was appointed burgomaster early in 1533 and threw himself into the movement for restoring Lübeck to her former position of influence. However, the movement eventually failed, and the citizens were compelled to make peace. The imperial court of justice at Speyer restored the old constitution, and in August 1535, the aristocratic party returned to power. Wullenwever was tortured, sentenced to death as a traitor and an Anabaptist, and beheaded at Wolfenbüttel.

SOURCES OF SONG AND POEM
EXCERPTS

All translations are by the author

❧❧❧

Excerpt of a folksong from the 17th century: "Es ritten drei Reiter"

Es ritten drei Reiter zum Tore hinaus,
Adé!
Feinsliebchen, das schaute zum Fenster heraus,
Adé!
Und wenn es denn soll geschieden sein,
So reich mir dein goldenes Ringelein,
Adé, adé, adé!
Ja, Scheiden und Meiden tut weh!

Three riders passed through the gate, farewell!
Their lady loves looked out of the window, farewell!
If we must be parted,
Then give me back your golden ring!
Death drives us apart, farewell!

Leaving breaks our hearts!
Farewell! Farewell! Farewell!

❧

A fragment of the famous Epitaph of Simonides, which commemorates the Battle of Thermopylae in 480 B.C. and the story of the ancient Spartan youths willing to sacrifice themselves for the greater good of their nation

Dic, hospes, Spartae nos te hic vidisse iacentes
dum sanctis patriae legibus obsequimur.

Cicero translated it from the original Greek in his Tusculanae Disputationes (1.42.101).

Oh, stranger, when you arrive in Sparta, tell of our pride
That here, obeying her commands, we died.

The notion of giving one's life for the fatherland became a cornerstone of Nazi propaganda. Heinrich Böll, a renowned novelist in the years following World War II, used it in a short story, titled *Wanderer kommst Du nach Spa*, in which a gravely wounded soldier is carried into a classroom turned into a makeshift hospital. The soldier recognizes the writing on the blackboard and realizes he is in the school he attended a few years earlier.

❧

A quote from a play by Johann Wolfgang Goethe, Faust, Part I, 1808.

Was du ererbt von deinen Vätern hast, erwirb es, um es zu besitzen.

Whatever you have inherited from your forebears, you have to earn
for yourself all over again to claim it as your own.

☙❧

Philipp von Zesen, 1619–89. Lyrics from a church song "Die
güldne Sonne"

> *Die güldene Sonne*
> *Bringt Leben und Wonne,*
> *Die Finsternis weichet.*
> *Der Morgen sich zeiget,*
> *Die Röte aufsteiget,*
> *Die Fimsternis weichet.*

> The golden sun
> Brings life and warmth,
> And darkness flees.
> As the morning rises
> With a rosy glow,
> Darkness flees.

☙❧

Excerpt of a marching song, *Wildgänse rauschen durch die Nacht*,
lyrics by Walter Flex, 1917, set to music by Robert Goetz
(1892–1978) in the style of a folk song.

> *Wildgänse rauschen durch die Nacht*
> *Mit schrillem Schrei nach Norden*
> *Laut hallt ihr Schrei, "Hab acht, habt acht!*
> *Die Welt ist voller Morden.*

> Wild geese are sweeping through the dark
> Northbound, with shrill wail into the morrow.

Harsh and loud their cry, "Oh hark, hark, hark!
The world is full of murder."

SOURCES

Bechstein, Ludwig. *Deutsches Sagenbuch.* ed. Karl Martin Schiller, Leipzig: Georg Wigand, 1853.

Böll, Heinrich. *Wanderer kommst Du nach Spa* ... Deutscher Taschenbuch Verlag: Munich, 1976 (first published 1950).

Llibre Vermell de Montserrat (Red Book of Montserrat) – one of the oldest extant medieval manuscripts containing music. It is a 14th-century manuscript collection of devotional texts containing, among others, some late medieval songs. The lyrics of the song *Vita Brevis* talk about the inevitability of death and the need to stop sinning.

Sachs, Hans, *Das Schlaraffenland.* Illustrated by Else Wenz-Vietor, Alfred Hahn's Verlag, Esslingen, 2001.

ACKNOWLEDGMENTS

Ann Howard Creel and William Greenleaf have provided me with incisive and constructive critiques at various points in the writing of this book. I cannot adequately express my gratitude for their professional advice and their words of support and encouragement. My brother Agostino von Hassell offered helpful comments and introduced me to relevant literature. Working with Michelle Lovi at Odyssey Books has been a pleasure. I am grateful for her support and her painstaking and meticulous attention to detail. I owe special thanks to my mother Christa von Hassell and her cousin Ingeborg von Zitzewitz, whose vivid stories and lived experiences inspired me. As always, I am grateful for my son Ivan's support throughout the writing process.

Dear readers,

I hope you enjoyed this book. I would be honored if you were to post a review on Goodreads or Amazon or any other site where you purchase your books.

Please visit my website at www.malvevonhassell.com for more information about this and other books. Also check out my historical fiction blog *Tales Through Time*, where you can find some maps, images, and sources of inspiration for *The Amber Crane*. I welcome questions and comments. You can contact me through my website.